Where the Skylark Flies

Denis S.J. Price

First Edition

First printed in the United Kingdom

Published by JustPublishOnline.com

Paperback ISBN-13: 978-1-8384170-0-0
.ePub eBook ISBN-13: 978-1-8384170-1-7
.Mobi eBook ISBN-13: 978-1-8384170-2-4

Author's Note

Some attitudes and vocabulary of the period are unacceptable in the 21st century, but their use is integral to the development of the story.

About the book

Tom Jorret, frustrated by the quiet inward-looking life of his Cornish village, tried by motorbike to live a life "responsible to no-one and responsible for no-one". But the coming of the War in 1939 took him to a remote corner of Africa where he not only had to take orders but suddenly found himself responsible for the lives and welfare of six African soldiers.

In his absence his village had to come to terms with the anxieties and losses of the War, especially when the nearby city of Plymouth was completely devastated by the Luftwaffe. The arrival of a Land Girl to work on the Jorret farm quietly gave Tom's family new hope.

'Where the Skylark Flies' paints a vivid and historically accurate picture of the fighting in a "sideshow" of the 1939-45 War and is written with compassion and humour looking into the lives of the villagers, with memorable portraits of Tom's comrades and above all, of the towering figure of the Gambian Lamin Bah.

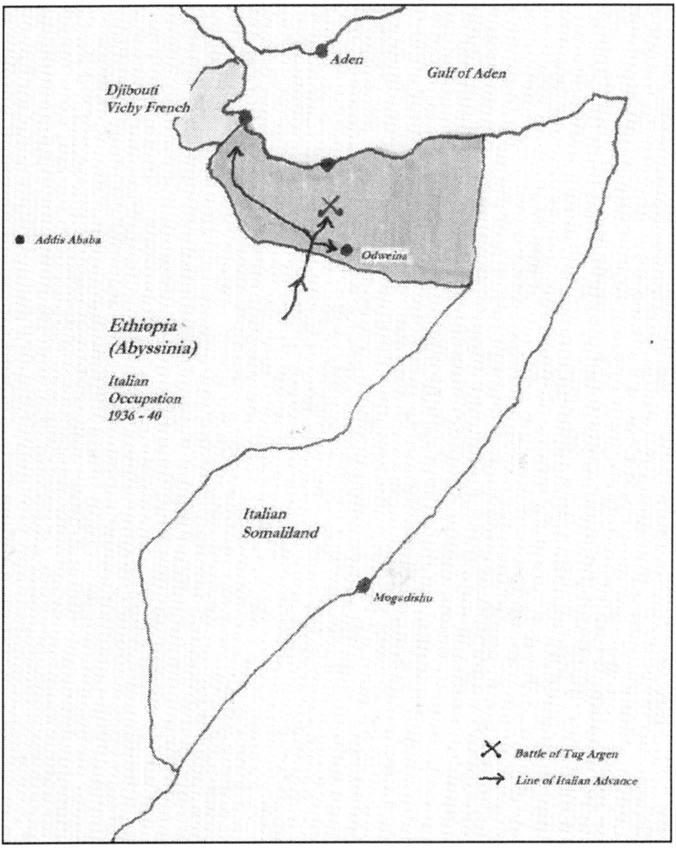

British Somaliland in 1940

Chapter 1

June 1939

For an extra few shillings a week the guests at Peter Jorret's hotel could look out to a magnificent North Cornish seascape; their view to the horizon would be interrupted only by the gaunt Gull Rock that stood out in the bay like a huge hump-backed whale.

Sand dunes (that shifted with the winds every winter) obscured their view of the expansive yellow sands fringed by their jagged black rocky cliffs, but if they craned their necks westwards, they could see the green Newmin headland stretching a quarter of a mile out to sea. A late-Victorian hotel stood massively alone on the headland. It had eighty bedrooms (several of which were said to have their own bathrooms) and its own nine-hole golf course (from which the inexpert golfer would lose his ball far out to sea on the Cornish wind).

Peter Jorret's Bay Hotel had no such refinements. He would often - always - remind his granddaughter Emily of that fact as she brought him his breakfast.

'Hard work's better than all that flummery,' he said. 'And where is that bloody brother of yours, eh? Why ain't he here?'

Emily looked down at her feet to avoid the sight of her grandfather, especially 'at a quarter before eight and not a second late', as every morning for years he had reminded her.

'Tom'll be working, grandfather.'

The old man's blue watery eyes looked up at her angrily.

'He's going to mend my wall,' he said. 'He told me he'd do the wall.' He gestured at her impatiently. 'Give us the eggs, then, girl.

Emily pushed the plate of bacon and eggs in front of him. 'I expect he will come as soon as he can,' she said.

'He keeps away, just like your father. Cares nothing for duty to us.' Emily poured him a mug of tea and spooned in two sugars. *Blood is thicker than water,* she said to herself. Whenever we don't do exactly as he wants. *We Jorrets've been here for generations, and what'll it come to? You'll see, when I've gone on.*

'Blood is thicker than water, and we'll see who remembers that when I've gone on. Generations we Jorrets 'a been here.' He took a forkful of bacon and continued to talk through it. 'But there's something else y'r brother Tom'd like to know. Look at that!'

He flung the *Western Morning News* onto the table in front of her. "Sit ye down and read that!'

Surprised - she never sat with him at the long breakfast table - she sat down abruptly and fished for her glasses from her apron pocket.

'There!' Jorret stabbed a finger at a headline: *Man drowned off Gull Rock.*

Emily read laboriously while her grandfather watched for her reaction.

'Oh my lord! It's Terry!' She stared horrified at the newspaper.

'That's right, Terence Samson, as was.'

'That's terrible! He's Tom's friend.'

'- *was* Tom's friend. And no credit to your brother. Should've had nothing to do with any Samson. Jorrets never had any truck with Samsons.'

Tears welled up in her eyes. 'How can you say that?' she said, in a rare show of spirit. 'How can you say that when that nice young man is dead? When he's drowned?'

'Oh, nice young man is it?' Jorret. 'He's only a year or two behind you.'

Emily read on, as quickly as she could. Twenty-four. *He was only twenty-four. Six years younger, and he's dead, and I'm already an old woman.*

'He'd swum out to Gull Rock. Got caught in the undertow by the cliffs, they think.' She took off her glasses and dabbed at her eyes.

'Silly young fool.' There was just a hint of compassion in Jorret's voice, and his fierce look softened. 'We tried it, one or two of us in the old days, y'know. But the tides were different, and all the sand's shifted along the Crannel there. But the best one who never gave up, he was y'r uncle Steve. Nothing c'd beat him, man nor beast nor sea, not till the blasted Huns blew 'im up.'

The old man in his stiff shiny black suit and waistcoat (even in the middle of summer) suddenly looked crumpled and beaten, the mask of severity slipped. Emily timidly stretched out her hand and covered his.

He looked up at her, and shook off her hand, but not roughly. 'No, that's all right, lass. It's jus' that, well, your uncle Steve, same age…No, you get on. They'll need you for the breakfasts.'

Emily wiped her eyes again and handed back the newspaper, pretending not to notice that there were tears in the old man's eyes too.

* * *

Emily took off her apron and smoothed down her dress before the mirror in the corridor. She stared miserably at the worn, lined sallow face, the black hair tied severely back in a bun and already tinged with grey. Forget about it, and get on, she told herself. People wouldn't notice she'd be crying if she put on her glasses.

The corridor connected the Jorrets' original house to the large extension that Peter Jorret had added cheap during the Depression. Built of granite from the Trescowen quarry, it provided comfortable rooms and a couple of bathrooms for up to a dozen visitors in the season, and made a good income for him. At three guineas a week for bed, breakfast and evening meal, with easy access to the beach, it was priced high enough to attract a more exclusive class of visitors, middle-aged folk from the North who came back for the same fortnight every year and had no time (and, truth to tell, not money enough) for the flunkeys and flummery of such as the Headland hotel, and at the same time didn't want their holidays ruined by noisy children.

Emily opened the door to the Bay Hotel kitchens where she found Mrs Penton busy over the stoves brimming with eggs bacon sausages black pudding smoked haddock and kippers. Mrs Penton was stout, perspiring, red-faced, in mobcap and rather grubby long apron, and unsmiling. The "Mrs" was in fact a courtesy title: she was unmarried and had a daughter of about seventeen called Pat who helped in the kitchen.

'Good morning, Mrs Penton.'

'Morning, ma'am. Wasn't expecting you just yet.'

'No, but the Master wants Pat to help in the house for a little.'

'Well, she's needed here.'

'I think it best if you run along, Pat. I'll help out with the serving, and Janice can help Mrs Penton'

Mrs Penton pursed her lips but said nothing. She was a good cook but knew there were plenty of other good cooks who would be glad of her place and didn't have the drawback of a daughter to find a room for.

Pat was plump and round-faced, but unlike her mother, seemed quite a jolly and carefree girl. Rumour had it that she had been out, as was euphemistically said, with several of the local lads, including Tom and Terence Samson. Emily wondered whether she ought to tell Pat about Terence.

'That's bad news, ma'am. About the Samson lad,' said Mrs Penton.

Pat obviously knew and looked sad, but not tearful, and went off to see to Mr Jorret, glad no doubt to be away from her mother.

'I know, Mrs Penton. Such a waste.' And no more was said about that.

Emily tried to put on a bright smile with the visitors as she took them their enormous platefuls of breakfast. They all knew her, calling her Emily, asking after her grandfather and passing cheerily patronising comments. They assumed she was always eager to see them, implying a close friendship and often offering her advice as to how she should conduct her life.

Then another fifty weeks would pass during which they would forget her completely.

(The wife) 'Did you know him, the young man who was drowned?'

'Yes. He was a friend of my brother's.'

(The man) 'Don't think we've had the pleasure of meeting your brother but do pass on our deepest sympathy.'

'Thankyou. Would you like some more coffee?'

(The wife) 'Oh yes please if it's no trouble. You look tired, dear; you shouldn't take on so much, you know.'

(The man jokingly) 'Must have her keeping fit, eh? Else we'll have to give a hand with the washing up. No, seriously, Emily, you shouldn't let old Jorret put too much on you, you know. We've both seen it, haven't we, Lil? Don't think he realises.'

'Mr Jorret has had to work very hard all his life. Anyway, I'll get the coffee.'

She could hear them discussing her in low tones as she went through the swing doors with the coffee pot. She caught the word *slave-driver,* followed by a loud *Shush* from her. But they didn't matter: as the old man so often said, 'summer visitors keep the bread in our mouths'.

As she refilled the coffee pot, Emily determined to take a couple of hours off and talk with Tom when he got back from work. She knew where she'd find him.

* * *

Tom Jorret had some work to finish off on the ornamental gateway to the Cornish Hotel in Newmin. The others had knocked off promptly at half-past five, but he hated to leave his work unfinished and worked his own hours.

He didn't think much of the design, far too ornate for this hotel and, although he didn't use the word, pretentious, with a stepped wall leading to decorated stone pillars surmounted by huge round balls. But it wasn't his business; he just did the work as well as he could, which was very well indeed.

Tom was a big man, not tall, five-foot-nine at the most, but typically Cornish in being built with huge shoulders and round body. At 27 he was muscular rather than fat, though no doubt, like all the male Jorrets, he would put on weight as he got older.

Tom's face was red, becoming weather-beaten, round and a little podgy. His short gingery hair was kept carefully clean and brushed. He was by no means a handsome man, but everyone when they met him would say the same thing, how *nice*-looking he was. His blue-grey eyes (beneath ginger brows already thickening) were kind and friendly if he liked you, and placid if he did not. It was an honest face, the face of a contented man who enjoyed life in a calm and measured way.

He was always neat and crisply clean. Even in his work cutting and shaping stone, he would keep his hands with their short stubby fingers carefully manicured, protected by gloves he would constantly discard and replace. 'My hands are my living', he would say. He habitually wore a blue cotton sun-hat and blue bib-and-brace overalls that he changed and washed whenever they collected dirt. His boots he cleaned and polished every evening; his tools, of the highest quality, he would care for immaculately.

Tom smoothed off a rough edge on the pedestal, stood back and with a grunt of satisfaction, wiped off his trowel and collected his tools. He stowed them carefully in a large leather pannier that he strapped to the back of his motorbike.

It took him very little time to cross the Crannel and get back to the farm: he always drove his bike far too fast. He locked up the bike and tools in his workshop with double padlocks, but instead of crossing to the Gustory Farmhouse where he lived with his parents, he walked briskly over the fields to a coastal path. He scrambled down to the beach and moved nimbly from rock to rock along the shoreline - despite his build he was remarkably light on his feet - until he reached a secluded promontory with the sea pounding the rocks below him.

He lay down on his back, his head pillowed on his rolled-up boiler-suit and stared into the almost cloudless evening sky. Far overhead a skylark climbed and climbed pouring out its song, and it was there that Emily found him.

Chapter 2

June 1939

Bob Jorret took his watch from his waistcoat pocket. 'Tom's late,' he said.

'Expect he's out with one of his lady-friends,' said Daisy sourly. Daisy was one of the female victims of the war; her "young man" had come back crippled by gas and had died (mercifully) in 1922. Since then she had had only one interest in life, the Jersey dairy herd in Gustory Farm. She didn't much like Tom, as he didn't help on the farm. Besides, he was alive; her fellow had been in his grave these 17 years.

'He hasn't been back to change,' said Annie, Daisy's sister-in-law, who *was* happily married, or at least contentedly married, to Bob (who had survived the war, having been a sergeant in the Service Corps). 'I'll just put his supper in the stove.'

Annie and Bob Jorret were both fifty-five, and they managed Peter Jorret's farm with Daisy, who was a year or two younger. It was proving too much for them, what with Emily always working (in the season at least) at the Bay Hotel, and Tom having years ago flatly refused to work for his grandfather.

When Tom left school at fourteen, everyone assumed he would work on the farm, not least as Peter Jorret had just acquired twenty of Samson's milkers and the herd was much more than Daisy could manage on her own. (The cows had to be brought through the village every time for milking, and then it needed extra help to get the churns on the platform for the lorry to collect.) The war had left the village short of younger men, like everywhere else, and Tom was already strong and well-built and fit for the heavy work. Besides, they had all been used to him helping out on the farm when not at school.

'There you are now, boy,' his grandfather had said. 'I'll find you a wage, won't be much to start with, but work hard and we'll see.' Peter Jorret paused to fill his pipe with shag tobacco. 'Who knows, one day when I've gone on, the farm might be yours. What d'you say?'

Jorret leant back in his rocking chair with a quiet smile of satisfaction on his face. Things would go the way he wanted them. The Jorrets had been here for generations, but he, Peter Jorret, had started off with nothing. Now the Jorret farm stretched all the way from the village to halfway up Pentire, and then there was the Hotel too. All done by guts and hard work and letting no-one stand in his way for long. Son Bob was not up to much, no spark, not like his brother Steve would have been, but young Tom…

'No, I don't think so,' said Tom.

'What? What did you say?' Jorret stopped in the act of lighting his pipe so that the match burnt down to his fingers. He flung the spent match angrily into the grate.

'No. I'm not going to farm,' Tom said steadily.

Jorret's face flushed with anger. 'You bloody well are, my lad! You'll do as you're told, or else you'll suffer for it!'

Tom made no reply.

Well?'

'I'm going to be a mason. Stonemason. Apprenticed to

Mr Henbury.'

'Mason? Who said? No-one said anything about mason to me. I'll see your father about that, and we'll soon stop that.'

'Ma's agreed. She arranged it with Mr Henbury.'

'Oh, so, *she's* behind it, is she? And who's goin' to pay for all this, tools and that, eh? I'm not goin' to pay I can tell you.'

'Ma's going to buy the tools off old Solly when he gives up. Solly's going to teach me, then give up. He's seventy.'

'So it's she been puttin' daft ideas in your head. Always against me, ever since she wed you're your father.'

Tom shrugged. He was never rude, but even at fourteen, just stuck to his guns. 'My craft teacher at school said. He said I'd got a talent for handlin' stone, and there's always jobs in the trade.'

And that was that. Peter Jorret was not used to being crossed (as he put it) by his family, except by Annie, and ever since then, Peter Jorret had said that Tom was an idle layabout, and Tom couldn't expect anything from *him* when he'd gone on.

* * *

Old Jorret was right in one sense: Tom was literally a layabout as he lay out on his secluded green bank. There, protected by the rocky shore, he would dream and watch the soaring skylark.

Emily at last came up to him, out of breath. She had to go across the fields and find the way through briar hedges to get to him, and it took her nearly half an hour.

'Sorry, Tom, disturbing you -'

'No. That's all right, Emmy. Sit down here. You look puffed.'

Tom leant up on his elbow and grinned affectionately at his sister. She had always stood up for him with their grandfather, even if she hadn't stood up for herself, and she and Tom loved each other dearly.

She sat down and clasped her hands about her knees.

'Tom, did you hear about Terry, Terry Samson?'

'Yes.' Tom's face was expressionless.

'Oh, why did he do it?' Tears welled up again and Emily wiped them away with the back of her hand.

'Fond of him, were you, Emmy?'

'I think all the girls were, a bit.'

Girls, thought Tom. Here's poor Emmy, thirty years old, heard nothing from her husband for years and worn to a frazzle by that old sod of a grandfather, and still thinks herself as *girls*.

'Yes. I suppose so.'

'Tom -' She hesitated, trying to find the words. 'D'you think he did it - *deliberately*?'

Tom sat for a time without reply. Then he got to his feet and gave her his hand to help her up.

'Come along here.' Tom led her to the edge of the clearing where they could look down on the black rocks encrusted with mussels. The weather was by no means rough, but the waves rolling up against some isolated outlying rocks washed them with a white spray.

'The high tide will flood all that to two or three feet.' He indicated a narrow stretch of sand leading to a series of inlets. 'Those caves there were smugglers' holes where they used to stash away the rum and all that. There was never any trace of them, the smugglers, no footprints or anything, only for a couple of hours at the most. So they rowed in the stuff just before the tide flooded the caves, then moved it out when the coast was clear, sometimes days later, see? But once they timed it wrong, and the customs men found three bodies close to a mile away up the coast. They'd been trapped in the cave, then washed out to sea when the tide turned.'

'But how'd they know, the customs, that the bodies came from here?' asked Emily. She peered down over the cliff, and she could see how the tide was already running along the shore.

'They didn't. They couldn't make it out. The men weren't just swimmers, they had all their clothes on, and knives and things. They weren't local lads either, from Redruth or somewhere, one of the towns where they could sell the stuff.'

'You mean, that local lads, like you - and Terry - knew?'

'Me? No. It was just after the war. Terry's dad told him, and we worked it out when we were crabbing along there.' Tom fell silent for a moment. 'Terry and me, we know - knew -all the crab holes. You've got to watch the tides when getting the crabs. And the undertow.'

'But if Terry knew - if he knew about the tides and that - why did -?'

For once the mask slipped and Tom turned on her fiercely, almost savagely.

'*I don't know, Emmy! I don't know!*' He quickly calmed down and patted her arm consolingly. 'Sorry, Emmy. Look: I must be getting back. So must you. The old bugger will be sending out the dogs.'

'You mustn't talk like that, Tom!' But she laughed nonetheless. She kissed him lightly on the cheek and set off across the fields.

He looked after her for a moment and waved as she looked back. He scrambled down over the rocks, skipping light-footed, despite his bulk, down to the shore and climbed the opposite cliff just as the water began to lap about his feet.

* * *

'The boy's still not back, then?' Bob Jorret was a mild-mannered man, no spark, as Peter Jorret contemptuously used to say, but he hated any disturbance to his routine. Supper was at half- past six, and not (he consulted his watch again) a quarter to nine.

Annie was drawing the curtains, even though it was still quite light.

'He's in his workshop,' she said. 'He's lit the lamp: you can see it from here. Expect he has some bits to finish off.'

Bob put down his paper and heaved himself from his rocking chair. 'I'd best go see what he's about. His supper's in the stove.'

'I wish you wouldn't fuss so,' said Annie, but Bob laboriously laced up his boots again and trudged off down the path.

Annie heard his boots crunching back up a few minutes later.

Well, I don't know. He's there fiddling with a bit o' wood. Says he's nearly done, then he'll be along for his supper. I told him it'll all dry up if he don't look sharp.'

Annie shrugged. 'He's twenty-seven, Bob, not seven. Don't fuss so.'

Tom got up from the bench with a grunt of satisfaction. He held up the piece of wood to study it by the light of his workshop window. It was a piece of flotsam, bleached white by the sea, carefully cut into the shape of a tablet about the size of a large exercise book.

He took the tablet back to the bench and pared down the top of the tablet so that the hard edge was completely smoothed off, and then fixed a small wire bracket to each side.

He then took the finest of his tools and scored faint lines on the surface, and with great patience carved an inscription:

In Memory of
TERRY SAMSON
1915-39

He stowed the plaque carefully into a canvas satchel he used for fishing, turned down the lamp and blew it out, shut the door and padlocked it, and strode up the path to the farmhouse for his supper.

Chapter 3

It was barely light when Tom got up the next morning.

He switched off the alarm clock before it rang: he normally did not need an alarm clock, but he wanted to make doubly sure that he woke and was ready in good time.

He took his bathing suit from the bottom drawer of the chest and put it on. It was new that year: it was of blue non-absorbent wool and covered his rather tubby body to just above the knees and just above the elbows.

Next he took the wooden plaque he had made the night before and threaded the white belt of his bathing-suit through the small wire brackets. He buckled on the belt so that the plaque was tied reasonably comfortably to his back with the smoothed-off edge uppermost.

Then he strapped his most treasured possession to his wrist: a Royal Navy waterproof watch with a large luminous dial.

He packed his underclothes, spare socks and a towel, two large pasties and a bottle of cider into his canvas bag. He put on a clean working shirt and trousers, boiler suit and a pair of tennis shoes, and as he stole out through the kitchen and left a note for them on the table.

* * *

It was light enough for him to follow paths a quarter of a mile to the west of the clearing where he always watched the skylarks. He stowed his canvas bag and his clothes into a niche in the rocks out of reach of the high tide, and, now only in bathing-suit and tennis shoes, scrambled back across the rocks to a point already being lapped by the spring-tide.

He sat there for fourteen minutes, consulting his watch in what seemed an endless wait, and then slipped into the sea. He at once settled into his stroke; it was almost leisurely in its rhythm, at once graceful and powerful. To his relief the plaque strapped to his back did not impede him; rather, it seemed to add to his buoyancy.

He made not straight for Gull Rock but for the mouth of the Crannel estuary; he knew how treacherous the Crannel currents could be. Only the other week, he had been out in the boat with Terry Samson to look for the shoals of pilchards, and it had taken all their efforts to pull the boat back to the river before it was dashed against the rocks along Pentire bank.

Tom had taken Terry out in the boat to try to cheer him up. He, Tom, had no interest in his grandfather's vendetta against the Samsons; as far as he was concerned, Terry was a friend of his and that was all there was to it.

Terry Samson had still been at school when his father had lost his farm, caught by the Depression owing a great deal of money on farm machinery. Backed by his wife's (Tom's grandmother's) money, Peter Jorret had moved in quickly, paid off all Samson's debts, then foreclosed on their farmhouse, leaving them with nowhere to go.

'Never understood why your grandfather had it in for us so much,' Terry had said as they rowed out of the bay. 'Wouldn't even let us rent the house, so my dad said.'

'It's a long story,' said Tom evasively. He watched his

friend's morose face as Terry pulled half-heartedly on the oars. Can understand him being depressed, Tom thought, no farm, living in that hut out on Pentire. But then he never tries at anything. Nicest chap, wouldn't hurt a fly. Good at soccer and swimming, good-looking, he supposed, the girls seem to like him a lot anyway, but he won't try at anything. Drifts from job to job ever since he left school.

'So how's the job, then?' But Tom knew: Terry was working at the garage but was just on the petrol pumps and blowing up tyres and washing the cars. Couldn't be bothered to learn the mechanics of it, too careless, so Freddie the garage owner said. Can't risk him getting things wrong in this business.

'All right. Freddie thinks I sh'd learn a bit about the engines but doesn't seem to want to let me have a go.'

'Better pull harder on the right, Terry. These currents 'll take us over too far.' Tom had thought of taking Terry on as his mate in the stone yard, and had even asked Mr Henbury about it, but he had just said it was up to Tom, and he, Tom, could see how he got on, and if Terry worked well he could have his wages every week. Tom had done nothing about it; he just wanted to do his own work as well as possible in his own time, and didn't really want the bother of someone always asking him what to do and, worse, not caring if he got it wrong.

Terry was still brooding about his father and Peter Jorret. 'Why did Mr Jorret chuck us out like that? They say it killed my dad.' (Mr Samson had died of a heart attack less than a year after.)

'Well, it was a kind of revenge, I suppose,' Tom said, and immediately cursed himself for having said it.

'Revenge?' Terry was so surprised that he stopped rowing and the boat immediately began to wheel about in the cross current. 'What d'you mean, revenge?'

'Not on you,' said Tom hastily. 'On the family, really. My grandfather is mad about *family*. I sometimes wonder if it's the only thing he thinks about: he has made the Jorrets the top family in these parts, so he says, and he started from nothing. We hear it all the time.'

'So what?'

Tom hesitated. 'Well the story goes that *your* grandfather really hated mine. Years ago, when they were both boys they used to fight all the time. Then the Samsons had the big farm and more or less ran the village and my grandfather was just a farm labourer, there wasn't any other work in those days, the eighteen eighties I suppose.'

He looked back over his shoulder. 'Look, let's pull over to those rocks and the current will take us in. Get ready to fend us off though. Don't want to damage my boat.'

Tom edged himself to the stern of the boat and used an oar as a rudder to steer into one of the coves on Gull Rock. Terry scrambled out and secured the boat.

The cove gave them some shelter and Tom took out his tin and filled his pipe, shielding the match expertly from the wind, and for a time they sat and watched the gulls screaming and wheeling about the Rock.

'Go on,' said Terry.

'What?'

'About grandfather.'

Tom took some time poking at his pipe with a dead match before replying. 'Not much to tell, really. Except that old man Samson was really hard. Knew that his men couldn't get any other work. Expected them to work whatever hours he wanted, and hardly paid them anything. Grandfather said he had fifteen-and-thruppence a week, and no time off except Christmas Day and Easter.'

'I suppose it was like that then.'

Tom re-lit his pipe. 'The worst was one Boxing Day. There was this plough-land out Pentire, and you know the wind there. Well, it was too cold to snow, my grandfather said, and he had to go out first thing. Can you imagine, out there at first light, *Boxing* Day? Then the afternoon the ploughshare broke and he had to come back, told the boss and thought that was that. Oh no: he had to take a new share out there again and there was a blizzard came up and my grandfather nearly died of cold. He never forgot it, and swore he'd have his revenge one day.'

'Why'd he go? I wouldn't have.'

'There was plenty of others were ready to have my grandfather's job in those days.'

Terry was showered with the spray as a larger wave broke over the rock. He wiped the specks of foam from his brow with a grubby handkerchief.

'It's all about money and jobs, isn't it?' he said bitterly. 'It's all right for you, you just keep - well, you've got all you want, motor-bike an' that, and I suppose you'll get our farm when old Jorret dies -'

'I don't know. I don't suppose so. I keep out of it. Always have.'

'Yeah. Keep out of it. You can afford to.' Terry angrily hurled a pebble into the sea. 'You can do what you like, you can chuck your job in any time you want an' go back to the farm. I have to do petrol pumps.'

'No. I like doing the job. No-one interferes with me, and I don't interfere with anyone else. I just do it.' Like the skylark, Tom said to himself: doing one thing as well as he possibly could. Nothing to do with anyone else, even other skylarks. He laughed out loud at the thought.

'What? What are you grinning about?'

'Sorry. I just had a thought. Thought I was a skylark.'

Even Terry laughed at that. 'Don't think you'd get very high.'

I don't know, thought Tom. 'I'll keep working at it.'

It was then that Terry said that one day he was going to swim out to Gull Rock and show everyone. Tom said that it wasn't worth it; several people had drowned trying it. It could only be done with very careful planning.

'You'd need to get the tides just right, and use the Crannel stream,' he added.

'I know all about that. There's no need for you to tell me. You think I can't do it. Everyone says I haven't the guts to stick at anything. Oh yes, they do, Tom; you think that too. No good denying it. Well, I have, and I'll do it, and then perhaps -'

'Perhaps what?'

'Nothing.'

'Well, I warned you. It's not just guts, Terry, it takes a helluver lot of working out.' Terry merely shrugged. 'Better be getting back, I suppose.'

They scrambled into the boat and rowed back down the Crannel estuary.

* * *

That was ten or so days before, and Tom had thought no more of it. Terry would get these ideas and never follow them up. Besides, it was no business of Tom's to tell people what they should or shouldn't do.

The cross-current that he had feared began to drag him to the mouth of the Crannel and out to sea. He had to concentrate: he had allowed his mind to wander as he pulled himself mechanically through waves that were already getting more choppy. Now it was a question of strength rather than just rhythm: he had to fix on a point on the rock to aim at and stick to his course.

But it would be no disgrace to turn back; no-one even knew he was attempting it. Why *was* he doing it anyway? He had no idea. He was not one for always trying to work out why people do things. He kept it simple. He didn't keep worrying about himself, or other people for that matter: let them sort out their own problems.

He was caught by a sudden surging wave which almost drove him backwards. He stayed calm: no point in fighting it. It was probably the seventh - he stuck to the view that every seventh wave was stronger - and the undertow would draw him back. Even so, his left shoulder-muscles, so used to holding the board for the mortar, were aching painfully at their unaccustomed strain. But keep going: soon be able to have that ten minutes rest on the rock.

In fact, by the time he got there, he calculated by his watch that he had only about eight- and-a half minutes before he had to begin the swim back. He was already very tired and lay flat on his back on a tiny stretch of sand, allowing the water to lap around his feet, only to feel the wooden plaque biting into his shoulder blades. Cursing, he untied it and looked about for somewhere to plant it higher up the rock. It took him nearly five minutes to clamber up painfully in his icy sea- soaked feet to a niche out of the reach of the neap tides where he could secure the memorial tablet.

He sat on the sand for an extra few minutes after all. The tide was turning; He had to take every advantage of that still phase before the tide was in full swell. All he had to do was to prevent the surge carrying him into one of the deadly coves where he was convinced Terry had met his end. *All* he had to do; he allowed himself a wry smile as he waded out and thought of the hour and twenty minutes that lay before him.

As he struck out with the same leisurely, rhythmic stroke, he thought of the time when his father had first taken him out to learn about the tides. Tom had been about ten or eleven; he was already a strong and practiced swimmer for his age, but Bob Jorret had always been insistent that Tom would never swim far out unsupervised. Tom had disobeyed him once, and been caught in the undertow, and it was the only occasion when his father had been so angry that he had taken him out to the shed and beaten him.

Those were the days when Bob was still lively, eager and fun, before he had been worn down by unremitting work on the farm and by the merciless demands of old Peter Jorret for greater and greater profit. Those were the days when he had taught Tom where all the crab holes were, and how to make the crab hooks, and how to help with the villagers with the drag netting, how to fish for the sea trout, how to shoot the rabbits for the pot. Together they had watched the stonechats in the thickets and the gulls swooping and wheeling and screaming around the cliff edges. They had trudged together along the coast to catch sight of the choughs and the cormorants. Together they had built the Cornish stone hedges round the farm fields and it was Bob (and Annie) who had scorned the common toys at Christmas and had bought Tom his first trowels and chisels instead.

His father was a different person then, thought Tom. Wonder if everyone changes like that: now all he does is slump in his chair with the paper before Annie wakes him for his supper. Annie doesn't change though: she's always been the same, always stuck to her own way of doing things, what she thinks best for everyone.

Tom suddenly realised that the tide was carrying him

near a dangerous rocky part of the shore, the place where swimmers could be fatally trapped. 'Always remember,' Bob had told him again and again, 'The tides go along the beach, not in and out from it.' He struck further out to sea to allow the tide to sweep him further up the coast to where, with luck, it would carry him to the Crow promontory.

Tom had hoped to come ashore on a more comfortable strand, but he was grateful enough at last to clamber onto the Crow rocks. The sharp edges and the mussels hurt his bare feet, but there was nothing for it but to scramble as best he could across the rocks to where he had left his things.

The morning sun was already hot and began to dry out his sodden skin, and Tom barely ate half a pasty before he fell into an exhausted sleep.

Chapter 4

Old Peter Jorret drove up to the farmhouse door in his Morris Cowley just as Daisy was coming in from milking. He gave her a curt nod as his only greeting.

'Where that blasted Tom got to then?'

'How sould I know, Pa? I've jus' been with the cows, ain't I? No-one's seen him all day.'

She went on round to the back door in her boots.

Jorret did not wait to knock but went straight through to the scullery.

'Do come in, father, please,' said Annie heavily.

'Where's the lad got to, then? I've had Henbury up at the hotel asking after him.' 'Mr Henbury's in the front room with Bob now. He says its important.'

'Why? What's up then? Young Tom walked out on him then? Thought he would.' Annie could not be bothered to refute this.

'Tom's been out all day. He left a note.' 'Note? What note?'

'That he'd be out all day. He'd finished the last job, and would we tell Jimmy Henbury.' 'If he's not working, he c'd do my wall, couldn't he?'

'He said you wouldn't fix a price for it.'

'Price? Price? For his own flesh and blood? Price for his own family? We'll fix a price for him when I've gone on, I can tell you.'

The old man scowled at her, but as Annie merely shrugged and made no reply as he ostentatiously fidgeted with his watch -chain.

'Can't wait all day.' Pause. He consulted his half-hunter "What's Henbury want anyway, that's so urgent?'

'I don't know. He's in there with Bob and Emily. You'd better ask him.' 'Emily? Emily? What the blazes she doin' here? She should be up the Hotel.'

'*I don't know.* Go and ask her.' She gave him a sweet false smile and went into the kitchen.

Jorret found them sitting round a cold tea tray. Bob grunted a greeting, took up the tray, and went out to the scullery.

'What are you doin' here?' he demanded of Emily in his usual fashion. "And what's this, Henbury? Followin' us round, are you?'

Jimmy Henbury was a small, wiry man, bald and bespectacled, about thirty-five or so. He looked more like a mild-mannered bank clerk than a jobbing builder. But his physical strength was famous in the local trade: they often told the tale of his lifting a steel joist off a man's leg trapped beneath it and holding it there until help came. It was said of him also that his appearance similarly belied his strength of character; he was a man of firm (if sometimes mistaken) opinions and was stubborn in keeping to them.

'On the contrary, Mr Jorret, you seem to be following me. I came here as I have important business with Tom and I asked Emily to come too.'

Jorret reddened with anger. 'My family! You don't interfere with my family without comin' to me first!'

'That's as may be. The fact is, Mr Jorret, there's a war coming, and we've all got to make new plans.'

'War? War? Who said there'd be a war? What's it to do

with Emily?'

Henbury assumed a look of mild surprise. 'I'm amazed Mr Chamberlain hasn't consulted you about it, Mr Jorret.'

Jorret merely snarled at him.

'No, seriously, Mr Jorret, the War Office are circulating lots of firms to stand by. It's no secret. So I'm getting some more men, fellows who are over the age for call-up.'

Jorret's mouth twisted into a grin. He jerked a thumb towards Emily. 'You must be desperate if you want *her* to be a bricky or somethin.''

'No, not a bricky.'

Emily cleared her throat nervously. 'Mr Henbury has asked me to do some secretarial work, keep the accounts and that.'

There was a silence while this sunk in.

'No. And that's final. She won't have time.'

'You don't quite understand, Mr Jorret,' said Henbury gently. 'I shall need her full-time.'

The old man was almost incoherent with rage. 'And you think I'd agree to that? And where d'you think she'll live? You'll have to pay me compensation for hiring some other woman. She's useless anyway, but she's family, an' we look after our own, even when that bloody Harris man wed her, bloody fool, an' he bunked off, we've had to look after her an' keep a roof over her head and feed her three meals a day an' you'll do all that, will you?'

Henbury removed his glasses and wiped them vigorously with his handkerchief. 'Mr Jorret,' he said, without raising his voice, 'I don't think you ought to speak of Emily in that way.'

He crossed to the tearful Emily and calmly put his arm about her shoulders. 'No, sir, it is quite clear from what you have said that Emily will be better working for Henbury and

Son as a full- time secretarial help. No doubt we can come to some arrangement as to finding a replacement, at least temporarily till the season's over, but as you think so little of her help at the Hotel, it should be all the better for you.'

They were saved from further outbursts from Jorret by the arrival of Tom.

He nodded to his grandfather, winked at Emily and slumped exhausted into the only vacant armchair. His normally ruddy round face was pale and drawn and his eyes were red with tiredness.

'What's all this then, Jimmy?' he asked.

Peter Jorret exploded in wrath. 'Where've you been? Everyone's been out lookin'. Never here when the family needs you. Emily says she's off with Henbury, somethin's goin' on there, no doubt, and you don't care a cuss.'

Henbury ignored him. 'I'd like a word, Tom. In private.' He turned back to Emily. 'It's all right, I'll see to it, Emily. Just want a word with Tom. If you don't mind, Mr Jorret?'

'Mind? I do mind, I can tell you. You come here and …' His voice trailed off as Henbury again removed his glasses and stared fixedly at him.

Emily seemed to catch some of Henbury's calm determined manner. She wiped her eyes and took the old man's arm. 'Come along, grandfather. We'll go and find some Scotch and I'll explain.'

Jorret looked up at her in surprise, but after a brief hesitation allowed himself to be led into the scullery.

'Now, Tom -' said Henbury when they were alone.

'Sorry I couldn't let you know sooner. Finished that hotel wall: rather daft, if you ask me, but I did what they wanted.'

'I know. Thanks. It wasn't that.'

'Needed some time, Jimmy. To myself.'

'I know. But - well, I've heard direct from the War Office,

and they're anxious about the defences up at St Mawgan; they're getting us and some others up there to extend the runways and build some gun emplacements.'

Tom whistled in surprise. 'They're sure there'll be a war, then? But isn't it all secret?'

'I don't know about that. But there's no point in keeping it secret, with dozens of builders up there.'

Tom pondered this for a moment. 'Where do I fit in? It's not my work, Jimmy. Anyone can mix a bit of concrete.'

'They want someone to read the plans. Someone they can trust. You'll have to sign something to keep your mouth shut.'

'You can do that, surely.'

'Yes, I shall. But I want two teams, and you'll have to take the other.'

Tom frowned. 'You know I don't like having anyone else when I'm working. No reason why they can't get it right without me. I'll do the fancy work if there is any.'

'Well, there won't be. Fancy work's finished: it'll be all war work from now on, you mark my words.'

'Can't think why you're so sure. About a war, I mean.'

'Then read the papers. They've played that Chamberlain man for a mug. The Air Force wouldn't be doing all that up Mawgan if they didn't think they'd need to. Anyway, Tom, you've no choice. Unless,' and Jimmy gave him a sly grin, 'you'd rather work under Jack Pender or someone?'

Jack Pender couldn't set one brick in line with the next, and so Henbury had put him in permanent charge of the cement mixer.

But Tom had fallen asleep.

'Then that's agreed, then,' said Jimmy softly, and left the room.

* * *

Emily let Tom sleep for an hour and then brought him a cup of tea and some saffron cake.

'You went out to the Rock, didn't you?' she said. 'Have they all gone?'

'Yes. Why?'

'Why what?'

'Why d'you swim out to the Rock? It was Terry, wasn't it?'

Tom held his head in his hands. 'I don't know, Emmy, and that's the truth. I just wonder if, well, if I could have stopped him.'

Emily put her arm round his shoulders. 'You can't take responsibility for it. People have to decide for themselves, even if they make mistakes. Like I did marrying John Harris.' 'Yes, but - mistake? When he drowns himself? I could at least have gone out with him, to make sure he did it right.'

'Have your tea. We'll talk about it later when you're not so tired.'

Tom sipped the tea, holding the mug in both hands, shivering a little. 'That's better,' he said at last. 'So...' He looked up at her, smiling. 'So you're leaving the old devil at last, eh? Good job too.'

'Jimmy says he'll find someone first. We think he ought to get a manager in and leave it to him to run. After all, he is seventy-five.'

'Pity the poor sod who takes that on, with him breathing down his neck all the time.' 'It'll all be different soon, Tom. Jimmy says there'll be another war.'

'I know. We've got to go and do some work on the airfield, Jimmy says.'

They both fell silent for a while with their own thoughts.

'I was thinking about Uncle Steve. I was eight. Grandfather

couldn't stop shouting about it. *My Steve's an officer,* he kept saying, *Told you! Better than the rest of you put together!*'

'Funny thing is, that everyone says that he was not like that at all,' said Tom. 'Uncle Steve just kidded everyone, tricked them all out of their money and that. I don't know, never knew him, so can't say. But that's what all the old ones say.'

'Grandfather worshipped him. Still does. Thinks that no-one comes up to scratch compared to Steve.' She paused. Her brow wrinkled in anxiety. 'You won't have to go, Tom? If there's a war, I mean. In the trenches? I couldn't bear that.'

Tom laughed. 'Don't think I could either, Emmy.' He took her hand. 'No, I've been thinking about it. If there *is* going to be a war one of the RAF chaps told me that I ought to sign on now, and you get some choice as to what you do and even sometimes where you get sent. Apparently once it's on the forms, they can't change it. I could go in the engineers or something, anyway not in the infantry like Uncle Steve, and get killed right away.'

'Oh, *Tom*! Suppose there isn't a war? And how d'you know they won't do just what they want when they've got you?'

'You forget I'm a skilled craftsman and they'll need that.' He sat for a moment in thought. 'Yes! Now I come to think of it, 'specially if I get to do some of those sites at Mawgan.'

Her brow wrinkled with anxiety. 'Anyway, where would you want to go, even if they let you?'

'Africa. I've always wanted to go to Africa.'

Emily laughed her high-pitched laugh. 'Africa! You are an ass, Tom! The Germans won't be fighting in Africa!

* * *

Tom set a fortnight aside to build a gun emplacement at the airfield.

He told the recruiting sergeant in Bodmin that he would not be available for another fortnight. He would sign on at the latest in the second week of August.

Chapter 5

They had set up a barrier at St Mawgan airfield and a sergeant in the RAF police stopped Tom as he drove up on his motorbike.

'Just got to check you off, sir, if you don't mind.' The sergeant was courteous, but firm, and there was a threatening-looking sentry behind him. 'Can't be too careful, you know, sir, in case, well, you know.'

He consulted his clipboard. 'What was the name again, sir?' 'Jorret. Tom Jorret.'

'Ah yes, Mr Jorret. You are to report to Major Johnson, sir, if you'd just sign here. I'll get a pass ready for you if you'd collect it when you go this evening.'

He pointed to a hut in the middle distance. 'You'll find the Major there, sir.' He looked enviously at Tom's motorbike. 'You can go on the bike, sir. That's a grand machine, that. I've got a BSA 500, but that's, well…'

Tom felt strangely nervous. No-one ever called him 'sir' and everything suddenly made him feel responsible and important.

A lanky soldier in grubby overalls was poring over some blueprints on a trestle table when Tom poked his head nervously round the door of the hut.

'Ah, you must be Tom Jorret. Johnson. George Johnson.' The Major held out a limp hand. 'Very glad you can help us here. Problems with all this sand.

Everything about George Johnson was long and thin: lanky thinning fair hair, long face, heavily lined, thin straight eyebrows, long thin nose. Keen eyes shone warmly at Tom through black-rimmed round spectacles.

'You know anything about guns, Tom?'

'Well, I do a bit of rough shooting, rabbits mostly, anything really, for the pot.'

'I really meant proper guns. Ack-ack guns. Artillery. No, of course not. Why should you? Perhaps you'd like to go on a course at Larkhill if we do all right here?'

'Well, er -' *What was he talking about? Course? Larkhill? How did he know about my skylarks? Not a hill anyway…*

'Well, we'll see how we get on, eh? Take a look at these plans here. Then we'll see the sites.' He glanced at his watch. 'Plenty of time now, then some lunch, so take your time.'

Tom studied the plans slowly and deliberately, muttering to himself, and once drawing in his breath sharply.

'What is it?'

'This one here, sir -'

'George. The name's George.'

'Well, this one will need a helluva windbreak.'

'What, trees? No time for that.'

Tom laughed. "It'll take you fifty years to get trees to grow there. No, you want a good Cornish hedge, nine feet high. You've seen them along the lanes.'

'It'll stand out from the air, Tom.'

Tom studied the map again. 'Well: why not run a track right the way along here' - he deftly pencilled in a double line on the map - 'and it'll be useful for your transport and act as a kind of cover.'

'Camouflage.' Johnson regarded Tom admiringly. He clapped Tom on the back. 'Just what I need. Let's go and look. We'll take your bike if you like. I'd enjoy that. I'll get it filled up for you later.'

Johnson put on an old greatcoat, stuffed the plans in a huge map case which he slung round his neck, and clambered onto the pillion as eager as a small boy.

* * *

It took them two and a half weeks (with overtime on Saturdays) to build the three emplacements.

George Johnson and Tom had taken to having supper and a beer at the Albion Inn a few miles from the site. Neither man was able to make light conversation, and they were often content to sit without a word.

George appreciated this, as although he was well enough liked in the Mess, he was not in any way convivial nor military, and was tolerantly regarded as an eccentric (as indeed he was).

His fellow officers could not understand why he had ever considered an army career. But he explained to Tom one evening that he had taken it up on a sudden rare impulse after an unhappy love affair.

'Not really an affair, Tom. No: just the opposite. She just wasn't interested and made it pretty clear.'

Tom regarded him with sympathy. It was unlikely that this vague and, frankly, rather shambolic figure would prove attractive to the opposite sex. He, Tom, had never bothered about it. If a girl had been happy to go out with him, then that was fine; if not, it didn't matter. Sometimes a girl would get serious and drop hints about marriage and he had to quietly but gently let her down. Only once had one girl persisted and refused to let go, and he had hit on the idea of taking her to tea with his grandfather, which he knew would be a disaster, and he had heard no more from her.

He jerked his attention back to George, who for once had had too much to drink and was telling him how he had some talent for maths at his Grammar School and had gone on to get an engineering degree in London. He was a bit lucky, he said, being just too young to miss the War. Then when he had had his "romantic set-back", as he called it, they had welcomed him in the Royal Artillery and, he said with a wry smile, 'they weren't so fussy about polishing boots and so on - bad enough, but not like an infantry officer - and I scraped through somehow.'

'D'you know,' he went on, 'in the army, it don't pay to be a specialist. You don't want to be too good at your job, or people can't spare you and keep you where you are. The regiments don't mind if the ordinary bloke gets moved away and promoted; it's the chaps who are really good at their job they want to keep.'

Tom said: 'But you're a specialist?'

George tapped out his pipe in the ashtray. 'That's why I'll never make General. But it'sdifferent in the Gunners. You're needed all over the place. And once the War Office get the idea you might be good at something - in my case, gun emplacements - they keep calling you in and sending you off to different places.

'D'you want another beer?' said Tom.

'Yes. One for the road.' George looked up at him earnestly as Tom brought the beer back to the table. 'Now look, Tom. I've got something important to say.' His speech was getting a little slurred. He peered at Tom myopically through his glasses.

'I expect it'll keep to Monday.'

'No, no, Tom. I've got something to say.'

Tom was getting impatient. He'd had enough himself and

had to get the bike back. 'Well?'

'It's this.' George took a deep breath. 'How'd you like a job with me? In Smalliland.'

'Smalliland?'

'SO mali-land.'

'Where's that?

'British So-maliland. Don't say you don't know where that is.'

'No.'

'Africa. Top right hand corner. Well, not top, really. More than halfway up. On the East coast. The Indian Ocean,' said George, with an air of triumph.

Tom pondered this somewhat fuzzily; his speech was beginning to get a little slurred too. 'D'you know, George,' - the name at last came easily to him - 'I've always wanted to go to Africa. Lions and giraffes, you know, and all the rare birds. Where the skylarks go to.'

'Skylarks? Don't quite follow you, old man. Don't know about skylarks. Nor giraffes. Maybe some lions. Camels, certainly. Lots of camels. Anyway, better talk on Monday when you're thinking clearer.'

With which George drained his glass, clapped Tom on the shoulder and lurched out to his car, a rather ridiculous Austin Seven in which he had taken out the driving seat and drove the car from the back seat.

Tom sat for a while trying to sort out what George could have meant. Finally, he shrugged, waved to the landlord and steered the bike carefully home.

* * *

Drizzling rain deterred Tom from taking his usual walk along the shore on Sunday morning. Instead he walked up from the farm to the hotel, where Emily was, as ever, delighted to see him.

'Give me your wet things.' She draped them over the clothes rack and hoisted it up. 'Like some bacon and eggs?'

'That would suit me fine. Emmy, I've something to tell -'

'Would you care for some tea or coffee?' Emily had slipped automatically into her waitress mode.

Tom grinned. 'Tea, miss, when you've a moment. No, Emmy, sit down for a moment. It's important.'

'I know. Jimmy told me yesterday that she wants to come. How did you know? We haven't told him yet,' she added, jerking her thumb towards the ceiling. 'He always has a lie-in on Sundays.' She sighed. 'He says it's his day of rest. Wish he'd make it all day instead of just a couple of hours.'

'Never mind that. What d'you mean, she wants to come?'

'Why, Jimmy's found someone. Manageress. Forty-ish. Used to run a place in Penzance, but couldn't stand the winters there with no-one about. Good isn't it? Anyway, what about you, Tom? Not joined up, I hope?'

'No. That is, I don't know. I may be getting a job in Somaliland. D'you know where that is?'

'Never heard of it.'

Tom went through to the guests' lounge where they kept a stock of books, mostly green paperback Penguin crime novels and sets of Georgette Heyer and other romantic writers. Some of Emily's old schoolbooks had somehow found their way onto the shelves.

Tom came back with Emily's old blue Philips atlas, with the vast expanses of the British Empire marked out in a startling red. He pointed to a red fist-shaped wedge of territory between the French and the Italian Somaliland.

'Can't think why you want to be going *there*,' said Emily.

Tom laughed. 'I won't be. It's just that Major Johnson's

got to go out there for some reason. But you never know… Anyway, how's the old man taking the idea of a new manageress?'

Emily took off her glasses and polished them on her apron. 'The odd thing is, Tom, he's quite smitten. Says how good it'll be to have someone smart and efficient instead of well, me, I suppose. He keeps saying how difficult it'll be to find the money, but he'll just have to find it somehow. Old skinflint.'

'Who's the skinflint, miss?'

Old Jorret had come down to the kitchen in his threadbare dressing-gown and carpet slippers. 'You'll see skinflint, miss, when I've gone on, I can tell you. What're *you* doin' here?' he demanded, turning on Tom.

'Hello, Grandfather. Just wanted a word with Emmy.'

'An' eatin' my breakfast, I see. That's a bob for that lot: you make sure he pays up, Emily. After all, 'e's goin' to charge me for the wall, ain't he?'

'I'll do the wall: you pay for the stone, and I'll get a friend to help me for nothing.'

'For nothing, eh? I'll believe it when I see it.'

'I'll order the stone and send the bill to you,' said Tom wearily. 'We'll do it as soon as you've paid the yard.'

Jorret shrugged and grunted.

'I take that as "yes and thank-you-very-much"?' asked Tom.

The old man managed a grimacing smile. 'Yes and thank you very much,' he growled. 'That is, if you do it.'

* * *

Tom got them to drop off some stone on the way to the airfield. George was eager (as in everything) to learn a new skill, and they worked at Jorret's hedge in the long summer evenings.

'Like a three-dimensional jigsaw,' said George tapping the last stones into place as Tom looked on approvingly.

'This hedge'll be here long after we've gone,' said Tom philosophically. 'We'll plant some St John's Wort and some fuchsias in the in-filling, and it'll soon be sprouting all kinds of things, you see. Let's see what the old man thinks of it.'

Peter Jorret was delighted but did his best not to show it. He was far more enthusiastic about the hedge having been built by an officer.

'My son Steve was an officer, you know, Major. Tom's uncle Steve. He would have gone on to be a Major too, they all said, but he got killed. 1917. Terrible loss that was for us. Would have taken over.'

'I'm very sorry to hear that, sir,' said George. 'So many wasted lives, so many young fellows.'

Peter Jorret pretended to peer intently at the stonework.

'We'll go and see what my granddaughter has for our supper, Major,' he said at last. 'An' some cider, eh? You too, Tom.'

Chapter 6

On the following Tuesday (18th July) Tom received a letter by the early post.

CONFIDENTIAL

Royal Artillery (Gunnery Emplacement Division)
The War Office
Whitehall
W1

Thomas J. Jorret Esq,
Gustory Farm
Newmin
Cornwall.

Dear Sir,

I am directed by the Principal and Board of the a/n Division to request your attendance for interview for the post of Assistant Construction Engineer (Emplacements) on Friday next 21st inst., at 2.45 pm.

I enclose a warrant for the first-class return rail fare from Newmin to Paddington (GWR) and you are requested to submit an account of further expenditures (luncheon, taxi fares, etc.) on conclusion of the interview.

I would be further obliged if you would complete the enclosed form and remit it to this office in the envelope provided by return post to indicate your intention to attend. In the event that you are unable to attend, I request that you enclose the rail warrant with your reply.

I am, Sir,

Your Humble and Obedient Servant,

JRM Wilkinson, CMG, MA, Deputy Under-Secretary.

'Goodness, Tom, that all looks mighty important,' said Annie.

'Got to go to London Friday. Leastways, that's what it looks like,' said Tom. "You look, Ma. And pass the marmalade.'

Annie took the letter and studied it at length.

'Goodness, Tom,' she said again before handing it to her husband. 'Well, I never!' she added.

'*Humble and Obedient Servant*, eh, Tom? You takin' on a butler, then?' said his father. 'What the blazes it all mean, lad?'

'I don't know. I'll ask George.' Tom tucked the letter into the pocket of his boiler suit. 'I'd better be off. I expect George'll know. 'Bye, Ma.'

Bob and Annie waited until they heard the motorbike roaring off.

'*Assistant Construction Engineer*!' exclaimed Bob.

'Well I never!' said Annie.

* * *

'Luncheon? Taxis? War Office?' demanded Tom.

'Don't worry. We'll be finished here by then and I'll be travelling up with you. I told you you'd have a chance to go to Somaliland with me.'

'Did you say that? You said something about Somaliland but - '

'Look, Tom, you're just the chap I need, and I told them so. Wilkinson's a silly little fart, to put it kindly, and insisted on an interview to see you're not tapping out messages to the Germans. You will have to go to Larkhill for a few weeks and I'll take some leave, then, off to Africa!'

'What's Larkhill?'

'Artillery place. Salisbury Plain. Learn about the guns.'

'Well I'm damned!' said Tom.

* * *

Tom put on the black suit he wore for funerals and Annie bought him a new shirt, tie and shoes in Truro. Despite his heavy build, he wore his clothes well and looked almost elegant, unlike George.

Major Johnson had put on uniform, which for most soldiers give them an air of smartness and efficiency. The leatherwork and brasses of his Sam Brown were well enough polished, his cap was new, and his trousers and tunic well pressed. But the clothes hung on him; they puckered around the shoulders, and they gave the appearance of somehow being draped over his long thin figure, fitting only where they touched.

The clerk in the ticket office regarded Tom with astonishment. 'You *sure*, Tom, you s'posed to 'ave a first-class?'

'That's what it says.'

'What if I gives you a second?'

'Give me what it says and shut up, Sid.'

It was quickly rumoured around Newmin that Tom Jorret had (a) come into money, (b) that he considered himself too good for the likes of us and (c) he now only went about with his Lunnen friends.

JRM Wilkinson's attitude was very different. Of medium height and slender build, immaculately groomed in morning coat and pin-stripe trousers, his hair neatly brushed over his ears with the regulation touch of grey, Wilkinson had sharp little eyes behind black circular-framed lenses which darted up and down disdainfully at Tom's Marks-and-Spencer's clothes. He carried a file bound in red tape.

'This way, if you please, gentlemen.'

He led them through carpeted corridors hung with nineteenth century portraits and eighteenth century landscapes and indicated to Tom to take a seat opposite the imposing doors of the interview anteroom.

'We are just a little ahead of time,' he said.

He gestured to George to accompany him, opened the double doors and ushered him through. Tom caught a glimpse of a long mahogany table at the end of the parquet-floored room.

If Wilkinson had hoped with all this to make Tom as nervous as possible, he quite failed. Tom sat placidly admiring the craftsmanship of the eighteenth century plaster mouldings. He had given no thought to the prospect of the War Office post, as he had no idea of what it entailed nor what he would be paid for it. He was quite content to take it or leave it.

A young official appeared from nowhere at precisely 2.45, carefully opened the double doors, announced Tom, and withdrew.

Tom took a chair facing three people at the table. Wilkinson sat importantly in the middle with a stern-faced lady secretary on his left and a Royal Artillery Lt.-Colonel on his right.

'Colonel Hope, Mr Jorret.' The Colonel leaned over the table to shake Tom's hand. 'Very pleased you could come. Geor - Major Johnson here says we ought to have you on board.'

He waved his hand towards the end of the table, where for the first time Tom saw that George Johnson was sitting slouched over a notepad. George looked up and gave Tom a welcoming nod of the head.

'Now,' said Wilkinson, 'we are very pressed for time, as no doubt you are also, and I think we should proceed without delay. What is your profession, Mr Jorret?'

'Master mason.'

'You live in Cornwall, I believe?' 'Yes. You wrote to me there.'

'Quite so. And you have lived there long?' 'Twenty-seven years.'

'And before that?'

'I was - born.' Col. Hope looked away, smothering a grin.

Wilkinson looked annoyed. 'I'm sorry, Mr Jorret. We have to ask these questions before making any appointment.'

Tom said nothing.

Wilkinson gave a false smile and did his best to look as if he were throwing in a casual, conversational question: 'Have you ever been abroad, Mr Jorret? To France or Germany, for instance?'

Tom looked at him in unfeigned astonishment. 'Abroad?' he said after a long pause. 'Twice. That is, to us Cornish *London's* abroad. My first visit *abroad* was in '35 to watch the Cornish Pirates play 'gainst Stepney Wanderers. We won 3-2. This is my second visit *abroad*. And with any luck my last,' he added.

Wilkinson went red in the face with annoyance. 'I do

insist that you take these matters seriously, Mr Jorret, if you are to be considered for this appointment.'

'I don't know if I want to be considered at all. I know nothing about it.'

With a great effort Wilkinson managed to bring himself under control.

'Do you consider yourself an expert on gun emplacements, Mr Jorret?'

'No.'

'But you built them in -' Wilkinson consulted the paper his secretary handed him '- in St Mawgan airfield?'

'There were no difficulties.'

'No difficulties! Do you realise how important such defences are to the gunners for whom we are responsible?' The Colonel winced.

'I'll tell you what, Mr Wilkinson, the best thing'd be for you to come down to Cornwall and see for yourself then you could make the changes you want,' said Tom, quite calmly. 'Then if you want, you could ask me again. But next time, tell me what the job is and what you're going to pay me instead of asking damn-fool questions.'

With this, Tom rose from his chair. George looked up in alarm and caught Col. Hope's eye.

To everyone's surprise, the Colonel burst out laughing. 'No, no, sit down again, Mr Jorret, there's a good fellow. I've got everything already for you.' He pushed a file of papers over the table. 'What we want you to do, and where, and salary and so on.'

Tom sat down again and turned the papers over.

'I know Mr Wilkinson's questions seem strange, but it's his job, isn't that so, Wilkinson? To make doubly sure that you're a safe man to entrust with military secrets, and the way you've answered was exactly what we wanted, isn't that so, Wilkinson?' He turned to the still fuming Civil Servant. 'Your clever questions, if I may say so, couldn't have winkled out more honest answers.'

Wilkinson almost beamed, instantly mollified. No doubt only he, and possibly his secretary, considered him anything other than a blundering ass. But he had unwittingly done his job.

'Now before we get down to details, perhaps Mr Wilkinson could get the map down and show us all the great importance of the British Somaliland in securing the sea-routes through to the Canal.'

Wilkinson with a condescending smile nodded to the secretary who bustled over and drew down a large roller-map.

He took up a pointer. 'We can see that we have friends to the North-West in French Somaliland, but if the balloon goes up -' (the Colonel winced again) '- we cannot be sure how Italy, under her Fascist regime and closely allied to Nazi Germany under the Axis agreement, will react if, as I say, the balloon were to go up.'

'You mean, if there's a war?' asked Tom, genuinely confused.

Wilkinson smiled down at him indulgently. 'Precisely, although we don't care to use such language whilst there is still - but I have said enough. See how our territory is hemmed into the Gulf of Aden by the Italian Somaliland to the East -' (he adopted a declamatory pose, brandishing the pointer menacingly) 'and to the recently acquired - nefariously acquired, I need hardly say - Ethiopia to the south. All in all, gentlemen, there is a potential threat to our national lifeline, and we-' (he spoke as if only he and Mr Chamberlain were making the preparations) 'and we must prepare for such an eventuality.'

He drew breath and made to launch into a stirring oration

only to be cut short by the Colonel. 'Absolutely, Wilkinson. That brings us to Mr Jorret's role, should he take it up.' He looked enquiringly at Wilkinson. 'Perhaps-?'

'Yes, indeed, Colonel,' said Wilkinson. 'Perhaps, Mr Jorret could retire to study the terms and conditions as set out by Col. Hope, with the Major, who of course is an interested party,' (he directed an ingratiating smile towards George) 'so that Col. Hope and I might confer?'

He called after Tom as he was half-way to the door: 'Mr Jorret, might I remind you that you are bound by the Official Secrets Act not to reveal the contents to any unauthorized person?'

Tom nodded and waved his hand without looking back.

'Fart, you're right,' he said, grinning at George as the secretary closed the doors behind them.

They pored over the documents for the best part of an hour until the secretary appeared again to summon them back.

'Tell him I've not done yet,' said Tom. The secretary pursed her lips. 'I'll come in when I'm ready.'

In fact Tom was very excited indeed at the prospect. He took care not to show it when he went back but signed the contract there and then.

* * *

'All a bit of a rush, old man,' said George. 'They want us to be off by the end of August, and you've got to fit in a week or two looking at the guns at Larkhill. And you've got all that kit to get from the Army-and-Navy. You'll need a tropical DJ too.'

'DJ?'

George was suddenly embarrassed. 'Dinner Jacket. You'll

need a summery one out there. Stifling evenings, I should say.'

Tom was annoyed and looked it. 'I've never seen the need for a DJ, as you call it, in my life. I'm damned if I'm going to spend good money on stuff like that.'

'Sorry Tom, but it's part of the kit and you'll find you need it when you get out there.

It's allowed for, anyway. And you'll need it for the mess at Larkhill.'

'Well, I'll see,' said Tom sulkily. 'I didn't intend to go to the Mess anyway.'

'Again, there's no option. You're not exactly in the army, but you'll have to work to army routine, and army orders, for that matter. The course only lasts a fortnight anyway. You'll just have to fit in with the others, I'm afraid.

'Others? What others.'

'Ten of you on the course. I've been collecting chaps for a few months.'

'What? Not all for Somaliland?'

George laughed. 'No, Tom, of course not! All over the place. No, no, it's my posting and, well, it seemed to fit in with you too. I had the idea you would like to, well, see a - a new world, away from Cornwall? Just for a spell, perhaps?'

How did he know that? Get away from it; fly free a bit. No responsibility for anyone.

Fly free a bit.

'Are there skylarks in Somalia?'

George shot him a puzzled look. 'Bit obsessed with skylarks, Tom?' He pondered this for a moment. 'Do you know, the army do more for birds and all that than all the nature-lovers. Apparently, the gunnery and shooting ranges keep the public off. Anyway, sounds as if there'll be some at Larkhill.'

Chapter 7

They had put into Gibraltar on the P&O cruise ship *Pevensey Bay* (which had already been commissioned as a troopship) when the news came through by wireless that war had been declared.

There was the inevitable muddle between the Army and the Navy as to whether the ship should return to England, but as the vessel carried vital stores and munitions, the order was at last made for the *Pevensey Bay* to continue as planned.

She also picked up a detachment of noisy West African recruits who had been enlisted in the King's African Rifles. These young men had come straight from their villages in Nigeria and the Gambia where they had previously had little prospect of escaping from the lifetime prospect of subsistence farming. Now they had the exhilarating prospect of adventure, travel and (for them) wealth. They kept a continuous chatter and noise until from time to time they were silenced by the grizzled English sergeant who had enlisted them.

The Sergeant was completely baffled by this non-stop vitality and noise.

'Can't understand it, Sir,' the Sergeant said to George, who had commented in his mild way about their noisiness. 'Not sure how we'll make soldiers of them.'

'I thought you recruited them.'

'Well, yes, me and the officer. They're fine chaps, quiet as mice in the Gambia, but once they're all together here on board, well, you can't hear yourself think.'

George let that pass without comment.

Tom enjoyed it, dressed in his Pith helmet and new shorts, leaning on the gunwale watching the wake as they made their steady way through the Mediterranean. He marvelled at the calm azure blue of the sea and at the cloudless skies, a different world from the wild crashing grey seas along his Cornish rocks.

It was after all the different world he had been seeking. He had not exaggerated when he had said that London was as near as he had been to a foreign country. True, he had escaped from Newmin every now and then on his motorbike to the other side of the Tamar, even as far as Exeter and (once) to Bristol. But he had never liked it: he found the people strange, and the food, and there was no sea.

Not that I've anything to complain of in life. Not like those poor devils down the tin mines, or worse, those coughing away their lives in the China clay pits, or worse still, those who couldn't find a job at all, and there were plenty of those. No, I've got my trade, a few hundred in the bank, but - to spend the rest of my life stuck on the ground hacking out little garden ornaments?

His true escape had been to watch the skylarks on the cliff edge, where he had no responsibility for anyone. And when he had fancifully told Emily that he wanted to go to Africa, it was as if he were skylarking himself, away from grubbing around on the ground, far away from responsibility for other people. And having to put up with mean-minded greedy people in order to make a living.

As he watched the white trail of the wake, his mind turned to the last but one work he had been commissioned to do. It was to be for a certain Mrs Violet Parr, or rather, Lady Violet Parr, as she was always insistent on having herself addressed, even though Sir Sydney had long since died of a serious liver failure, no doubt indirectly attributable to Lady Violet.

Lady Violet, long, thin, sharp-featured, unpleasant and in consequence extremely lonely, had sent for him for a commission in what she called her grounds.

A gardener raked over the gravel as soon as Tom had driven up the drive.

Lady Violet scowled at his motorbike. 'I would prefer you left that machine in the lane next time,' she said. 'Now, Jorret, you have been recommended to me as an able and conscientious craftsman.'

'I must bring the bike to the house as it carries not only me but also my tools, Lady Violet.'

She snapped back. 'That we shall discuss later, Jorret. If you work for me, you must do exactly as I say. I want that clearly understood.'

'I understand what you are saying, yes,' said Tom carefully. "Now, let's see just what you want done.' He took his old haversack from the pannier of his bike.

She summoned the man with the rake. 'Take Jorret round to the summer house.' The man touched his cap and gestured to Tom to follow him.

'Wait there until I come.' She went back into the house.

The lawns were beautifully kept, and Tom could see two other gardeners at work in the shrubbery. Tom lingered to admire the stone figures of birds round the pond: there was a hunched heron, a stork and a group of egrets.

'Mustn't keep 'er waitin', Jorry or whatever yer name is.' These were the only words the gardener uttered before he left Tom to wait by the summerhouse.

He inspected the stonework whilst he waited, making

notes of the erosion and the quality of the carving, grimacing every now and then to himself. When she still had not arrived after twenty minutes, he sat down in the summerhouse and lit his pipe.

At last, he was confronted by a bald portly figure in morning dress. He consulted his watch: thirty-five minutes had passed.

'Workmen are *not* permitted in the summer-house,' said the bald figure imperiously.

Tom stayed where he was. 'She has kept me waiting for thirty-five, no, thirty-six, minutes. 'Who the hell are you?'

'I am in the employ of Lady Violet. I am instructed to give you directions for your work.' Tom stared at him for a moment.

'Then if you are in her employ, go back and tell her that *I* am not yet in her employ, that I have been waiting, and that I will take directions only from her -'

'I shall report your unsuitability to her ladyship -'

'- only if she is with me in ten minutes.'

There was no reply to this other than a red-faced spluttering noise before the figure stalked off.

Tom waited a further carefully timed ten minutes before he made his way back to the motorbike. He had the small satisfaction of seeing the bitter angry face of Lady Violet peering at him from the hall window as he left.

Tom did not mind: he shrugged his shoulders, and pitied the unfortunates who had no choice but work for the ghastly woman. She made them all unpleasant too, it seemed. Too much wealth seems to make people bitter, he thought. Lady Violet used her money to run people's lives and make them as nasty as herself.

Not all that different from my grandfather, I suppose. Not that he was nasty like Lady Violet. At least grandfather worked hard and the old miser provided for the family. The family, yes: the Jorrets. Why did he keep on about the "family" when he obviously didn't like any of us? He didn't think any of us were any good. The only one he ever thought anything of was his uncle Steve killed in the war and who by all accounts had been a pretty bad lot. None of us are any good compared with him.

No, I'm much better off out of it, especially now Emmy has got herself fixed up with Jimmy Henbury. Don't think Ma minds me going off, either; I've the idea Ma's rather pleased for me, and as for Pa, he couldn't care less one way or the other.

'There you are, Tom. Been looking for you,' George said. 'You should come forward with me: we're in sight of Port Said.'

* * *

The *Pevensey Bay* was soon making its way through the Canal. The strangeness of the scene: the throngs of shouting Egyptian workers on the waterside, the appalling smell, the dozens of little smacks all in danger of being crushed by the troopship, the extraordinary noise which carried into the middle of the Canal, and every now and then the cadavers floating alongside: dogs, even a camel and, to Tom's horror, more than one human, about whom no-one but he seemed concerned.

'Can't do anything about it, old man,' said George, shaking his head sadly. 'No-one takes responsibility. But that's the way of it, I'm afraid.'

Tom turned away in disgust: but he was thinking of Terry Samson.

They came to a clearer, cleaner stretch of the Canal, the

water reflecting the cloudless blue of the sky. Tom and George sought the shelter of the awnings. Not so the Gambians who, whooping with delight, so much excelled at the deck quoits that none of them could win.

'Those fellows could shoot the flea off the back of a dog,' said George thoughtfully. 'They'll make good gunners.'

'Or riflemen?'

'Too excitable, too eager. They'd get themselves killed too easily. No, they'd be better with the regular steady rhythm of sighting, loading, firing, unloading.'

Tom looked about him at the calm of the scene: the only sounds came from the throbbing of the engines and, of course, the shouts of the Africans.

'Not that there's much chance of getting shot as far as I can see.'

'No: we'll be away from it. They're not fighting in France either, apparently.'

'Funny that the only time appeasement's working is when war's declared.' Tom surprised even himself: he was not accustomed to making such observations, indeed, not accustomed to thinking at all on such matters.

'I wouldn't say that to the Poles. The French have a saying: *reculer pour avancer plus* - take a step back so you can move forward better. I assume that's what the Germans are doing. They'll wait for the spring now. You'll see.'

Tom made no reply, but when he got back to his tiny cabin he reached in his case for Emily's Phillips School Atlas and studied the *Europe in 1922* maps.

He drew a pencil line east of Warsaw from the Baltic to the most northerly tip of Hungary. 'Bloody hell,' he said. 'They can go where they like now.'

He stripped off, but the stifling airless heat would not let him sleep. And for the first time he thought longingly of the high winds of the North Cornish shoreline.

* * *

There was a hot sea breeze just offshore, but once they put into Berbera the heat was unbearable. The sweat soaked Tom's khaki drill shirt and shorts within seconds, and he was grateful that he had to do nothing but slump into the back of the Austin staff car which had been sent to meet them while a gang of cheerful KAR fellows manhandled their kit into the back of a three-tonner.

'Takes a little while to acclimatise, Tom,' said George. 'We won't get to work for a week or so. By the way, you've been made Acting Captain, Royal Engineers. Had to do that I'm afraid. If they caught you in civvies, you could be shot as a spy, you know.'

Tom had just energy enough to ask who "they" were. 'Well, any putative enemy.'

Tom was no wiser. He had no idea what putative was, and could not be bothered to enquire further.

'Only twenty minutes or so, and we'll be there,' said George. 'Cooler in the mess and then we'll have a stiff G-and-T.'

Tom stared out at the rows of sandy-mud houses interspersed with the occasional square whitewashed building. The scene rather reminded him of the Wild West towns of the cowboy films he had seen at the Odeon in Newmin, but before long he had fallen into a drowsy, headachy sleep.

Chapter 8

Emily tried to write every few weeks, but there was very little to say.

Nothing seemed to be happening in the war, she said, and the papers were calling it a "phoney" war, with pictures of soldiers going out on patrol and not meeting any Germans.

I expect you get the papers anyway so it can't be a secret about the things that have been going on at sea. We've all been told to wear our gas masks, not wear them of course but keep them in little cardboard boxes over our shoulders. I expect you have them too. I hope they're feeding you alright, Tom, everyone here's alright because of the fish and Pa goes out a lot now for rabbits on the green, and even Granddad goes *with him sometimes. He's much better now as some rich old people from London have moved into the hotel for the duration and he don't have to bother with getting guests in at all now. And you ought to hear him going on about YOU Tom! Telling everyone about you being a CAPTAIN in the ROYAL ENGINEERS, just like Uncle Steve who would have been if he hadn't been killed. Everyone sends their love and Pa and Ma are quite well and just hope you're safe and you'll be back soon. Lots of love Emmy. PS Jimmy sends his love too. He's doing very important work now.*

Tom was not used to receiving letters, and certainly not used to writing any. But he found himself with a great deal of time on his hands: the working day started at 5.00 am and virtually ended at 11.00, save for a desultory hour or so when the burning heat of the day had faded a little. He therefore tried to answer Emily's letter sitting sweltering under one of the great slow-moving ceiling fans in the Mess. He sat there sucking his pen in frustration until, to his embarrassment, he saw George Johnson looming over him.

'Sorry, Tom: didn't mean to pry.'

Tom grunted. 'Trouble is, nothing happens here. Emmy says that nothing's happening there either. You wouldn't think there was a war on.'

'You could tell her about the hills and the sand and the camels, I suppose.'

Tom felt the clammy sweat along his back despite the fans. 'Yeah. And the heat.' 'Nothing like Cornwall, eh? They'll be interested in the Gambian chaps, too.'

'Never know what I can write without it being censored.'

'Leave it to them. They'll blot it out if it's secret.' George grinned. 'It's hardly a secret that there are Gambians in Somaliland. We don't mind Adolf knowing that.'

So Tom tried to tell Emily about the Gambians - *jolly chaps, all black as the ace of spades, always laughing and yelling. There's not much to do Emmy* - the next line "because we're always waiting for supplies" was blotted out - *so they play lots of football so I join in until it gets too hot. You won't believe it Emmy but I've lost a stone and two pounds since I've been here.*

What Tom did not tell her was that he and George and some of the Gambians had been reassembling an abandoned 25pdr Field gun. The Quarter-Master Sergeant -Major told them that it had been written off some time ago and one of the Sergeants had been court martialed for having allowed it to tip down the hillside onto some rocks.

'What happened to him?' Tom asked.

'Well, they couldn't be sure about it, so he was bumped down to Gunner and sent back home. Anyway, sir, you and those black chaps are welcome to it if it'll keep them happy. It looks a mess, but I don't think there's a lot wrong with it apart from bust axles. Then it rusted up in the rains 'cos they couldn't get it out. Had to get a tank over and tow it out in the end.'

You won't believe it, Emmy, but they don't know what these Gambian chaps are doing here. They were supposed to go and join another lot in Kenya but typical army they lost all their papers and so they're stuck here with nothing to do but drill and train and clean up some stuff here that we found. The sergeant who brought them over is an old chap who should have been retired but he has been kept on for the duration. He looks like old Roberts in the village, you remember, Grandfather's cowman, but he's much smarter of course and keeps his hair very short and all that. Sergeant Jamison, he's called, but everyone just calls him Jock, or sometimes ruder names.

'I just don't understand these fellows, sir,' Jock said wearily. 'They like drill so much than when they've done it in the morning they say do we have to stop now, sarge, and I'm knackered, sir, what with the heat and that. But they all shout at once and they don't seem to understand *discipline*, sir, they just keep shouting. When one of them gets it wrong, right turns instead of left or something, they all start laughing and kind of mob him and I just have to say they'll all go on orders, but then they form threes again and just say we got to do it all again now.'

It was towards the end of May before the Battery office at last got some official news about the Gambians, or rather, about the Nigerian contingent to which they had been attached. A troopship was on the way from Aden to transport all the Nigerian soldiers to Kenya where they were to join the King's African Rifles 1st East African Infantry Brigade.

The six Gambians who were left gathered round the steps of the battery office, for once all talking in whispers. After a while the lanky figure of Major Johnson emerged, contriving to look even more unsoldierly in his pith helmet, khaki drill shirt and long droopy shorts.

One of the Gambian soldiers stepped forward; he was obviously their leader, (probably because he was the tallest). He gave the Major an immaculate salute, which Johnson returned with a smile and what could only be described as a sloppy wave.

'Yes?'

'We was wonderin', sir, now that lot have gone, sir, what we doin'? Don't get on with them, anywise,' he added inconsequentially.

'What would you like to do, Lamin Bah?'

'We been talkin', Major, and we all say, stay here, with you an' Tom and even Sergeant Jock, he's not bad, y'know, Major.'

* * *

'Well, come on, George: what did you tell him?'

George added another ice cube to his gin-and-tonic before looking up with a mischievous grin. 'I told Lamin Bah that they were staying, they had my word on it.'

Tom gasped. 'Surely you can't just do that. Or did you have orders?'

'No. No-one at the War Office has the faintest interest in who they are, where they are. Or what they are to do.

And what's more, they - and we - are the last people the WO wants to worry about now. So I decided.'

Tom shook his head wonderingly. 'And what *are* they going to do?'

George paused for a moment before replying. 'They are going to be a gun-team. We'll train them.'

'*WE?*'

'Yes: you and me. You'll be gun commander, of the 25pdr.'

'That's crazy. I can't be responsible for a gun, let alone these Gambian chaps, even if...'

Johnson thumped the bamboo table in the nearest he ever got to anger. 'Responsible? Of course you are responsible. They will look to you to lead them and you will bloody learn to be responsible. It don't matter about duty, or anything like that, you understand me, but you can bloody well be responsible for someone else other than Tom Jorret. These fellows - oh, never mind.' His temper evaporated as quickly as it had arisen, and he broke off as if the effort of so long a speech had exhausted him.

Tom stared at George in amazement. He could think of nothing to say, and so said nothing. There was a long silence as they sat there toying with their glasses, eying each other.

All the same, he's right. Then with a sudden rush of guilt, and awareness: *Terry, Terry Samson. Could have saved him. Responsible.*

'You're right,' Tom said. 'I'll do it.'

George leant forward and patted his friend on the shoulder. 'Knew you would. No need for me to - no need for all that… Sorry, Tom.'

'No. Had to be said.' Tom pushed his glass over the table. 'Your turn, I think. Scotch.

A double.'

'Yes. You'll need it,' said George grimly. 'You know what's

happening Tom?'

'In France, you mean?'

George called the mess waiter over and waited till he had brought the drinks and was out of earshot. 'They're pushing us into the sea, Tom. Got it from Jackson at HQ. France is done for, he reckons.'

Tom sat silent, toying with his glass.

'There's worse, Tom. Even if we hold on in France, the Italians will come in. They always come in on the winning side.'

'What they *think's* the winning side.'

'Right. Makes no difference, they'll come in, and it won't be long before they're coming up from the south at us. Or from the East, for that matter. And we've got about two men and a donkey.'

'And a two-point-five and a gun crew.'

'Exactly. I expect they'll send us some more chaps from Aden, but even so…'

They took their drinks along the sand track from the mess to the Battery Office to inspect the huge wall map.

'There. They'll come up from the plains there. Ethiopia. Mussolini will complete his great East African Empire.'

'God! They're all round us!'

'Yep. We'll need your gun all right. But I tell you what, Tom. Why don't we take some leave and go up to the Karkaars for a few days and see if we can see anything of them along the coast there.' He pointed to the mountain range which ran along the Gulf of Aden to the frontier with the Italian Somaliland.

'Bloody hot.'

'No, they say it's much cooler in the mountains. We can take Rachid with us to translate and he could drive a bit,' (Tom grimaced) 'and we can leave the Gambians to Jock for a few days and they can grease up the gun. We'll look out some dummies and he can start them on some basic gun drill.'

'We'll never do it, sir,' said Jock with his customary gloom. 'These chaps 'll blow us all up, you mark my words.'

'Old Jock's really proud of those chaps, you know, Tom,' George said later. 'They're so keen they exhaust the old bugger.'

'Eeyau, that's who he reminds me of.' Tom looked blank. 'Oh, never mind.'

It took them a couple of days to get the new gun crew started and to get the stores and weapons for their trip. Rachid was delighted to get away from his wife for a few days.

It was before dawn on the second of June 1940, when they set out.

Chapter 9

The fifteen-hundred-weight climbed the twisting road into the Karkaar Mountains. Tom rather wished that he were driving: he was used to steering along narrow rocky coastal paths with his truck sliding on the stone chips and shale. But these mountain roads were three, four times higher than any that the Cornish coast could offer, and Rachid was swinging the wheel with an easy nonchalance, oblivious to the dizzy precipices that every now and then opened up to Tom's alarmed gaze.

It was some seventy miles from Berbera to Burac, but it took them the best part of four hours. George was in no hurry and was quite content to pull off the track when opportunity offered so they could train their binoculars on the vultures soaring magnificently overhead, their plumage a silvery white catching the golden rising sun.

Tom had a sudden wave of homesickness 'The last time I was doing this I was watching the skylarks.'

'They'll still be there when you get back.'

If I get back. 'They'll be the same: I won't.' *Wonder how they're all getting on, haven't heard for ages. Hope the farm's keeping going and the old devil isn't making everyone's life a misery. It was all right when I was there, he just blamed me and Emmy for everything.*

'Think of it this way: how would you ever have seen

British Somaliland if the army hadn't paid you to do it?'

'Well, I've seen it now.' Tom grinned. 'Now lets go home.'

'Not till we've seen what the Eyeties are up to.'

Burac lay on the plateau at the foot of the mountains. It had a few dozen square sand houses and a vast market square in which merchants had their stalls of oranges, dates, figs, and tired-looking vegetables. Here and there camels dozed waiting for their masters to strike their bargains over rolls of cloth or cooking-pots

Scrawny cattle with protuberant haunch bones wandered aimlessly in front of the truck as it edged forward. A swarm of Arab urchins who had appeared as from nowhere crowded noisily round the truck.

'Jackson told me on no account stop in Burac,' said George. 'Before you know it they'll all be climbing in the back flinging all our stuff out.'

'No police or anything?'

'What d'you expect? Half a dozen English bobbies? No, the Commissioner just leaves these towns on the plains to get on with it. There's a few local chaps if there's any violence. It's more on the plains you find the robbers. They raid the towns sometimes. Used to take off slaves, they say.'

Now he tells me. 'So why are we here? The British, I mean?'

George shrugged. 'It's the coast. We've had Aden for years. Jackson'll tell you: trading post a hundred years ago. Then they opened up the Canal and we wanted to keep the Germans out. Keep the routes to India open, no drugs or pirates, that kind of thing.'

The road through the mountains was comparatively cool, but the plain on which Burac stood was of baked-hard sands scattered with stones. For the past fifty years successive troops of engineers had supervised Somali labourers in the laying down of a hard beaten road, which was lined at intervals with piles of the large flint-like stones.

'They used to stone people to death with those here,' said George. 'Still do, I'm told.'

'Explains the Sunday School story,' said Tom.

'What was that?'

"Let he who is without sin cast the first stone". About the only thing I remembered. Used to go off crabbing on the Sunday till Pa caught me once and dragged me back to the Chapel. Miserable old bastard, that fellow who ran it. We used to sing the hymns all wrong, and then he would belt us for it.' He mopped his brow with a large spotted handkerchief. 'God, it's hot, George.'

They consulted the charts.

'We turn west soon and then we make for the mountains again. Should be cooler then.'

In fact, by the time the road had reached the foothills, the heat had become unbearable, up to 43 degrees centigrade. They took the first opportunity to turn off the road along the stone- strewn baked earth to find some shade in the rocks.

Both men were exhausted. Neither would admit, however, that he thought it unwise to go on.

They managed to find something of a cave in which they could get the bonnet of the truck out of the sun. They moved up into the shelter of the rocks to try to catch some sleep until the sun was lower.

Tom gulped down some water. It was unpleasantly tepid.

Like grandfather's tea. Wonder how the old skinflint's doing. Watching Emmy like a hawk spooning the tea from the caddy: "You go aisy on that tay, maid. It'll have to last us.' Then his silly chuckle and the same old joke: 'Came all the way from Indie, that tay, so you go aisy on it.' India: that's why it's so hot. God, the heat: throbbing through my head. Indians: must be Indians in these rocks. Tom Mix: he's the cowboy'll sort'em out. All these rocks along the shore. But can't hear the sea. No sea. No skylarks. Where's the sea?'

'It's all right, old man. Drink some water.'

'George! Where the hell..? I must have dropped off...'

'Touch of the sun.' George regarded him anxiously. 'Look: I'll put a little salt in the water. Drink it up. Not too much, mind. Aches in the legs?'

'A bit, yes. Sorry about this.'

'No. We've overdone it. Here...' He slopped some water from the jerry can onto a towel. 'Wrap this round your head.'

By the time Tom woke from a fitful headachy sleep the sun had dipped below the mountains and the rocks they were sheltering behind were in complete shadow. The temperature was dropping like a stone, and George suggested they ought to make a little headway.

'If you're feeling up to it?'

'Yes. Much better.' Tom suddenly sat up. '*Quiet a moment, George! Listen*!' Something was moving below, by the truck, just out of sight.

'Thieves, probably,' George whispered. He groped for his pistol and eased back the hammer. Rachid was already alert and had armed himself with a long curved-blade *kukri* that he had bartered for in one of the Berbera markets.

'I'll get round behind them,' Tom whispered. He clamped the magazine into his .303 rifle. 'Only, don't shoot me by mistake. Three minutes.'

George watched admiringly as Tom, the rifle slung across his back, skipped nimbly despite his bulk across the rocks.

'Give him another minute or two, Rachid.'

They could hear faint muttering voices from the direction of the truck.

At last George signalled to Rachid to move on, and they began to edge cautiously down across the rocks.

Suddenly they heard the engine of the 15cwt roar into life. 'They've got the truck! Come on Rachid!'

Rachid reached the ground first and ran lithely towards the truck still 200 yards away; George was stumbling clumsily across the rocks and had just reached the sand when he heard the shot ring out.

'God! *Tom*!'

By now it was nearly dark. George could only dimly discern two long-robed figures running away headlong. He dared not shoot at them for fear of hitting Rachid, but he could just see Rachid stoop and hurl a stone at one of the retreating figures.

It must have caught the man between the shoulder blades and he went down like a felled pine-tree. Rachid retrieved his *kukri* and stood threateningly over the screaming Arab.

'The other, sir? Shall I chase?' 'Leave him. We must find Tom.'

'I'm here. Behind you.' Tom gave a strange nervous laugh. 'Like the pantomime.'

'Thank God! You all right, Tom?'

'Bit shaky. I think I - killed him.' He giggled again. 'Didn't think at all, just took aim and phow! Shot him. Got him in the head. Like the rabbits on the green, but not rabbit really. Dead - *man*, this time.'

'Where, Tom?' George took a length of cord from his pocket. 'Tie his hands behind him, Rachid, and leave him.' He put his arm round Tom's shoulders and could feel him trembling. "Where d'you shoot him, Tom?'

'In the head. I told you. In the truck..'

The truck had not moved, but its engine was still roaring.

The body had slumped over with the impact of the shot, it's right knee pressing grotesquely across the accelerator.

Tom sat down heavily on the sand. He unclipped the

magazine from the rifle and stuffed it into the pocket of his drill shirt.

'I don't want to see him. The one I - shot.'

'You had to, Tom. We'd all have died out here else.'

Rachid said: 'I lift out the body, sir? Need help, sir.'

'Of course, Rachid. You stay there, Tom.' A thought suddenly struck him. 'What about the other one, Rachid? The one you tied up? Can't hear him at all.'

'He's all right. See to him later, sir.

They dragged the body from behind the steering wheel and laid it out in front of the truck.

George surveyed the cab. 'We'll have to clear this up, Rachid. There's blood all over the seat. Let's see to the other one first.'

They took their torches, and could see the man lying face down, his hands tied behind his back. He was completely still.

'He's dead, Rachid! You killed him!' 'Had to silence him, sir.'

'Yes, but -'

'What else to do with him, sir?'

Tom had joined them and peered at the body.

'Another dead? I suppose it was necessary.' Strangely, he felt a great deal better to know that he was not the only - killer.

George knelt down and rolled the body over. Its head lolled uselessly on the shoulders.

'Bloody hell! Tom, Rachid: look at this! Italian!'

The slate-grey tunic and trousers (although ill-fitting) were clearly those of the Italian East African force.

'Not Italian, sir,' said Rachid. 'Askari, deserted from Ethiopia. There are many on the plains here.'

'Poor devils,' said Tom.

'Yes. But they would have killed us, Tom, if they'd caught us,' said George. He looked down at Rachid who had started to divest the corpse of its clothing. "What the hell are you doing now?'

'Put the bodies on rocks for vultures. Cloths can clean the van.'

Tom stared at Rachid with admiration not unmixed with a *frisson* of fear at his cold- hearted efficiency. He had the uneasy feeling that if he needed to Rachid would treat him without compunction in just the same way.

They dragged the bodies along the path and with a concerted effort flung them as far as they could onto the rocks.

'Just white bones tomorrow,' said Rachid, expressionless.

Tom stared at the corpses draped grotesquely over the crags. *So much for human life out here. Or anywhere, if we're honest.*

'Come on, Tom. We've been here too long. There may be others. There was a third one, anyway, who got away.'

They did what they could to clean out the cab with as little water as possible, and used the rest of the clothing to cover the seats. This time Tom insisted on driving, and they crept forward with sidelights. There were no signs of any Askaris, or indeed any other human, as they followed the road north-eastwards to the township of Erigave in the foothills.

Erigave was larger than Burso and more important.

'Jackson told us to take care at Erigave. The Italians have lots of merchants here. At least they say they are merchants.'

Tom gave George a quizzical look: he had said nothing about this when they had set out. *I thought we were on leave; thought we were looking for skylarks. Now we are looking for Italian agents and fighting off marauding gangs. Apparently, the responsibility for the safety of the British Empire is on my shoulders.*

'Why? What's up?' asked George.

'Nothing,' replied Tom testily.

'It's only a few miles north to the coast.' They climbed to a vantage point and studied the terrain to the north through their binoculars. 'You can see the pass from here.'

Tom also searched the rocks to either side for Red Indians - he still had the old cowboy films of Tom Mix in his mind. *Simpler then: you knew who was on your side and who the bad guys were.*

'This is about the narrowest part of the Karkaar chain,' George was saying. 'We go off east.' They studied the maps again. 'There. The road peters out to a track,' - Tom grimaced - 'but we should be all right. Only a few miles to the border.'

They guarded the truck whilst Rachid was given some money and sent into the town to find out what he could. He returned after a while carrying a large wicker basket.

There were lots of Italians there, he said, but they were certainly not all merchants.

He had the feeling that they were trying to stir everyone up against the English.

He grinned. (It was the first time Tom had seen him smile at all.) 'I bring you both a basket, sirs.'

He whipped off the cloth with a flourish.

There was a huge platter of steaming goat and rice and a bottle of what turned out to be execrable Kenyan wine.

They all three fell upon it with great whoops of delight, and Tom revised his opinion of Rachid.

Chapter 10

Emily rushed into the sitting room. As usual, all the windows were open, and despite the warm June sun outside, inside the room was draughty and chilly.

Old Peter Jorret sat there in his black three-piece suit. (Sometimes if it were really hot sitting in the garden, he might take off the jacket, but never the waistcoat).

'I've got a letter at last!' Emily shouted.

'Why d'lad always write to you then? Don't he know I be the head of the Jorrets?'

'It's to everyone, grandfather. Look, he says, *Dear everyone*.'

'Give it 'ere, then.' The old man squinted at it, fiddled with his glasses, and grunted with annoyance. 'Never could make out the lad's hand.'

'I'll read it out loud, father,' said Annie. 'Emmy, you get us all a glass of the cider. I expect you've seen it, haven't you?'

Emily nodded and rushed off into the scullery.

'Now then,' said Annie, adjusting her glasses. 'He says, "*Dear everyone at home, I hope this finds you all well and busy for the war effort. We don't get any fighting here but just train and we have some very good fellows from Gambia*" - ''e told us all that last time,' grumbled the old man - '*and we have been polishing and greasing on old gun we found which we have already been practising on. So if the Eyeties come in which George expects we'll be ready for them. I expect you can see from the maps (sorry Emmy I pinched your maps) where they'll be, and George and me are going out to have a look next week.*"'

'What's 'e mean by all that?' demanded Jorret. 'Why can't 'e tell us what 'e means by all that?'

'It's all secret. He's not allowed,' said Emily, who had returned with a large jug and a tray of glasses. 'Here, have your cider.'

'They're diggin' the trenches, I'll be bound. Like your uncle Steve in the last lot.' Jorret fell into a melancholy reverie.

'No, father,' said Annie. 'Listen. "*It's all sand and rocks and mountains here, and much hotter than it ever was even in last August on the beach. We've heard the news from France is very bad, but I expect you know all that. Food is not bad. We get lots of rice and goat meat and they bring some stuff up from Kenya, coffee and tea which they grow a lot of there. It's good that Mr Churchill's in, isn't it. George says that Mr Chamberlain was very good in the peace, health and that, but no-one in the government liked him as he always ignored them and went on his own. Tell Grandfather that it's now official: I am a Captain in Royal Engineers with the King's Commission and they're sending the certificate thing to you for me. I had to have this otherwise if the enemy catch me they could shoot me as a spy. I've been riding on camels quite a bit. George is very well and sends his regards. Your ever-loving Tom.*

'Read that bit again, maid, about the King's Commission,' said Peter. 'That's what Steve got, that's his certificate I got in the sitting-room. That was the old King George gave him that. George the Fifth.'

The old man glowed with pride at mention of the King's Commission. 'I ought to 'ave that certificate, I'm head of the

Jorrets, an' it'll go with Steve's certificate.'

'We're proud of the lad, too, dad,' said Bob, suddenly; he had as usual been sitting puffing his pipe in silence. 'The certificate goes up on *our* wall. Ain't that right, Annie?'

'We'll see, when it co-' Her glass suddenly crashed to the floor. 'Oh God! What on earth…?'

One huge explosion was following another, getting closer to the farmhouse. They could hear the Heinkels almost overhead as they broke off southwards, followed by an angry (and ineffective) Ack-Ack barrage.

'They've found our Dunkirk chaps at the Pengale camp. Poor devils,' said Bob. He got up and calmly knocked out his pipe in the grate. 'I'll take Tom's bike and see if I can help.'

The others sat staring and fearful.

'No Bob! They might come back!' said Annie. She was still pale and shaking.

'How d'you mean, Dunkirk chaps?' Peter demanded.

'There's hundreds of them back from France up at Pengale, some without a stitch to their backs, and dozens of them hurt, Grandfather. The Germans must have found them,' said Emily. 'You take care, Dad.'

'They won't be back, Annie.' Bob spoke with a calmness and confidence which startled his wife. 'They've barely enough petrol to get them back to France, I should think. And our chaps'll be chasing them, you'll see. Anyway, put up a pasty or two and a thermos and I'll be off.'

* * *

It was gone three in the morning before Annie heard the motorbike returning.

'Whisky, Annie.' Bob slumped into his chair, grey-faced, smeared with mud and blood.

'God, Bob, are you hurt? I'll get some -'

'No, Annie. Later. Stay here, by me.' Annie sat down beside him and rested her head on his knee, something she had not done for years. 'Not my blood. It's those poor chaps. Annie, I've been pickin' up arms and legs and -'

Bob began to sob. 'Got to get back, Annie. Have a bath and get back.'

'I'll get that whisky. Here,' she put a blanket over his trembling shoulders. 'Sit there a bit and warm yourself. I'll get that whisky, then you can tell me.'

'Jimmy was there, Jimmy Henbury.' Bob gulped down some whisky. 'That's a bit better.' He took a deep breath. 'D'you know, Annie, Jimmy was marvellous. Organised us all, calm as you like. Should have been a general or something. Told me to come home and get some rest. "Not much use so tired," he said. "Get some rest, Bob, then come back." Emmy was there too, Annie. Cool as a cucumber. You'd have been proud.'

'Proud of you, too, Bob.'

Bob was suddenly calmer. He put his glass down and took both her hands in his. 'D'you know, Annie, it was the first time for ages I've been any use. Annie, you *would* have been proud of me, wouldn't you? Wouldn't you?'

'You know I would. I always am, if you did but know it. I'll go and run a bath.'

Bob stretched out his arm and took her wrist.

'Annie,' He looked at her anxiously, almost shyly. 'Won't you come and do my back, like you used to?'

'Now just you come along, stupid. Of course I will.'

Annie had never really liked the hair on Bob's back, but now she took pleasure in soaping it to a lather.

'Those poor chaps were back from Dunkirk. OK, that's just right, Annie.' He closed his eyes and lent back in the bath while Annie ran in some more hot water. 'One of them told me they'd all been strafed on the beach by the German planes and lots of them just lay there and no-one could do anything as the Germans kept coming over machine-gunning. It was a miracle anyone got off the beach at all. Then they come back here safe up at Pengale, just get new kit and that and sorted out. And then the buggers come back and bomb 'em again.'

'How on earth did they know? Where they were, I mean?'

'They have these flying boats, Dorniers, an' they track our boats. And Jimmy says that they know all about the Coastal Command place at Mawgan, and came looking for it, and saw all the troop trucks. Pretty clever, if you ask me.'

Bob slowly began to towel himself down, then sat down heavily on the bathroom stool. 'Pretty bloody clever, those buggers, Annie. Don't see how we'll ever beat them.'

'Oh, we'll beat them all right,' said Annie.

'You always say that when we've got to get the corn in when it's rainin' cats and dogs.' Annie laughed. 'Yes, and that's just it. We always do.'

He put on a clean check shirt, corduroys and boiler suit. 'I'll jus' lie down for a bit, Annie.'

'I'll bring some tea up in a couple of hours.'

Bob shook his head. 'Forty minutes. Not a sec longer. It's important that I'm there.'

* * *

Emily didn't know how much she would be allowed to tell Tom about the raid on Pengale camp. She told him of everyone's - especially Peter's - pride in Tom's commission. Then she thought she would risk the censorship man. Let him decide, she told herself.

Anyway, Tom, - she had consciously decided that the only way she could write to him was to pretend that she was just talking to him as she used to on the headland - *anyway Tom, we were really proud of your Pa when there was a raid on some of our fellows at the camp you know where and Jimmy, who was wonderful, and I did some helping there too, but your Pa saved the lives of two of the soldiers who but for him would have bled to death and he spent all night searching for the wounded boys and bringing them back to the hospital tent and he and some of the soldiers including a young officer who was covered in blood all did what your Pa said and they dug out some men with their bare hands from a hut which had been blown to bits.*

Emily sat back sucking her pen. She wondered whether this would upset Tom and he would worry, so she wrote that everyone was quite OK and now they were ready there wouldn't be any more raids, Jimmy said.

Pa was very upset afterwards, Ma said, and couldn't eat anything and said he didn't know how we'd ever win against the Germans. And do you know what Ma said, with people like Tom and Jimmy and you, meaning Pa, and those brave soldiers, we can't lose. I'm going to train as a volunteer nurse after that night as I could have helped a lot more if I'd known what to do. Jimmy said I was marvelous anyway but I think he was just trying to cheer me up, and Jimmy thinks nursing would be a good idea. I don't have to do it full-time, just when needed and can carry on helping Jimmy with the building business. Any way we got Grandfather doing a lot more with the vegetable garden now you're not here, Tom, and he's got quite keen and produces some lovely stuff and it gives him lots to grumble at - he says he gets no credit, everyone else fighting and nursing or whatever and here's me slaving away at my age with my bad back - you can just hear him, Tom, can't you, but he really enjoys doing something to help. He spends most time down with Ma at the farmhouse and Ma has made up a room for him and I think he's much less awkward and nasty than he used to be now he's got the hotel off his mind. So the war does some good in a funny way. It makes everyone pull together, as Mr Churchill says.

* * *

Emily's letter got to the Officers' mess while Tom and George were still in the Karkaar Mountains, or rather, in the foothills running eastwards from Erigave. The track to the border with Italian Somaliland was littered with boulders and was more suited to camels and donkeys than their 15cwt, but after their recent experience they could not leave the truck and go on foot.

'Can't see anywhere to turn round anyway,' George muttered. 'We'll just have to bash on to the border.'

Forty minutes later, having crawled forward in second gear, they caught sight of splodges of red paint on the hillside. Round the next sharp bend they came to an impenetrable row of barbed wire coiled along crossed beams. A footpath wide enough for a camel led alongside it to a small compound, in which stood an open-sided shed with a corrugated iron roof.

Two soldiers appeared from the shed brandishing sub-machine guns. They were stripped to the waist, and one had a cigarette stuck between his lips. They had obviously been taken by surprise at the sound of the truck and looked extremely nervous. Even, Tom thought, trigger-happy…

Chapter 11

'We can't reverse,' said George. 'They'll just open up. Probably miss, but we can't rely on it.'

He opened his holster and drew out his pistol, keeping it out of sight below the steering wheel. 'We may have to fight it out, but it will probably cause an international incident. Excuse for Italy to come in. Think of that, Tom. We're going to start a war.'

'Better not,' said Tom. He turned round to Rachid in the back. 'Give me a sten, Rachid. And get the other one loaded. And give me a bottle of that whisky from the hold- all.'

To George's astonishment, Tom flung the empty stengun through the open window of the truck. George watched as he stepped cautiously out onto the dusty track to be greeted by a torrent of unintelligible Italian.

Tom moved slowly towards the frightened soldiers, his arms raised in surrender. One hand, however, was brandishing the whisky bottle.

'We come in peace,' said Tom, (still with the notion of Tom Mix and the Indians in mind).

The young soldiers continued to level their guns uncertainly towards him as he approached the barbed wire and proffered the whisky to them. The coiled wire was far too thick for them to reach the whisky, so after a voluble high-pitched discussion, they gestured to Tom to come round to the footpath.

Tom turned and signaled to George and Rachid to join him, and they too, arms raised, came into the compound.

The young Italians saw with relief that they were unarmed. They made no attempt to take the whisky, but somewhat to George's alarm, waved their guns at him, obviously telling them to stay where they were. They then turned and went into their hut, slamming the door behind them.

Rachid appeared unmoved by the situation. But George and Tom exchanged anxious glances: they were unarmed and caught in an enclosure with two young half-trained soldiers who might easily panic with disastrous consequences.

The youths suddenly reappeared, laughing, in their cotton uniforms, one wearing insignia George took to be corporal's stripes.

They were carrying not their automatic weapons, but carafes of rough red wine and a selection of mugs and glasses.

One of them attempted some English. 'No warra,' he shouted, repeatedly.

'No war,' repeated George, laughing with relief. He then thought to try some Latin. 'Pacifico Inglesa, Italia. Amare opera, vinum.'

The boys roared with laughter. 'Tosca!' yelled one and attempted a snatch of an aria. Then sticking out his chest and with a dramatic gesture, the corporal announced 'Il Barbiere di Siviglia' and intoned a reply in a quite acceptable tenor.

A little competition ensued in which George joined. 'Gilbert and Sullivan!' he said, to the complete bewilderment of the Italians, not helped by his indifferent rendering of a half- remembered verse of the Major-General.

Rachid (who refused all drink) stared at them impassively; Tom sat down heavily in the shade of the hut and watched them all, quite bemused.

He remembered the whisky. He offered it to them again, shouting 'Take - the- bottle!' but the Italians were suddenly serious and started to chatter to each other and made emphatic gestures of refusal.

Rachid said: 'I think they fear that the officers will find it and they find out about you too and -' He drew his finger across his throat.

'No. You all go,' said the Corporal, fearful again.

George offered his hand. 'Amicitia,' he said. 'No war.' He pointed to the plains to the southeast, and grinned. 'No exercitus. No milites hoc loco.'

Whether they understood him or not, it was evident that that there was nor could there be any useful purpose in a concentration of troops on that eastern border.

They all pushed back the barbed wire barrier so that Rachid could turn the truck round. The soldiers embraced each of them in turn and waved to them from their compound.

'No warra!' they shouted after them.

'Poor fellows,' said George. "We shall have to shoot them if we see them in a few days' time.'

'I shall not shoot them,' said Tom gravely. 'They are decent fellows and have done no harm to anyone.'

George made no reply but concentrated on negotiating the stony track back to Erigave.

* * *

The melancholy Sergeant Jock presented himself at the lobby of the mess hut as soon as they got back.

'Bad news, sirs,' he said, the downward curves of his greying moustache emphasizing the gloom of his visage.

'Sorry to hear that, Jock,' said George. 'Pleased to see us back, eh?'

'That I am, sirs,' said Jock, with a suspicion of warmth in his tone. 'That's just it. There's a new Brigade Major, come from Aden, and he's tryin' to get our lads sent off. Doesn't like them on the gun, sir. Says they're bad for discipline.'

'Why so? They've been misbehaving, Jock?'

'Not a bit of it, sir. They've been drillin' me - that is, I've been drillin' them, like, on the two-five, until, well, long after hours, an' the new Major don't like it. Thinks they're plottin' something.'

'Plotting? Never met more honest fellows. Open books. We'd better see him. Let's get the kit stowed. Send some of them over to lend a hand, Jock.'

'The new Major says you're to go as soon as you gets here, sirs.'

'Does he indeed?' George started to unload the truck, handing his holdall to Rachid. 'Do as I say, Sergeant. Get those men here to unload this truck at the stores, and go with them to check the stuff in for me. Captain Jorret and I are going to get some tea and brush ourselves up.'

'What shall I tell Major Brimshaw, sir?'

George paused. 'Tell him that you have delivered his message, that I thank him for it, and that we are in the Mess -'

'- and we'll be along directly,' added Tom.

* * *

Brushed up or not, they hardly looked smart and soldierly officers as they presented themselves to the new Brigade Major. Even with his uniform beautifully cleaned and pressed by his Gambian batman, Joni Kru, the khaki drill shirt and shorts were draped over, rather than worn by, George Johnson. Alongside him, standing to his undrilled attention, was the neat, shorter and burly figure of Acting Captain Tom Jorret, whom ignorant observers could have described as corpulent.

Major Brimshaw regarded them with ill-concealed displeasure. He had cold, hooded blue eyes beneath bristling ginger brows. His ginger hair was cropped like an RSM's with only a hint of grey over the temples, and his thin upper lip sported a neatly trimmed Clark Gable-like moustache, except that it too was gingery. He stood up from behind his desk when they had formally presented themselves, and was almost as tall as George Johnson, but superbly built and obviously extremely fit.

His handshake was firm to the point of painful. He gestured to them to sit down whilst he perched himself on the edge of the desk.

'Now then, gentlemen, I have been seconded here to help prepare for the Eyeties when they come. I think you should know that I shall look for the highest standards of smartness and efficiency from my officers-' (It did not go unnoticed by Brimshaw that George had raised an eyebrow at this, but had said nothing) 'Oh, indeed, gentlemen, I have to use my seniority if and when necessary, should it be so.'

Yes, Headmaster, no, Headmaster. Funny how people who get a bit of authority feel it necessary to tell everyone about it.

'Now I've had the opportunity to look through your files during your -' he paused and stared at them fixedly, '- during your absence, for which I would be grateful for an explanation?'

'Leave. We took some leave.'

'And you took one of our vehicles? And an interpreter?'

'Correct.'

'By whose authority?'

'Clearance from Colonel Jackson. We did a recce. Unofficially.'

'This is the kind of thing we must stop gentlemen.'

'I've no doubt the Italians will soon be stopping this kind of thing.'

Brimshaw grunted. 'And what was the object of the "recce"?'

Johnson got to his feet. 'Look here, Brimshaw, if we're going to work together, you will have to learn how we do things here. Of course we will submit a full report tomorrow to Colonel Jackson and Intelligence, for what it's worth. In the meantime, I suggest we meet later and have a G and T. Good day to you.'

Brimshaw flushed with anger. 'Just one moment, Major Johnson. You may be expert in your field, as no doubt is Jorret here, but if we are to be an efficient fighting unit you will both have to knuckle down to some discipline. And that applies to those black soldiers you have apparently been training on a Field Gun. I shall put a stop to that, I can tell you. And that doddering old sergeant - he can go home right away.'

'Those soldiers from Gambia have made themselves into just such an efficient fighting unit under Sergeant Jamison as even you could demand. As for Sergeant Jamison, he has signed on for the duration, and that is all there is to it. Now you can come for a drink with us, or not, as you please, Brimshaw.'

Jock was waiting for them outside, and had no doubt heard only part of the exchange, as Major Brimshaw had a very loud voice, and George Johnson a very soft one.

'Is it goin' to be all right, Major Johnson, about the boys and the gun an' that?'

'Don't know yet, Jock, but yes, I'm sure we'll work something out.'

Jock looked at his most woeful. 'Don't want to part with 'em, sir, not after all that work an' that. I thinks they like it 'ere, too.' He heaved a great sigh. 'Oh, nearly forgot,' he added. 'There's some letters for you, sirs. I kept them back from pryin' eyes, so to speak, but left them in your mess, sirs.'

'I don't think poor Jock cares for our new Major, Tom.'

'Not sure I do, for that matter.'

Tom had two letters, a rare one from Annie, and the other, of course, from Emily. He decided to put them aside until after his gin-and-tonic.

Chapter 12

6th June 1940

Dear Tom,

Hope you are well as this finds your Pa and me, just to tell you some bad news. Your Auntie Daisy died, very sudden, just as she was sitting down pulling off her boots. I know she was never happy, Tom, she just loved her cows and didn't really like any people. The funeral's Thursday. Then would you believe! We just heard that poor Mr Harris was killed in France three weeks before they all got away at Dunkirk. The officer wrote a nice letter to Emmy but you can imagine she was very upset even though they hadn't seen each other for so long, only for a few months after they got married, which your Grandfather said was such a mistake, which I suppose it was really. Emmy had to have a few days off but Mr Henbury didn't mind and was very kind, brought her flowers and that. I think they may get together now, which would be very nice even though its sad about poor Mr Harris, it does free Emmy from worry about what became of Mr Harris. He must have been called up. I told your Grandfather off, he would keep on about poor Mr Harris not being like Steve and you, and Emmy in floods of tears. Your Pa says all the animals are fine, though we had to have old Cowslip put down, she was a good milker in her day but got ill when she was so old. But what we'll do without Daisy I just don't know. Your Pa 's going to advertise for a Land Girl you should just hear what your Grandfather says about that! Won't have silly ignorant girls on the farm, seems to forget that I've been on the farm all these years. The Farmers Union says its mad too but the government started up the training before the war and so we'll properbly get one. Just as well you're not here or we'd have some larks I bet! Only joking of course, we do so want you back safe and sound. With love from your Pa and even your grandpa if he'd admit it. Your loving Ma xxx

Tom put the letter down and took another sip of gin. 'Emmy's husband's been killed, at Dunkirk,' he said.

'Sorry to hear that, Tom.'

'Yes. She hadn't seen him for years, though. Funny chap, didn't want to do anything at all. Something in Insurance, I think. No-one could understand what Emmy saw in him. Grandfather thought he was just after Emmy's money, till Harris realized she hadn't really got any, unless the old blighter gave it her, which he wouldn't.'

'There are some ladies,' said George, 'who are only keen on fellows they can look after. Someone they can take responsibility for. Some bounders trade on that, you know.'

Bounders? Where does he get these words from? Can hardly describe that spineless chap - wait a moment, he might have been brave at the end, who knows? - as a bounder. But Emmy was only keen on him because he pretended to be keen on her.

'You may be right. He wasn't a bounder, though.'

'Perhaps Emily thought that at last someone was taking her seriously, was that it?' George summoned the mess waiter and ordered some more drinks.

Maybe that's it. Never thought you had to have a reason for being fond of someone. Or not fond, for that matter.

Tom slit open Emily's letter with a table-knife: he could not stand an untidy envelope. His grandfather always opened them with his finger. Tom liked a neat edge.

'Gentlemen! Gentlemen, your attention please!'

The burly red figure of Major Brimshaw had burst into the Mess. 'The balloon's gone up, gentlemen!' he bellowed. (There were six officers in the Mess.) 'Mussolini has declared war on Britain and France, and British Somaliland is now a war zone.'

He could not disguise the relish, almost glee, in his voice.

Johnson muttered sotto voce to Tom something about the professional soldier who wanted not to keep the peace, but the opportunities of war.

Brimshaw gave George a withering look. 'Now, we must get straight down to work, gentlemen. No muttering, if you please. Teamwork, gentlemen, teamwork! The time for gins and - holidays - is over. Colonel Jackson has ordered an O-group for ten hundred hours tomorrow morning, the 11th June. You will attend with all relevant material. That is all.' With which he strode out.

'We'd better cut across and have a word with the Colonel about what we found - or didn't find, Tom. Mind you, he'll have a shrewd idea where they'll be coming from, but we can confirm they won't be coming from the east at least. And what of their poor soldiers, eh, Tom? We'll have to shoot them after all.'

* * *

The Intelligence Officer Colonel Jackson, who like Major Brimshaw had been seconded from the KAR, stood before an enormous wall-map, pointer in hand.

'I shall not take your time with a history lesson,

gentlemen.' Nonetheless he did so. 'Forty or so years ago the Italians suffered the only defeat of a European power at the hands of a native African people, at the battle here.'

He pointed to the town of Adowa close to the border of French Somaliland. 'The French had fallen out with the Italians some years before and supported the Abyssinians with arms and training - and in doing so consolidated their hold on Djibouti.'

'But you know all that.' (Tom knew none of it: he determined to consult the Phillips School Atlas again.) 'So four years ago Mussolini revenged that defeat and conquered Abyssinia with machine-guns, aeroplanes and mustard gas against the tribesmen. Now Musso is going to expand his new Roman Empire here at our expense, and probably get his revenge on the French at the same time. So we anticipate he will drive to the coast very soon.'

Jackson looked gravely around the room. 'I cannot disguise from you all that we are faced with a serious tactical situation, for when he strikes he will heavily outnumber us. But there are several points in our favour. We do not know how the French will turn out. The Germans are in Paris without a fight, but what will become of the French colonies? Will they, and our neighbours along the coast,' - here he pointed to French Somaliland - 'and Djibouti in particular, will they resist the Italians? I suspect they will.'

He then turned to Ethiopia. 'And here is the country he seized only three or four years ago, a country seething with hatred against Italy for her incomparable cruelties, a conquered people only demanding the call to rise and seize Mussolini by the throat.'

Inspired by his own rhetoric, Colonel Jackson put down his pointer and gestured wildly to his somewhat bemused audience of officers. 'Soon their leader will return, aye, and the Italians will have no place to hide from their wrath.'

He caught Brimshaw's eye and coughed. 'Oh yes,' he added lamely. 'Valuable allies there, French and Abyssinians.' He referred to his notes. 'The Camel Corps scouts have identified the great concentration of Italian forces in Degeh Bur and the plains to the north of the township. We have seen no troop movements to the east from the Italian border: indeed, two of our officers have confirmed the Camel Corps report that the country is impassable for large numbers, and it makes no strategic sense for an Italian attack from that direction.'

He nodded towards George and Tom and went on: 'they add an anecdotal note that the ordinary Italian soldiery is probably ill-prepared morally and physically for war. On the other hand, we have confirmed the presence of highly trained Fascist Blackshirt units and an Alpini battalion in the forces at Degeh Bur. Many of the other units are drawn from local Askaris, but they should not be underrated. Any questions so far?'

'Yes, sir. What numbers are we talking of?' Jackson paused.

'Approximately two hundred and fifty thousand,' he said.

Long low whistles of alarm greeted this answer.

'But remember,' he added hastily, 'this force is split between four sectors, of which ours is, well, er, only one,' he ended lamely.

He shuffled his papers. 'Remember too,' he added, '70 per cent of the forces are locally recruited and trained, and many of those are simply for keeping order, not fighting units. A great deal of their armoured equipment is obsolete by our standards. And their rifle, for instance, is known as the '91 - it was designed in 1891!'

Jackson looked about him with a grin, but there were no

answering smiles.

'Gentlemen: we don't know when, or if, they will strike at us. They may well go for the Sudan, or Kenya: bear in mind that it is prestige as much as strategy that governs Mussolini's thinking. I shall circulate a memo - top secret, I need hardly remind you - of what we know of their strengths and equipment (machine-guns, etc) in greater detail.'

Tom and George made their way back to the Mess in gloomy silence, broken only when they had their drinks before them.

'It's very well for Jackson to say their men are locally raised and so on, but so are ours, all the KAR, ' said Tom thoughtfully.

'Oh, I don't know.' Johnson grinned. 'We have some Gambians.'

'Brimshaw won't be able to send them away now. And we'll need the gun.'

'Send who away?' Brimshaw had come up to their table unnoticed.

'Our Gambian gun-crew,' said Johnson coolly

Brimshaw grunted. 'Already sent to the War Office to have them transferred to the KAR in Kenya. They can join the rest of the Nigerians there.'

'They're not Nigerians, they're Gambians.'

'Same difference. They'll run away just as fast.'

George put out a restraining hand as Tom, flushed with anger, half rose to his feet. 'We'll see about that soon enough, Brimshaw,' said George mildly. He fished in his pocket and brought out a crumpled message form. 'I have clearance from Colonel Chater. Message reads: Keep them here. Need every man jack. Jorret I/c 25pdr. Chater.'

'Show me that!'

Brimshaw studied the message and turned to Tom.

'Right. You're responsible for those Gambians, then. I warn you - one step out of line on the King's Regulations and I'll - well...'

'Brimshaw! Do sit down and have a drink...'

'Time enough, Johnson, when we've licked those bloody wops!'

George grinned. 'OK. I'll hold you to that.' Brimshaw nodded curtly and turned on his heel.

Tom waited till he had gone and turned on his friend. 'George! When did you get that message from Chater?'

'Sent Jock with a memo first thing this morning and Chater was good enough to get the reply to me before the O-group. Was going to break it to you gently - You're I/c a 25pdr field gun in what Brimshaw calls the War Zone.'

Tom sat silent for a long moment.

'God!' he said at last. 'I've forgotten Emmy's letter!'

Chapter 13

There was an atmosphere of studied panic in the Mess.

One of the Camel Corps lieutenants told George and Tom that they had fewer than 1500 men to defend the whole of British Somaliland. The Camel Corps and a Northern Rhodesia battalion made up the whole force, with only a few guns and Bren gun carriers to ward off an estimated 25,000 Italians from Ethiopia, should they come.

'They'll come all right,' said another. 'Wouldn't you? If you had a quarter of a million men in East Africa, all used to the terrain?'

'Divided into four sectors, remember,' said George, without conviction.

'Well, perhaps they'll go for the other three then. Anyway, it's all right for you artillery chaps, blasting away from the back.'

Tom had just settled down to read Emmy's letter when they were summoned to report to Colonel Chater's HQ. Chater was the commander of the Camel Corps and assumed temporary command of all the defence forces.

'We're getting some KARs from Kenya and, from Aden, a battalion each of the Punjabis, Rhodesians and the Black Watch. In the meantime, we must defend with all the guns we can muster, Major Johnson, against an advance on Berbera though the Tug-Argen pass. We shall rely on the

French to safeguard our right flank: I have conferred with General Lengentilhomme who has a considerable force at his disposal to bar any Italian advance on the coast to the west.'

Chater and Johnson pored over the map, making preliminary plans for the siting of the few guns that were at Johnson's disposal. It was clear even to Tom that Colonel Chater was over- confident of their ability to withstand a determined Italian offensive, with such an overwhelming superiority in numbers and expertise over the Somalian terrain. Colonel Chater, indeed, as commander of the Somalian Camel Corps, was obviously concerned with reconnaissance and skirmishing and (as he freely admitted) could not contribute to a static defensive war except on the fringes.

'But it might not come to that,' he said. 'I'm sure the Italians will go for Djibouti. If they have that, they'll be in a position to threaten all our shipping through to the Suez Canal. But the French have all the men and arms to keep them out.'

'Berbera, surely, would do just as well for them, strategically?' 'Well, we'll see.'

On which unsatisfactory note George and Tom spent the next weeks in a desperate attempt to build the emplacements for the defence of Berbera.

Tom also had to prepare himself and the Gambians for the probability of fighting. He began to feel the pressure of overwork in the stifling heat, and relied more and more on the Gambian crew to build the emplacement for their field gun, which they sited on a hillside commanding the road leading north to Tug Argen.

They made Lamin Bah up to full corporal.

'It's all very well, Lamin Bah, but you must quieten them

all down. It's not a game. Once we open fire on them, this emplacement becomes a target, and we could all get badly hurt.'

'I tell them all that, Tom, sir, but they very keen, sir, an' dyin' to fight them Eyeties for you and the Major, sir.'

'Not for us, Lamin Bah, it's for…' *What the hell IS it for? Why are these young men from the other side of Africa going to risk their lives fighting the Italians over this God-forsaken stretch of rocks and sand?*

'We protect Smaliland, Tom, sir, because you and the Major say so.'

Tom suddenly felt a crushing weight of responsibility. *Only a few months ago contentedly watching his skylarks, not responsible to anyone and responsible for no-one, after all if Terry Samson wanted to risk his life, who was he to stop him? Now…*

'Our job to protect you and the Major, Tom, sir,' added Lamin Bah.

Tom patted him on the shoulder. 'And ours to protect you fellows, Lamin Bah, and get you back home safely one day.'

Lamin Bah pulled a face. 'No, we really happy here, Tom, sir, useful and important.'

'You might be, Lamin Bah, but what about the others? Don't they all want to get back to Gambia?'

Lamin Bah sat down on the concrete wall of the emplacement and thought for a while. 'Don't know, some do. We have plenty money to send back. Girls here no good, Tom, sir, dangerous. Joni Kru likes to stay here, and Frelli, but the others homesick sometimes, happy most of time. So don't know, sir, but money good, and uniforms.'

I was a pleasant uncomplicated fellow like Lamin Bah taking things as they came. Now I'm here sweltering in this bloody heat in a rocky desert, which God knows why we occupied in the first place. The Somalis don't seem to mind: they just get on with their miserable lives whether we're here or not...

'A word, Captain Jorret.' It was Major Brimshaw again, bristling, red-faced and running with sweat. 'Dismiss, Corporal!'

Lamin Bah leapt to his feet, saluted smartly, and marched off, with that exaggerated arm swing the West African soldiers always use.

Brimshaw returned the salute cursorily. 'Look here, Jorret, you are far too pally with these fellows, sitting down and chatting like a - like a couple of old natives in a kraal or something.'

'He's an excellent man, and keen as mustard.' *Why am I beginning to talk like Brimshaw? Keen as mustard?* 'And it's bloody hot, so we find some shade.'

'That's all very well, but when the balloon goes up-' *it's gone up once already, surely,* '-you're going to need the tightest discipline or you'll find those black fellows scampering off.'

'Brimshaw, why are we here?'

'Why are we where?'

'Here, in Somaliland, fighting the Italians.'

Brimshaw looked as if someone had punched him in the stomach. 'What? What? The heat must be getting to you, Jorret. You must pull yourself together, man. Think on it, Jorret, or you'll not have the spirit for a fight when it comes to it.'

'When the balloon goes up?

'Exactly. Stiffen the sinews, Jorret. Ours not to question why, ours but to -' Brimshaw realized that the quotation could hardly do much for morale, so he stalked off, muttering to himself and shaking his head.

Tom took another look round the emplacement. He grunted with satisfaction to see the immaculate condition in which the Gambians had left it.

He started up the motorbike he had borrowed from the Signals and drove over to their encampment. They had found a relatively shady site to pitch a large sand-coloured bell-tent (which dated, Tom noted, not from the Great War, but from the Boer War).

They were playing football, three-a-side, in the heat.

Tom called them together. He was fearful of being pompous, but he had somehow to give them some idea of the danger they were in. What would Brimshaw say? *You've done a grand job, lads. Thanks to you, we'll be able to hit them for six when the balloon goes up.*

'Look, -er- when they come, we've done all we can, but, well, we might have to - might be wounded or even - killed.' They all sat there grinning at him, all teeth and round black eyes.

Joni Kru said: 'No worry, Tom, sir. We ready and willin.' They all laughed uproariously at this.

Tom shook his head in amused bafflement. 'OK. I'll join in if I may.'

In fact, Tom had been quite a good footballer, and he was a little put out when they all "accidentally" fed him the ball, or pretended to be beaten by his runs, or persisted in deferentially passing the ball to him all the time. When they started to applaud even his inept miss-kicks, he called a halt.

'Look, it's too hot for me. I'll referee from the shade.'

He sat and watched while they ran joyously about with great athleticism, and he gave up awarding free kicks as the most blatant fouls (which would have done credit to Truro thirds) were greeted with hoots of laughter and derision.

Now they're going to kill and be killed by those Italian

fellows we met at the border post.

After a while he slipped away and drove off on the motorbike to the Mess to read Emily's letter.

* * *

The letter was more than a fortnight old.

Dear Tom,
I expect you've already heard that Mr Harris was killed in France. I didn't know what to think, Tom, because I was terribly sad and felt terrible because I didn't even know he was fighting and I hadn't heard for so long. It's funny but he was my husband but I can't remember him and I only had that old photo of you and him on the beach, him still in his collar and tie and bare feet and rolled-up trousers. I feel it's all my fault that everything went wrong and he just went away as I knew he was short of money and grandfather wouldn't help him when he thought he would. It was good though that he liked me enough to marry me, Tom, even though he couldn't stay long, and now he's killed.

Tom put down the letter down on the table, still partly unread, and cupped his head in his hands. He thought of Emily's joy when she was going to be married, and everyone else's failure to welcome Mr Harris. (He suddenly realized that he didn't remember Harris's Christian name, and Emmy hadn't even used it in her letter.) Everyone knew, except poor Emily, that Harris did not love Emily in the slightest: his affection for her was clearly no more than lukewarm. Yet Emily was blaming herself for the failure of the marriage!

Tom turned almost unwillingly back to the letter.

I had a very nice letter from his officer.

Corporal James Sydney Harris, RAPC

Dear Mrs Harris,
I expect the War Office has already informed you the sad news that James was killed in action but I am writing to tell you that you can be sure that he died instantly and did not suffer. Our Headquarters personnel all fought very bravely to cover the retreat of our unit but they were overrun by the enemy. It may be some comfort to know that it was owing to the courage of soldiers like James that so many of our troops were able to get back from Dunkirk.
Yours very sincerely, Bernard Wilson, Capt. RA.

It was very good of Captain Wilson to take all that time to write when he must have been so busy. I never thought of Mr Harris as being a brave man particularly, he was always very quiet, but we can all be proud of him now, can't we?

We are going to get a land girl to help with the farm and she arrives Tuesday. I wonder what she'll be like? Do hope that you are well and liking it out there, Tom. Pa and Ma and Grandfather all send their love, your loving sister Emmy.

George Johnson joined him, and Tom showed him Emily's letter.

'What d'you make of it, George? A good letter from this fellow Wilson. Hope I don't have to write any like that, to Gambia.'

'Yes. Good for him. Not a standard letter and must have been a comfort.'

'D'you think it's - true?'

'Who knows? Probably. Possibly. But it's true as far as

Emmy's concerned, and that's what counts.'

Once again an excited Major Brimshaw burst in on them.

'This is it! The balloo- ' This time he caught the expression on their faces and cut himself short. 'No, gentlemen, the Wops have attacked our air bases in Kenya, and there are ominous troop movements on the Sudan frontier. And, gentlemen, in Northern Ethiopia. Chater's men have reported that the Wop armour is massing north of Degeh Bur.'

Chapter 14

In some ways it had proved a false alarm.

'I am afraid, gentlemen,' Chater told them the following afternoon, 'that there have been some casualties. The Italians attacked our airfield at Wajir in Kenya with three bombers at dawn and four of our KAR men were killed, and some wounded when a fuel dump went up. We lost some aircraft too, but reports are still vague on that.

'I have to tell you, gentlemen - and this is top secret - that we are receiving reinforcements. We are getting another Punjabi Battalion, and the 2nd Battalion Black Watch. They should be deployed by the first or second week of August.

'Major Johnson, you will position the East African howitzer battery on the Mill Hill flanking the Berbera road?'

'Yes sir. We have chosen the positions. But four Howitzers, sir -?' He spread his hands in a gesture of resignation.

Chater grinned. 'Ah, but you have Tom's Gambian field gun. No, seriously, there are plans for more artillery to come from Aden. It's all a bit of a rush, though, gentlemen, but I know we can send these fellows packing if they come.'

He crossed to the wall map again.

'But although there is a considerable concentration of Italian forces some twenty miles inside the Ethiopian border, my men are certain there are no signs of any enemy reconnaissance vehicles, let alone scouting parties, advancing northwards. That being so, we should stand down for the time being, but be ready to take up battle stations if and when we have further indications. But for now, we must assume that their offensives will be towards Port Sudan and in Kenya.'

Even Tom with his scant knowledge of military affairs thought that Col. Chater was rather like one of his camels in avoiding the sandstorm. He kept his misgivings to himself but over their gins George raised the matter anyway.

'I have a feeling Aden will be replacing old Chater and let him get on with his camels.' 'Now how d'you know that?'

George shrugged his shoulders and grinned. 'Well, Chater really hasn't much idea about troops in the field. He admitted as much himself. Aden are bound to send someone with a bit more rank if we're getting these infantry units. There's a company of the Punjabis will be digging in on your hill, incidentally. You'll have to keep your chaps from shelling them. They are sending some Black Watch too, when they come. If they come. But it'd be quite a nice touch, sending the Black Watch to look after your fellows, eh?'

'I don't know what they'll make of the kilts.'

'No. I don't know what to make of them either.'

They sipped their gins.

'There's another thing,' said George. 'Rumour has it -'

'Ye-es?'

'Rumour has it that one of the Punjabi company commanders - your company actually - is staying back in Aden. Fever or something. So HQ had to find someone else for the time being, and who does HQ want to get off their backs?'

'Not Brimshaw!'

'The very man, experienced, confident, a great soldier. It's only a rumour, mind. But he's meeting the troopship tomorrow. So they say.'

'*They*, I suppose, is your friend Jackson?'

George grinned and mimicked Brimshaw's booming voice. 'Not at liberty to say. But when the balloon goes up, you'll be reassured that he will be by your side.'

* * *

George was right. Brimshaw's company headquarters were uncomfortably close to Tom's emplacement. Indeed, Tom had the suspicion that they were sited as much to give the Major a chance to keep an eye on him and his crew as to supervise his own men.

'Had a peek at your man on guard duty, Jorret,' said Brimshaw. 'Not alert enough. Have a word.'

'There's no duty roster as such: I prefer that they shelter from this mid-day sun.'

'Not good enough. I might have been anyone, coming on him unawares.'

'He wouldn't think you an Italian spy, sir. I'm sure of it. We are all used to seeing you about.'

Brimshaw gave him a sideways look. 'Ye-es. Very good. But I think I'll give the man a little drill practice. See how he shapes up.'

Tom looked at him in astonishment. '*Drill practice, sir?*'

Brimshaw bared his teeth in what passed for a grin. 'Thought that'd make you sit up Jorret. You're too soft with these useless so-and-sos. Vital part of our defences here. Must be on the alert.'

'Yes, but really, sir… The Eyeties are *miles* away.'

'All the more reason to keep on the *qui vive*,' replied Brimshaw, and to Tom's amazement, the Major put down his swagger cane on the emplacement wall, and marched across to where the unfortunate Gambian (rifleman Bari Din) was sheltering from the sun.

'*You there!*' bawled the Major.

Bari Din jumped to his feet. 'Me, sah, Major sah?'

'*Yes, you sah! Come here! At the double, man!*'

Bari Din looked thoroughly alarmed, and in his haste, fumbled with his rifle, dropped it, made to pick it up, hesitated, and finally abandoned it to sprint over to Brimshaw and stood rigidly to attention before him.

The Major was now genuinely angry. '*What d'you mean by it, lad? Don't you know, your rifle's your best friend, lad? Go and get it!*'

Din sprinted back for the rifle, and, terrified, rolled his eyes at Brimshaw. '*Look to your front! ATTEN - SHUN!*'

Bari Din responded immediately: Staff-Sergeant Jock's long hours in the sun had paid off: the Gambians all drilled superbly. Brimshaw then screamed a quick-fire succession of orders to which Din responded impeccably.

Brimshaw, already sweating profusely, walked across to and put his swagger cane down on the emplacement wall.

'*For inspection, PORT ARMS!*'

The Major took the rifle, checked the safety catch, and clicked off the magazine, which he handed back to the soldier.

'What's your name, lad?'

'Rifleman 77 O7 Bari Din, sah.'

'How many rounds you got there then, Gungar Din?'

'Two live rounds in magazine, sah, four live rounds in pouch, safe and sound, sah.'

Brimshaw squinted down the barrel to check its condition. A grunt testified the Major's somewhat reluctant approval. He tossed the rifle back to Bari Din who caught it deftly.

By this time the others had gathered round to watch. Swinging their legs, they sat in a line along the wall. Joni Kru nearly sat on the Major's swagger stick and, grinning, passed it behind his back to his neighbour. Soon it was being smuggled between them in a laughing hunt-the-thimble game.

Inevitably, to their horror, the cane slipped over the wall into the gun pit.

'*Right then, Gungar Din. ATTen -SHUN! PRE-sent ARMS! SLO-OPE ARMS! A-BOUT TURN!*

FORward MARCH!'

Bari Din was now enjoying himself hugely, while the Major stood roaring his commands, with the shirt clinging to his back with sweat, until finally he had had enough.

'That'll do, then, Gungar Din.' He spoke almost kindly. 'Don't let me catch you idling again, or you'll be doin' drill all day.'

Bari Din saluted smartly and turned to find his comrades. But they were nowhere to be seen.

'Ought to have learnt me lesson in Kenya with the Rifles. But they mustn't let you see you can't take the heat as well as they can. Give these black fellows an inch an' they'll take a mile, Jorret.'

'I suppose so.'

Brimshaw took off his Pith helmet and mopped his brow. 'Now where did I put that bloody stick?' He looked about him. 'I know! It was on that wall, wasn't it? Wasn't it? Just where your bloody men were sitting? What've they done with it? You find it, Jorret, or they'll all be on a charge! They've stolen it, haven't they? Rank insubordination! My God, I'll have their bloody balls for this!'

'I expect it slipped into the gun-pit,' said Tom.

But at that moment Joni Kru had appeared up the steps.

He carried Brimshaw's swagger stick under his left arm. He saluted smartly and with a broad grin, all white teeth, handed the stick to the Major in ceremonial fashion.

'I the honour to present it you, Major sah.'

'And what the devil've you been doing with it?'

'I didn't think it would've gone far,' said Tom.

Brimshaw managed to take control of himself with a visible effort and snatched the stick from the laughing Kru. 'Right. Now get out.' He waved the stick in acknowledgement of Joni Kru's salute and turned back to Tom.

'I tell you, Jorret, that's typical of these bloody useless buggers. Think everything's a joke. No discipline. God help us when the Eyeties come.' He fell into a brief reverie, and then to Tom's astonishment, clapped Tom on the shoulder. 'Yes: when the Eyeties come. A day or two now, Tom. Not much doubt about it. Might be our last chance to get together in the Mess before the balloo- before the Eyeties come. Appreciate it if you'd be there. George too.'

He set off back to the infantry lines, but turned back. "'Warned you, Jorret: you can't trust that lot. You'll see. Hope not, but you'll see.'

* * *

Emily tried to pin the paper down as she skimmed through the *Western Morning news* for the umpteenth time.

'There's nothing. They don't even mention Africa. Just the bombing and that. They don't even say anything about the bombing on Penhale.'

'No: they wouldn't. Don't want the Germans to know how serious it was.' Jimmy Henbury tried in vain for a third time to light his pipe. 'Blast.' He put his pipe back in his pocket. 'They don't want our own papers to say anything about it, either. Bad for morale, if they knew all those poor beggars from Dunkirk had been shot up like that.'

The waves were crashing against the rocks, and every now and then spray would be blown into their faces even on their perch on the cliff edge.

'Anyway, I think we'd better be getting back now, Emmy. I've a lot to do before I go.'

'No. Just a little longer. I love it here. I always think of Tom, watching the skylarks. It's so peaceful.'

Jimmy grinned and gave her a little peck on the cheek. 'Peaceful? Just look at that!'

A huge wave broke it's back against the cliff, in a storm of white spray.

'No: I don't know how to say it. There's no war. It's how things should be.'

'Yes, I know, Emmy. And will be again,' said Jimmy. 'But we'd better go.'

He gave her his hand and helped her to her feet and put his arm about her as they made their slow way back to the farm.

Chapter 15

It was not so much nervousness at the thought of the fighting that worried Tom: it was just that he could not stand doing nothing. Just waiting about. He longed to unpack his masonry tools from his kit and just carving something out of the rare sandstone he had found.

Now he was sitting in the Mess waiting again, for Brimshaw and (he hoped) George to turn up.

He stared gloomily at the untouched gin in front of him, and felt in his pocket for Emily's most recent letter. He turned the envelope over and looked at the King's head on the stamp. Handsome bugger, he said to himself irreverently. I'm supposed to die for him, King and country.

He began to read the letter for the sixth or seventh time. *I still don't know, Tom, if Jimmy and me should get married, not with Mr Harris going. (He's been gone for ten years, you daft maid, thought Tom, so what's the difference?) Grandfather doesn't like him, Jimmy I mean, Jimmy says it's because he stands up to him and doesn't let me get bullied, and he says that he's after my money, which can't be so as I keep telling him because Jimmy's very successful in his building and I haven't any money anyway, at least none worth marrying me for.*

Barmy world, thought Tom. Here's me in this God-forsaken heap of sand and rocks waiting to get shot by

Italians, and there's Emmy on *her* sand and rocks worrying about getting married because, well, because of the late Mr Harris.

He wearily put the letter on the table and consulted his watch. Where have they got to? Waiting again: waiting for Brimshaw, waiting for the Eyeties. It would be another ten days before the Wops attacked - at least, the latest reconnaissance reports from the Camel Corps still insisted that the Italian attack couldn't come in the next ten days. Tom was beginning to doubt whether they were coming at all. It was all right for the Gambians, he thought: they loved to laze about and play their peculiar kind of dice or endless games of Euka Tom had taught them with his packs of cards. They just never thought about time. And once I was like that, Tom said to himself.

Tom had had to stop them polishing the gun. On the contrary, they were shocked and almost rebellious when Tom made them camouflage it with sand-coloured paint, ruining their gleaming paintwork, so he got them to paint it to look like a pile of rocks and they spent hours on it with considerable skill and patience. He just had to hope that that and the camouflage netting would be enough to hide the emplacement from the Italian spotter planes that flew over unchallenged.

He turned back to the letter. *Grandfather keeps talking about "making his arrangements". He's sent that funny woman packing and got a man in to do the Hotel, I don't know why. I expect he thought she was after his money, which she probably was. But what he keeps on about is what's going to happen when he's "gone on". The nice old man from Hancock and Lawrence has been out three or four times because there's all kind of difficulties about Death Duties or something.*

Then came the shock. He read it over and over again. *But*

do you know what, Tom? You remember Terry Samson, your friend who was drowned? (Do I remember him!) *Well, you know we were getting a Land Girl to help us? A Sally SAMSON applied and we've taken her on! She's a cousin or something of Terry and she saw our advertisement and knew it would be us, so she wrote to Pa and we didn't dare tell Grandfather. He thought it was terrible for us to have a girl here anyway and he would have had a fit if he knew it was a Samson! But she's very nice and works very hard and Pa and Ma think she's just what they need. So what do you think of that, Tom? Who'd have thought a Samson would help run the farm!! We have long chats you know where when she has time off and she loves the skylarks too and I tell her about how we used to sit there and all about poor Terry that day.*

George arrived with Brimshaw at last.

'G-and-T, George?' asked Tom. 'What can I get you, Major?'

'A pint. Thanks. It's Terence, Tom. Major Terence J. Brimshaw, KAR, MM.'

He gave a bitter laugh. 'You two are the only friends I …' His voice trailed off. 'It's good to have real friends at last. It's Terence.'

Tom looked at George in blank astonishment.

Terence. It would be. He covered his embarrassment by summoning the waiter and ordering the drinks. *A real friend? I hardly know the man. Poor devil: all this military stuff must be some show. And he, Brimshaw - Terence- looks an absolute mess. Even his bristly little moustache looks bedraggled. What's happened to the poor chap?*

'Everything all right, er, Terence?'

Brimshaw gave a low groan. 'No,' he said. 'It's not all right. I have been a serving officer for twenty-one years. Risen from the ranks, Tom. Did quite well in France in '18 and they gave me a medal for it and when all the subalterns got shot up again at Amiens they moved me up a notch just before the end of the war.' He paused and regarded Tom with his beady eye.

'Well, I would have thought - that is, credit -' George said lamely.

'Still had years to run but no regiment wanted me,' Brimshaw went on, ignoring him. 'Didn't fit in. Not Sandhurst. Not Public School. So they moved me about to Div HQ to do all those admin jobs, which were beneath the *real* officers. . Then they shunted me out to India for a bit. Tried to introduce some bloody discipline but they thought I would upset them, so they sent me to Kenya. KARs. Then they seconded me here to bloody Somaliland.'

He took a gulp of his beer and slammed the glass down in disgust. 'Bloody muck they serve here.' He snapped his fingers for the Mess waiter. 'Take this rubbish away and bring me a Worthington. Two. And don't shake them. Bring me the bottles and I'll pour them. And bring these gentlemen more gins.'

'They'll just slop in the sediment if you don't watch them,' he explained. 'Bloody natives. You can't trust them to do the simplest thing. Can't trust them at all, in fact.' He fixed George with a beady eye. 'Take that Rachid fellow, for instance. Did you know he's run off?'

'Rachid? What d'you mean, run off?'

'Your interpreter friend. He's gone off with dozens of them into the hills. Linked up with lots of other natives, so they say.'

George and Tom exchanged glances.

'I'm not surprised,' George said after a pause. 'Rachid as good as said that he'd have the English rather than the Italians, but he'd much sooner have neither.'

Brimshaw gave a snort of contempt. 'What? Let them run their own show? Cut off the noses of anyone they don't like? They'd string us up as soon as look at us if we let up, you mark my words. And we'd be bloody lucky to just get away with being strung up, I can tell you.'

George regarded him sadly. 'Yes. You may be right. But Rachid and his friends might not let that happen. We don't know.'

'Well, I do,' said Brimshaw. 'We can't change 'em.'

'Neither, it seems, will they change us.' George spoke in his usual quiet and flat tones, but Tom could see his friend's annoyance behind the words.

Tom himself said nothing. He had long come to the view that in matters of politics it was useless to argue against a man's prejudice. Politics was a matter of emotions rather than reason, and he kept out of it.

George was saying that all Rachid wanted was to be left alone. 'Let the English and the Italians fight it out and when they've all done, we'll have our country back: that's how he sees it.'

'Well, they can have it, and good riddance. What d'you think, Tom? Leave it to the 'em, or what?'

What do I think? I think I'd like to be back in Cornwall carving a bit of stone or watching the skylarks on the field by the cliffs. 'Well, I think we ought to leave them to it,' he said slowly. *It's not my responsibility. He's not my responsibility either: can't see why he thinks me a friend. But I can see why the Officers' messes all got rid of him, even if they agreed with him. Not the right sort at all. Not out of the top drawer, I bet that's what they all said.*

'Anyway, Terence,' he said. 'You didn't say why you're feeling a bit low.'

'I was just explaining. It's happened again. Just getting

on with the Punjabi lot, getting them straight, when they said I had to go back to Berbera HQ as soon as they find a replacement. As soon as there's fighting, they bring me out.' He toyed with his glass moodily.

He looked up and stared hard into Tom's eyes. 'And fighting's what I'm good at, Tom. It's when I'm as good as the next man. Better than most, much better. Showed it in France, didn't I?'

* * *

A few days later, on July 23rd, the first Italian spotter planes flew over the British positions on the hillsides overlooking the Tug Argen.

The cumbersome Caproni biplanes flew over unchallenged by the British units apart from some sporadic wild and futile shooting from the Somali irregulars. (They seized any opportunity to fire off their long-barrelled rifles.) When the Gambian gun crew grabbed their rifles Tom forbade any firing: it would only give away their position.

The planes did their tour and chugged back to their bases in Ethiopia.

Tom was concerned about Brimshaw's mental state, so he took the opportunity to go across the four hundred yards or so to Brimshaw's company HQ.

He was halted by a fierce Punjabi guard. 'Halt! Who goes there?'

'Friend. Captain Jorret to confer with Major Brimshaw.'

'Advance friend and be recognized!'

Brimshaw's obviously back on form. Playing by the book: quite right too, I suppose.

No need to have me escorted to his dugout with an armed guard though.

'Terence -,' began Tom, putting out his hand.

'I'd prefer you stick to rank, Captain Jorret. Vital to keep to procedures when the balloon goes up. Chain of Command.' Brimshaw's face was brick red again, and his eyes beneath the bristling ginger brows glowed with excitement.

Bloody hell. Glad he's on our side. 'I'm concerned about air cover, Major,' said Tom. 'Their reconnaissance planes will have us all mapped at this rate. Can't our Air Force chaps do anything about it?'

The Major's look was scornful, almost contemptuous. 'What, Jorret, call up the RAF from Biggin Hill or wherever? Don't you think they're busy enough?'

'No. But - '

'Our nearest Air Strips are in Kenya and the Sudan, Jorret. And those old crates would hardly have time to take off before the Eyeties have bombed us to bits. D'you know what they've got there? Hawker Harts, Hawker Furies and everything else is even older. No, as far as the Air Force is concerned, we're not important enough.'

Tom was just digesting this gloomy news, not made easier by his knowing nothing of the planes in question when a dispatch rider came in (escorted by the Punjabi guard).

'Message for Major Brimshaw, sir. Sign here sir, if you please.'

'And how do you know I'm Major Brimshaw, lad, and not some Eyetie spy?'

'I see you're a Major, sir, from the crown, and I recognize the moustache, sir.'

Tom tried to hide his grin while Brimshaw muttered something about insubordination and dismissed the DR.

'It's from Johnson.' Brimshaw read and re-read the message in increasing rage. 'Why can't he follow procedures? He's not writing to his girlfriend! It could have fallen into enemy hands.'

'Why, what does he say?'

Brimshaw wore an expression of utter disgust.

'It says: Please inform Tom, but your CO will have official confirmation soon, that the French Somaliland forces have gone over to the Vichy lot and will co-operate with Musso. Means our right flank would be completely exposed if they attack so expect the worst. GJ."

'Expect the worst! What the hell does that mean? Sloppy ill-disciplined mothers' meeting stuff, Jorret.'

Nonetheless they got out the maps: they saw that George was quite right.

Chapter 16

Brigadier Arthur Chater, commander of the Somaliland Camel Corps, now found himself given overall command of the British and Commonwealth land forces in British Somaliland.

He drew down the wall map.

'I cannot disguise from you, gentlemen, that the situation is serious. The enemy number some 25,000 men, with two light and two medium tank squadrons, three batteries of field artillery, air cover which, as things stand, we are unable to challenge, and considerable reserves of experienced forces in occupied Ethiopia.'

To Tom's surprise, Chater said: 'I have asked Major Johnson to survey and to do a sit-rep on our units which, I need hardly say, are for the moment in prepared defensive positions.'

George shambled forward, his khaki drill shirt crumpled and sweaty. Tom could hear Brimshaw's snort of disgust behind him.

'Well,' he said, as if greeting guests to a dinner party. 'You know we're up against it. Jolly grateful to our Nyasaland KARs, and the Rhodesian and Punjabi battalions. They've all taken up defensive positions in the hills behind the Tug Argen. This is the only way the Eyet- the enemy - can come with wheeled and track vehicles when they make for

Berbera. The road runs along dried-up riverbed, the Tug, so we've got our artillery and heavy machine -gun people enfilading that road.'

He looked about him vaguely. 'Any questions so far?'

Brimshaw stood up. He was, as ever, red-faced and spluttering with suppressed rage 'Does that mean, Major Johnson, that you propose to abandon Hargeisa?'

George looked appealingly to Chater.

'No, Major Brimshaw, that is not our proposal.' The Brigadier, tall, distinguished-looking, remained calm and courteous. 'You will see from the map that Hargeisa controls the vital road north to Berbera. But just south of Hargeisa there are reasonable tracks that will take enemy transport westwards and north towards Zeila on the coast. It was our expectation that the Free French would be able to defend our right flank on that west track, but now Djibouti has declared for neutrality that is no longer the case. We have few resources to defend that flank, but the terrain is difficult for a mass of infantry and the Camel Corps with some Illalos will skirmish and harass the advance. We must plan for a holding action at Hargeisa followed by a phased withdrawal to our Tug Argen lines.'

Brimshaw grunted. 'Major Johnson speaks of artillery. Cannot that be brought forward to resist the enemy advance across the plain?'

'No.' George still spoke gently. 'Major Brimshaw, our artillery consists solely of the East African Light battery, namely, four guns, 3.7 inch howitzers,' - here he grinned at Tom - 'and one highly trained and efficient 25-pounder Field Gun. We have no anti-tank weapons, and no air cover. Therefore, I cannot risk our guns at Hargeisa.'

There was a stunned silence.

When he was asked about support from native forces,

George was of the opinion that, far from giving support to the British, Somali tribesmen would more likely fight against them in the attempt to rid themselves of all Europeans, 'despite,' as Chater put it, 'our benevolent and humane rule'.

'Now I have drawn a gloomy picture, gentlemen. But I need hardly stress that our immediate objective must be to maintain a high level of morale and to delay the enemy by all means possible. Our strategic objective will be to halt the enemy advance until considerable reinforcements, already preparing, arrive from Aden and our armies, with the support of Ethiopian patriots, will undertake the expulsion of the Italian regime from East Africa.'

With which Churchillian flourish, the Brigadier strode from the room. The officers sat stunned: the only sound was of the slow pulse of the ceiling fan.

* * *

'Now, George, now Tom,' said Terence Brimshaw, showing his teeth in an unaccustomed smile, 'we won't have many other chances to chew the cud as friends before the…'

'…balloon goes up,' said George, unable to resist it.

'Exactly. So we must swap ideas off the record. Speak our minds, whatever we tell the troops, eh?'

George knocked his pipe out into the ashtray. 'I don't think there's much to add, Terence, to what Chater has said.'

'No, I didn't mean that. Though, what he didn't say was what a lot of pansy soldiers the Eyeties are. Useless. I'd sooner have some of your lot, eh, Tom?'

'So would I,' said Tom.

'You're wrong, Terence,' George studied the bowl of his pipe intently and begun to clean it out with a scraper. 'Some are very fine troops. Lots of 'em have experience in Ethiopia.

No doubt brave lads too. Can't rely on their being feeble when it comes to it.'

'An Italian bullet hurts as much as a British one, I should say,' said Tom.

'And there'll be a lot more of them,' added George.

Terence gazed moodily into his beer. 'Yes. I'll be a goner this time. Feel it in my bones.

Shan't be sorry. Left it with you, Tom, to make the arrangements.'

Tom stared at him blankly. 'Make the arrangements?'

'Yes. Told HQ, signed the form and that. When I cop it.'

'Well, I'm not sure -'

'Only friends I've got. Only friends I've ever had. Take me as you find me, you see. Don't look down your noses. "Jumped-up bastard: what's he doin' in our Mess?" None of that with you, Tom, or you, George.'

George made a futile attempt to light his pipe to cover his embarrassment. Tom studied the beer mats. *Poor old Brimshaw. And I've done nothing to help him along. Never really gave it a thought, and now, he calls me a friend. Not much of a friend, Terry…*

'Well, Terry - Terence - I, well, I really, er, appreciate that,' he stumbled, 'but what d'you mean, arrangements? Besides, I'm more likely than you to - cop it.'

'Oh no you're not. It's all settled, then?'

Before Tom could answer, Brimshaw turned to Johnson. 'D'you think there's life after death, then, George?'

George positively started in his seat at this, but again Brimshaw allowed him no time to answer. 'You know about these things. Only know what the Padre says, and that's in one ear and out the other. Lot of guff anyway. But I've been thinking about it a lot recently. You learned about it all, at University and that.'

Brimshaw fixed his beady eye on George, who was outwardly preoccupied with re-filling the pipe with yet more tobacco. Inwardly, Johnson knew that he could not shrug this off: it mattered desperately to Terence Brimshaw not so much that there was an answer but that his question was respected. And it was a perfectly reasonable question if you thought you were going to be killed in a few days' time…

'I don't know. Thought about it myself, but not for years. Nobody knows, really. There's a story I did read once, though.'

He drew a deep breath and looked Brimshaw steadily in the eye.

'Well, go on then,' said Brimshaw impatiently.

George gave up any attempt to light the pipe and laid it carefully on the table.

'Well,' George said. 'There was a storm in the night, and a group of soldiers were sitting round a huge log fire. This fire was in the middle of a great open hall, as was the way in those days, and the hall was lit with the flaming torches in kind of iron hoops hung from the walls. It was the way they did it in those days,' he added apologetically.

'All right, go on.'

'Anyway, the soldiers were warm and the hall was well lit. There were gaps in the walls near the rafters to let the smoke out and suddenly a sparrow was blown in from the dark and flew straight across this great hall and out the opposite side.'

George said no more, and all three sat round the table thinking. 'Is that it? Long time ago, was it?' asked Terence at last.

'Oh yes. A long time ago, a thousand years or more. But the point was that the soldiers were asking the same as your question. Perhaps they had to fight soon. But they didn't know the answer either, so one of them said, that we are like that sparrow: going from the dark, flying briefly across in the light, then back into the dark again.'

Suddenly self-conscious, George fumbled with his matches and at last succeeded in lighting his pipe. The others sat silent.

'Calls for another drink,' Tom mumbled at last. *Yes: remember that old workshop on the Zelah road. Mr Trelick teaching me how to shape the stone: worked all hours, then to the pub for beers and pasties. Always said the same thing: Eat drink and be merry for tomorrow we die. Never forgotten that.*

Instead of calling the waiter, Tom got to his feet, and George and Terence watched him as he threaded his way between the tables to the bar.

'Tom's lost a lot of weight,' said George.

'What does he think about it?' Terence asked.

'About what?'

'You know. The sparrow and that.'

'I don't know. He's never said.'

'Don't suppose he worries about things like that. Just goes his own way, and never worries about things.'

George did not care for talking about people, let alone his friends. 'I think he is content with his stone-carving and looks forward to getting back to Cornwall.'

'Do you think he would teach me, stone-carving?'

Poor old Brimshaw: he wants to share other people's lives, George thought. His own is so pointless...

'I'm sure he would, if you ever get the chance,' he said.

The Mess waiter arrived carrying an ice-bucket with champagne and Tom followed him with the glasses.

'Here,' said Tom. 'Eat, drink and be merry, for tomo-' He caught George's warning eye. 'Well, who knows, eh?'

'Will you teach me stone-carving, Tom?'

Tom pretended to fiddle with the wiring round the neck

of the bottle, swearing under his breath, giving himself time to recover from this startling request. In the end he handed the champagne to George.

'You do it, George. You're used to it.' He sat down heavily. 'Of course I will, Terry - Terence - when we get out of here. Pleased to be of help.'

George turned the bottle away from the cork with practiced ease.

'I've never had champagne,' said Terence. 'Always refused it. Not a wine-drinker at all. Is that a promise, Tom? If - well, you know, if I don't cop it.'

'Don't think he'll be able to help much if you do, Terence,' said George dryly. 'Mind you, depends what the sparrow found on the other side.'

He charged their glasses.

'Well, we can drink to happy sparrows if we don't meet again, eh?'

Damn the sparrow: it's the skylark I want to see again.

Terence gulped down some champagne. 'Don't like it,' he said.

'Neither do I,' said Tom.

'Well, I do,' said George. 'Anyway, it's the spirit that counts.'

* * *

The following day Chater's scouts reported that the Italians were concentrating on the Ethiopian border to the south of Hargeisa. Major Johnson did his final tour of the artillery - the four howitzers and Tom's Gambian field gun, all of course standing to.

'They're already evacuating some of the civilian staff and non-combatants to Aden,' he said. 'They say it's a precautionary measure, but it don't look as if we will be able to beat this lot off for long when they move.'

Tom said nothing.

'Don't know when we'll meet up again, Tom. Best of luck, old chap. Best of luck to your Gambian chaps.'

'Of course.' They shook hands, and Tom stood and watched with his binoculars until George's staff car wound out of sight up the mountain pass.

The pass ran between mountains, which rose to more than four thousand feet. Tom scanned the boulder-strewn rock faces to the east of his emplacement. He had long ago concluded that the Italians would need their crack Alpine troops (of which they were known to have a battalion) to scale those heights, and such an exercise would be pointless in view of the overwhelming forces they could command in the centre.

What he did not reckon on, however, was the alarming sight of numbers of Somali tribesmen gathering on the mountainside.

Can't believe how quickly they're moving over those rocks - rather like me when I'm crabbing, but I wouldn't be carrying those sacks and those bandoliers and long-barrelled rifles. And kukris. These fellows must know every bloody track and cave in these hills. Like I do on the Bay. Calling each other -god! gives you the shivers, those wailing calls to each other. Echo across the rocks for miles. They're gathering like those swarms of gulls round the harbour when the fishing boats come in.

He scribbled a note for Brimshaw on his field message pad and ordered one of the Gambians to run across with it.

"Somali irregulars in force on eastern flank. Must have machine-gun support. Jorret."

Chapter 17

George had brought Emily's latest letter to Tom with him.

Tom had stuffed it into his pocket unopened. Unusually for him, he was beginning to fuss about details, checking the ammunition bunker over and again, nagging the crew about supposed gaps in the camouflage, and constantly scanning the hillsides for the Somali irregulars. He equipped two of the gun-crew with binoculars and loaded .303s to try to ascertain the numbers of the tribesmen who, as George had said, were definitely hostile. He thought of Rachid, always cool, deliberate and detached in his work, but making it quite clear that he looked forward to the day when the British would leave. He would be sure to help to drive out Europeans, be they British or Italian, when the opportunity presented itself.

Tom cursed himself for his nervousness. The Gambians' sensitivity to his mood was uncanny: they seemed to pick up every nuance of voice or manner regardless of his calming words to them.

He regarded the oncoming battle itself not with fear – he was confident he could face danger – but with the nervousness that comes with his not being in control of a situation. Other people were taking all the decisions. Moreover, he was taking responsibility for others when, again, he could do nothing to ensure their safety. He could not bear to think that any of "his" Gambians should come to harm: they were not, not even in the most far-fetched way defending their own country. (Neither, Tom thought, was he. But he did not deny that it was his duty, as Grandfather constantly said, "to do his bit".)

He gave a heavy sigh, slumped into a chair, and immediately got up again. One more check on the sentries, then read Emmy's letter.

'Everything OK, Joni?'

Joni Kru leapt to his feet and saluted smartly. 'Everything fine, Captain Tom, sir. We keepin' sharp eye on Smalis, Captain Tom, isn't we, Samuel?'

Samuel gave Tom a huge grin. *He looks about fifteen, with his unmarked round face, gangling limbs and his mass of tight black curls. Probably is fifteen. Or less. Old Jock said he never could get a straight answer when he was recruiting, and they would swear on the Bible to anything that came into their heads. Fifteen. Might be dead next week.*

'Any idea how many there are, Samuel?'

'We counted 63, Captain Tom, an' then we said there are two or three lots gatherin' on the plain, 'bout same size, addin' up to two hundred. Maybe.'

And those are the ones we can see. Cowboys and Indians, and we are the Indians, and we know how the film always ends.

* * *

The letter ran to four sides of her spidery handwriting. It was dated 17th July, and remarkably had taken less than a fortnight to reach him.

Dear Tom,

We haven't heard from you for ages I hope you're alright but there's nothing in the papers about where you are so we suppose it's still all quiet. How are the Gambian boys? They sound so nice and friendly and it must be very nice for you and George to have them there. Do you think they'll ever come to Cornwall when it's all over? (Tom suddenly felt both sad and ashamed at this: he wondered how Grandfather would react to six "darkies" in the village…) *We would like to thank them for looking after you. Perhaps we'll be able to give them some real Cornish cream and pasties legally then! They're supposed to be forbidden because of rationing but we can't throw it away when we've got too many eggs and that. We usually send what we can up to the camp and Newmin Hospital of course. Some inspector came all the way from Plymouth to say we weren't legal and we'd be prosecuted.* (She had written persecuted first but had crossed it out.)

Do you know he had a car! Well anyway Ma just ignored him at first, then Pa came in for his tea and Tom I've NEVER seen him like that, he was so angry, and said he'd run him down to the beach and throw him in the sea, then Ma said don't do that as they're laying mines down there and Pa will blow himself up, she didn't mind about the inspector.

Tom laughed out loud: he could just imagine his mother with pursed lips bustling past the man asking him politely to get out of the way, then deliberately going backwards and forwards as he tried to step aside. It was her usual technique when people annoyed her: he remembered her keeping a curate like that for nearly ten minutes until Pa and Emmy had to leave the room before they exploded with laughter.

Then you'd never guess what, Grandfather came in. "Who are you? Why aren't you in the army? They'd even take the likes of you now, clean out the lavatories an' that, you could do your bit." The inspector-chap got all huffy and said that he was in a reserved occupation doing vital war work, and then he got it all from Grandfather, how Steve was a lieutenant in the War and got killed for the likes of him and now he had a grandson (he actually said "son" first) who was a Captain fighting the Italians in Africa and that's what war work is and he'd report him for malingering and speak to an important officer in the Royal Artillery (I suppose he meant Major Johnson) who'd get him put in prison if he tried to stop us sending our stuff up to the troops in Penhale Camp after what they'd been through in Dunkirk and if Mr Churchill ever got to hear of it he'd have him shot as a fifth columnist.

Honestly Tom I felt quite sorry for the man and when he said to Grandfather that he would be reporting the matter I thought that Grandfather was going to hit him and we got quite frightened that Grandfather would have a fit or something. Well, he said, that is Grandfather said " you yellow livered blank blank blank" and I can't write the words Grandfather said, if you won't fight the Germans you can fight me an' I wouldn't give much for your chances cause I'm only 80 next birthday (he isn't, actually). Anyway, he made off for his car as quick as a dose of salts.

Tom was about to turn the page when a 15cwt drew up along the stony track that the Engineers had laid from the Punjabi positions. He stuffed the letter back into his shirt pocket.

Major Brimshaw leapt out of the truck.

Tom smiled to himself as he went to greet him. George had described Terence Brimshaw's moods as 'droopy moustache' or 'bristly moustache'. Brimshaw's manner was certainly of the latter description.

'Right-ho, Captain Jorret. Couple of Brens for you. Stacks of magazines, so you should be all right here.'

The Service Corps driver saluted Tom and handed him a clipboard. 'Sign here, sir, and here, sir please.'

Tom hesitated. 'Just a moment. Major, I don't have the men for the bren-guns. I just can't spare the gun-crew.'

'Just check the stores, Jorret.' Tom took the pencil. 'No! Before you sign for them. Procedures!' They walked round to the back of the truck. 'Thought I'd wangle some extra stuff, Jorret. Sacks of rice and dried fish for the Aficans, extra corned beef for us. Not cordon bleu but it may be needed. We keep the 15cwt too, and the driver. Good, eh?'

'Well, that's very good, Terence. Thanks. But the Bren gunners?'

'I have four volunteers from Battalion HQ. Too many pen-pushers. You know one of them - old sergeant chap, should have been demobbed ages ago. Scotsman. Says he knows your Gambians.'

'What? Jock Jamison?'

Brimshaw gave Tom a disapproving look. 'Right. *Sergeant* Jamison. Old soldier in many ways, but said he couldn't stand just making out duty rosters and wanted to see action, so here we are?'

'I'm really pleased to have Jock with us. My Gambian soldiers' -Tom spoke with heavy emphasis - 'think the world of him. But who'll be i/c the bren-gunners?'

Brimshaw bared his teeth in a grin. 'I will. No need for me with the Punjabis. Spare prick at the wedding, eh?' He patted the pistol holster at his side. 'Looking forward to a scrap after all this marking time, I can tell you. By the way, I won't insist on rank here, Captain Jorret; I've just got myself attached by HQ to be i/c infantry side of things. Won't interfere with the gun unless you're put out of action.'

'We've had months of training here, Terence, so they'll carry on very well without me if need be.'

Brimshaw regarded Tom wearily. 'You just don't get it, do you? These bloody fellows are all right while you're watching them, but give them an inch, especially under fire, and, well…' He rolled his eyes to the sky.

'Well, we'll soon be seeing about that. But, Major Brimshaw, I must make it clear: I will not tolerate any interference with my command.' Tom found himself speaking with a severity that astonished himself as much as it did Brimshaw.

The Major went red in the face, but restrained himself, turned on his heel and stumped off, saying he would supervise the unloading of the stores.

'Good! Thank you, sir,' Tom shouted after him. 'Please sign for them, Major.'

* * *

Tom found himself shaking. *Strange, I can handle anything except, well, other people. Why can't I be left alone to do what I can do?*

He turned back to the letter to calm himself. It was in a different ink and had been added a day or two later.

Sorry, Tom, I had to stop to feed the cows as Annie wasn't well, summer cold or something - nothing serious. Jimmy's away in Plymouth building air-raid shelters. I don't think that's a war secret, as the papers say that the Germans have already built lots of shelters in Berlin and places.

But do you know what? That inspector man sent a letter which we couldn't understand all the language of except that under Ministry of Food regulation 589/40 or something - I can't remember it all as Grandfather put it straight in the stove - subsection something or other an exception could be made in our case and we could receive a copy of the relevant regulation from His Majesty's Stationery Office, on the payment of 1s.2d though what the King has to do with it I can't imagine.

Talking of air raid shelters, Tom, they sent round pamphlets a few weeks ago showing how we could dig some shelters in the garden - Anderson shelters or something - and Jimmy burst out laughing and said he'd already checked our cellars and he sent some men in to shore them up for us and we needn't worry. He didn't think they'd bomb us anyway, though they might try on St Mawgan. He's far more worried about Plymouth. He keeps getting called away on meetings and he is afraid he and the others won't have time to get it ready if there's a big attack.

Sally - Sally Samson - and I have such fun, when we can get some time off and we go on the walks round the cliffs and watch the gulls and - you've guessed it - the skylarks. She's really lovely with fair hair and blue eyes and red cheeks, she's really a country girl, quite big and strong though and can lift her side of the milk churns and when Pa tries to help her with the heavy stuff she sends him away and even Grandfather's quite smitten though we've STILL not told him she's a Samson!

I MUST stop now Tom or I'll never get it posted, but every Sunday the church is full and Rev Pentol who had retired but Rev Foster has gone off as a Chaplain in the Navy, anyway every Sunday Rev Pentol reads out a list of names of our men who are fighting, and your on it of course, to pray to keep everyone safe, and I asked that they put George's name on it too and Rev Pentol agreed. I don't know that it makes any difference because poor Mr Treharne's son's ship went down with all hands from Dunkirk. But it shows that everyone's thinking of you all the time, dear Tom, and Pa and Ma and Grandfather and everyone send all their love, Emmy.

Tom was just re-reading the part about Sally when the first rifle-shots rang out from the hills to the east.

Chapter 18

Sammy rushed excitedly up to Tom. He was carrying his rifle and Tom nervously looked to see that the safety catch was on. It was.

'There's shootin', Captain Tom!' He gestured wildly towards the hills. 'Over there!'

'Yes. I heard it, Sammy.'

'Not shootin' at us, Captain Tom. They shootin' in the air, and then, we think, some started shootin' at each other.'

'Right, Sammy. You get back. I'll be straight over.'

'The Major says no need, but -' Sammy hesitated, '- but better you come as well, Captain Tom.'

'Major Brimshaw's there already, Sammy?'

'Yes, sah. An' Sergeant Jock, sah.'

Tom swore under his breath: Sergeant Jock had not yet reported to him, and, Tom thought bitterly, he could see how Brimshaw was asserting himself. *No need for him to go - when his left flank was already under some kind of threat!*

He seized his sten gun and clipped it to the motorbike and roared over to where he had posted his guards. He was met by Jock Jamison, who saluted smartly and gave him as near to a grin as he was capable of.

'Pleased to be of service here, sir. Wi' the lads. The Major said you asked for me special, sir. Pleased to be of service, sir,' he repeated.

'What, Major Brimshaw said that?'

'Nae, bless ye, sir, Major *Johnson*: he saw I could nae sit there filling the triplicate forms.'

'Well, we're really pleased to have you, Jock, though I'm afraid we're in a bit of a pickle here.'

'We are indeed, sir,' agreed Jock gloomily. 'I see that. We are indeed.'

Brimshaw bustled over. 'Ah, Captain,' he said, cursorily acknowledging Tom's salute, 'I told the rifleman that you could stay put. Everything's quiet.'

'What d'you make of all this shooting then?'

'Tribal stuff. Paying off old scores, I'll be bound. Now the British hands lifted a bit, they'll all scramble for being top dog. Seen it before, in India.'

'We-ell,' said Tom doubtfully. 'They seem to be gathering in some numbers. And they know every rock, every pass in the mountains. And they'll move pretty quickly.'

Brimshaw took him to one side, out of earshot of the men.

'I've set up the Brens so they'll have to come through the crossfire. Should be enough.' 'Except we should be fighting the Italians. What happens when they come?'

Brimshaw went into a fatherly Sergeant-major mode and took Tom's hand. 'Well, lad, we just do what we can. If they are too many for us, well, there are too many for us.'

And for the first time, Tom was glad that Terence Brimshaw was there.

* * *

'I thought you would be used to this, Lamin,' said Tom, trying to ward off the flies with a fly whisk a Gambian had made for him.

‘Not like this, Captain, even in August. Gambia a great river, with trees and forest and canoes on the water, sah, no, not like this like bakin’ in oven, sah.’

Lamin Bah got languidly to his feet and peered out of the cave.

‘Thought I heard it, sah. Another wop aeroplane. Two, maybe three.’

Tom could just make out the throb of the Capronis.

‘Comin’ this way, sah.’

‘Yes. They’re much too high to see us, though. 5000 feet if they want to clear the mountain. But something’s brewing, Lamin. They’re getting busier.’

When the planes had gone, George Johnson rang on the Signals line.

‘They came over the border before dawn, Tom. Chater’s men have met up with their scouts and they’ve taken a prisoner but he won’t talk. But Chater knows what they’re up to. Over.’

Tom gestured to Lamin Bar to wind up the receiver set.

‘How on earth does he *know*?’ Tom forgot his procedure, but Johnson answered anyway.

‘I’ll be with you tomorrow and put you all in the picture. Out.’

* * *

‘It’s pretty clear though: they’re coming in three columns, one moving west to seal off the French - not that they need to - and we can do bugger-all about that. Then the one to the east is presumably to secure their right flank at Odweina, probably in reserve. Chater thinks these are poor troops comparatively. A lot of them are Askaris, bloody good fighters in themselves but just as likely to shoot at the Eyeties

-or each other - as at us. But it don't matter, Tom, Terence, 'cos we can do bugger-all about *that,* either. Anyway, they crossed on the early morning of the day before yesterday-'

'- the Third of August,' said Terence. 'My birthday.'

'Congratulations,' said George dryly. 'Celebrate it some other time. But they're already moving in on Hargeisa. The Camel Corps and some Northern Rhodesian lads are holding them off a bit, but they're moving up armour and, well, you know, we haven't any anti-tank stuff and that's that. Our chaps'll have no choice but withdraw to our lines on Observation Hill.'

'Not the Camel Corps, surely?'

'Don't know what Chater will do with them, to be honest, Tom. They'll do what they can, and then disperse, I suppose.'

'Like the poor old Poles, cavalry charging the Nazi tanks,' said Terence.

'I think Chater hopes to get at their supply lines a bit. Anyway, the Wops' obvious route to Berbera is past us and we have to hold out long enough for the reinforcements to come over from Aden. We're getting some guns, apparently,' he added with an enthusiastic grin.

The glances Tom and Terence exchanged did not escape George.

'Oh yes,' George went on thoughtfully. 'Some guns. Soon be on their way. Bit of paperwork to do first, I've no doubt. And,' he added brightly, 'they're sending us a new boss: Major-General Reade Godwin-Austen.'

'Hope he can fire a Bren,' said Terence sourly.

'When? When's he coming?' asked Tom.

'Should be here by the end of next week.'

There was a silence. Brimshaw studied his fingernails

'Major-General something Godwin-Austen, eh?' said Terence at last.

'Reade. Reade Godwin-Austen.'

'The name scares the shits out of me. Don't know what it'll do to the Eyeties.'

'He got an MC in '17, Terence, like you.'

'Oh no: mine was an MM, not nearly so important.

'So Reade gets a *General* before his name. I've just got the *Major* bit.'

'Yes. So have I. But believe me, Terence, we're better off without the General bit.' George was suddenly animated, his eyes angry. 'Here's our *Reade*, responsible at a moment's notice for beating off an army five times as big as ours, not counting their reserves, without any guns except for a second-hand 25-pounder field gun and four howitzers to face squadrons of light tanks and armoured cars, all in these God-forsaken sands and rocks in hellish heat. Oh no, no time even for his round of cocktail parties, Terence. Not really for the likes of us, Terence.'

Tom was taken aback by George's bitterness: it was the first time he had ever seen such feeling behind his friend's imperturbable manner. Their little East African army had been left virtually defenceless, abandoned as irrelevant, and George's anger showed.

Terence leant across and took George's hand, just as he had done earlier with Tom. 'We're all scared, George. Scared shitless. Just have to do what we can when the time comes. Helps a bit when you're going out to bat, to be scared. Anyway, Major,' he asked briskly, 'what are you going to do when they come?'

George scratched in the dust with his stick. 'Won't be here: sorry I can't be with you here.' Tom knew he meant it: George never said anything he did not mean.

'I'll be with the howitzer lads,' George said. 'Probably won't be back for a while. But remember, Tom, no firing until you get the signal unless you're under direct threat, in which case the howitzers will already be out. Now,' he said to them both, 'You've got all your non-essential kit ready to get back to Berbera?'

They nodded.

'Except this,' said Tom. He handed George a small heavy holdall.

'What's this?'

'It's to go to Terence here if he survives me. Otherwise you have it.'

'Right. But what's in it?'

'Tools. My special stone-carving tools. Guard them with your life, George.'

* * *

Emily had written Tom a long letter but it did not get to him in Somaliland.

...we didn't have any idea what it was all about. Grandfather came and told us we must all be ready to go into Newmin Tuesday morning at eleven o'clock and we had to put on Sunday best! There was Grandfather in his old black funeral suit, waistcoat watch-chain and all and his bowler hat which he never wears and Jones' big taxi came! Grandfather sat in the front with Mr Jones and started to tell him the way and Mr Jones got quite cross and told Grandfather off and said he'd been driving into Newmin for thirty years and didn't need any help and he knew exactly where Hancock and Lawrence's offices were thank you. So now we knew where were going! Ma whispered it was probably the old devil's will at last after all his threats.

Anyway, to cut a long story short it wasn't the will exactly and we still don't understand it all except that he's made

EVERYTHING over to YOU! "My grandson's a Captain in the Gunners you know". He said 'Gunners' as if he'd always been an army man himself and even dear old Mr Long who was doing all the legal stuff couldn't help smiling at it. I thought you were in the Engineers anyway and that's not the same is it? When I say everything he's kept a lot of money back of course and he said that he's going to continue to let out the hotel and keeps his flat in it but pays you a nominal rent whatever that is, and even Pa and Ma are supposed to pay their rent over to you. Mr Long tried to ask what would happen if anything happened to you but Grandfather got quite angry with him and went on about Steve being an officer and got killed but that was against the Germans in the trenches and you were against the Italians.

Anyway, Pa and Ma both had to sign papers and Mr Long called in his clerk Joe Kitson who's only about twenty-five. You know him he lives out Bedruthan way and cycles in every day. Grandfather got up and asked poor Joe why he wasn't in the army and Joe was really upset because he's got those thick glasses and he was rejected as C3 and says he's an Air Raid Warden anyway. Joe had to come in as a witness and Grandfather said that if he could see our signatures then his eyesight and couldn't be that bad could it? And poor Joe was nearly in tears when Grandfather started up again about Steve, but Mr Long asked Joe to get us all a glass of sherry himself included so it all passed off all right.

But when it was all done Grandfather started up again about how it was a pity that his grandson had to work with those blacks when there were all those British who ought to be fighting for King and Country. Mr Long in the end said that he had fought in the Navy in the last war and he was sure that he would like to go out again as "doubtless you would again, Mr Jorret, were it not for our age" - those were his very words, pretending that he thought Grandfather had been in the war too, and he had no doubt about Joe's courage but he would put the others in danger with his bad eyes so he must help all he can in other ways.

Well must close now as have to put the blackout up but we're all really glad that Grandfather's done this Tom and perhaps he's got some good sense after all and we all send our love and we're praying that you and George and the Gambian soldiers all keep safe. Emmy. PS It's so nice to have Sally Samson here and she wants to be included in all our good wishes to you.

Chapter 19

The observation post Tom had built for himself gave him a panoramic view of the mountainside as it fell away to the south and west. Both at ground level and (he hoped) from the air, it appeared as just another outcrop on the rocky slopes. But it was cunningly hidden too by having been built in a hollow on a reverse slope which at the same time concealed the emplacement without restricting the gun's field of fire.

But as George Johnson pointed out, however the 25pdr was calibrated, Tom's field of fire onto the Tug Argen was severely restricted. There were two, possibly three, stretches of the track which were not themselves sheltered by outcrops of rock, and the third was so narrow that it would need extreme accuracy, and luck, to hit.

Everything seemed unreal. An eerie silence hung over the hills. After two days Hargeisa had already fallen to the Italian armour: and even sporadic gunfire had died away. On his left flank (defended by Terence Brimshaw's lonely bren-gunners) there was no more furious shouting, no more wild shots in the air.

It's the quiet before the storm, as Ma always used to say, when even the sea breezes had dropped, and the sea had barely the strength to lap against the rocks. And she was right: within a few hours, the winds would be lashing against the window pains and the force of the gusts make it almost impossible to open the farmhouse door with a sack over your head you would fight against the storm to give the cows their fodder and when it was all done you would be blown back shivering and soaked - streamin'-leakin', as Grandma Jorret used to describe it - back to the farmhouse, to sit there wrapped in towels and blankets trying to warm up before the kitchen range. Cold and wet! Can't even begin to imagine it…

Tom jerked awake as George rang through on the field telephone.

'Bad news, Tom. They're re-grouping in Hargeisa and have taken Odweina. Worse - they've sent an estimated 30 tankettes and at least twenty armoured cars with truckloads of infantry straight up the west tracks to Zeila and for all we know they'll have taken it by now.'

Tom could not grasp the significance of this. 'Haven't the faintest idea what a tankette is.'

George's voice was unusually edgy and sharp 'For God's sake, Tom, wake up! Tankettes: little tanks, things without turrets, vaguely like our Bren gun carriers, only not nearly so good. Even if they break down, there's nothing we can do about them because *we have no guns.* But my point is that if - when - Zeila goes, they can move along the coast tracks to Berbera. They'll need to reinforce, and we should be able to keep them out of Berbera for a bit, but…'

'… we'll be buggered here stuck in the middle of these bloody mountains and the wops all round us, that's what you're saying?' said Tom, forgetting all procedures.

'Right.' George paused. 'Tom, what's the situation to your east?'

'All quiet at the moment. But there are hordes of them. In the hillsides. Remind me of those great waves of starlings that used swirl about in the evenings at home.'

George laughed. 'Very poetic, but luckily they can't fly.

Hopefully they'll wait and go for the wops.' He paused. 'Look, Tom, I'd better come down. Chater thinks you're too exposed there if the Somalis turn nasty.We'll move some Punjabi fellows over to prepare some positions.'

Now they tell me. Just as well George knows about us; doubt whether we're on the HQ lists at all. Brimshaw's right: can hear him mocking the Staff officers now. "What?" they'll be sayin' in the Mess, "Who's this Jorret fellow then? Gun? What gun? Not on the establishment here, sorry. Anyway, you'd better get down there and see for yourself, George. 'Nother sherry first? No? Cut along, then."

Tom grunted and turned back to his binoculars. He picked out the Bren gunners in their rocky emplacements, Brimshaw alert and scanning the hillside, Jock nodding in the shade. *Bullets kill the brave as well as the frightened: I wonder if that's what Terence Brimshaw wants, to die heroically. He's certainly chosen the right place to do it.*

In fact, the first shells fell nowhere near them, still at least two miles to the south. . Tom swung the binoculars on their mounting to follow the shell bursts raking the ridge. He could see the rock and sand shooting into the air long before he heard the thumps of the explosions. The Northern Rhodesians who had pulled back from Hargeisa must have been the target of the Italian gunners.

George had guessed that the Italians would move cautiously. They had taken two days since capturing Hargeisa, presumably to regroup, and now they were no doubt moving up the mountainside - 'infiltrating', George called it.

Suddenly the howitzers on the Mill Hill opened up.

The battle was way below Tom. George had said that the defence was so thin that one of the hills was held by a single company of the Punjabis, and if the waves of Italian infantry were to storm their hill, then however well our fellows fought, they'd never hold out.

Tom ordered the gun detachment to stand to, but his Gambians were there before him; they were already in position, with Lamin Bah in his seat ready to adjust the sights, eagerly looking to him to give his commands.

Is this what a battle is? Are the men down there dying and screaming? But I can do nothing to help them. I can't see them. Only puffs of smoke, columns of smoke. And the great flashes lighting up the sky even in this hellish scorching sun. That sounds like a barrage of mortars, now the double boom- crump of shellfire. Rattling of machine-guns, volleys of rifle fire. Echoes through the hills make it sound just like the continuous crashing thunder that used to roll round the Newmin Bay. Poor devils.

He screamed at the number 4 to load.

Then he saw them. A cortege of enemy turretless tanks was crawling through the very stretch of the Tug that was perfectly in his sights.

His first two shots fell well short. Lamin Bah quickly and coolly made the adjustments and signaled to Tom that he had done so.

Tom gave the order to lay down a barrage, and the Gambian team worked swiftly but unhurriedly, as calmly as on the range. Tom himself felt curiously detached. It was as if he were above the battle, stolidly indifferent to those suffering under the bombardment he had commanded.

George Johnson's staff car came to a screaming halt in the compound. George, all long limbs and flapping shirt, lollopped over to Tom.

'They've taken the Punjabi hill. We're counter attacking, but there's no real chance.

All we can do is to blast away blind and hope to make a

mess of their supplies.'

Tom made a large traverse and ordered the elevation.

'More, Tom. Our chaps are pulling back: mustn't risk them."

Tom ordered the new elevation. The Gambians, grim-faced, their naked torsos running with sweat, worked steadily and rhythmically, loosing off the 25 pounder round every two minutes until George suddenly screamed out to cease fire.

'We can do no more here, Tom. We've no idea where our fellows are getting to. Daren't risk them.'

Tom ordered the crew to stand down and rest.

'I'll get Jock and Brimshaw back.'

He trained his glasses on Jock. The soldier he had brought with him from HQ was changing the barrels on the Bren, when Tom saw him slump suddenly backwards: it looked as if a ricochet hit him in the shoulder.

Jock gave him a quick glance, then seized the barrels and flung them spinning down the mountainside in front of him. The gun itself followed, bouncing down from rock to rock into a gully.

He crawled over to his comrade and clapped on a field dressing before attempting to drag him by his webbing, face up, to the emplacement.

Jock was gasping for breath and nearly purple in the face.

Frelli, (the skinny Gambian Tom had put down as fourteen or fifteen) leapt up shouting, 'I go help Sergeant Jock!'

Frelli scrambled over the parapet and raced the two hundred-odd yards to where the wounded soldier lay. The reverse slope no longer hid Frelli's lanky figure, but heedless of the shots about him, he seized the soldier's webbing cross straps and dragged him groaning over the rough ground.

Tom and the crew hastily made a gap in the sandbag wall to the north side of the emplacement and the whole crew stood and screamed encouragement to Frelli as if they were watching a 220-yard race.

Frelli somehow reached the safety of the emplacement unscathed and willing hands hauled the wounded soldier in. But meanwhile Jock had been able to crawl hardly more than a few yards before collapsing on the ground panting, and no sooner had Frelli seen the man safe than he turned and raced back to help the old sergeant.

Jock raised his head and tried feebly to wave him back.

Even through the rattle of rifle shots Tom could hear Frelli: 'I comin' Sergeant Jock!'. Jock staggered a few more yards towards him before collapsing again. When Frelli reached him he was doubled over in pain.

Frelli seized Jock's wrist and flung the burly 12-stone Scotsman over his shoulder like a sack of coal and, again to almost hysterical dancing and shouting, reached the gap in the sandbags and laid the old sergeant down as gently as he could on the ground. Tom snapped an order for two men to get a second stretcher and knelt to give Jock first aid.

But Frelli shook off the whooping congratulations of his friends, and went to sit alone, shaking, his head in his hands.

He looked up tearfully as Tom approached him and laid a hand gently on his shoulder. 'Sergeant Jock dead, Captain Tom, I know. Dead. I feel sudden weight on shoulder. Dead. I should go quicker, Captain Tom.'

'He had a heart attack, Frelli. There's nothing anyone could have done. You saved a man's life, Frelli. You would have saved Sergeant Jock too if he hadn't been so ill. I've never seen such bravery.'

I left it to that boy while I watched, and it was my responsibility: I should never have left those two out there.

Frelli's large black eyes were filled with tears. 'Heart, Captain Tom?'.

'He was old and ill. All he wanted was to be a soldier and fight bravely, and he was a proud man, and proud of you, Frelli, and all his friends.'

Here's old Jock, here's this boy, taking responsibility for their friends without a second thought, risking their lives for them, and there's me, always the skylark, singing my own song watching them all. You take over, George, now there's some risk to our soldiers. Oh my God! Terence Brimshaw and Sapper Lyons are still out there. Get them back. My responsibility. Should never have allowed them-

Tom braced himself and made for the gap in the sandbag defence that the boys were busy re-stacking.

'Leave it! I'm going out! I've got to get the others back!'

Bari Din threw down the sandbag he was stacking. 'No, Captain Tom. You needed here. I go. Major Blim is my friend.'

He gave the others his wide grin, and before Tom could stop him, had skipped nimbly over the pile of sandbags.

'Wait! Bari Din! The Major must have a written order. Here -' he scribbled a note on his message pad: "*Withdrawal imminent: return to base enclosure without delay. Jorret C/O Emplacement. 15.33 12/10/40*"

Tom knew the Major would stay there if the correct procedures were disregarded.

Chapter 20

Tom's letter was dated 25 July but took over a fortnight to arrive at the farm. As usual he could say only that he was well, and hot, and how the sand and rocks and the sunshine where he was were so unlike the sand and rocks and bright sunshine of the Newmin beaches - not to mention the wind. He went on:

We don't see as much of George as we used to as he's always busy helping out at HQ but he's just the same, tall and thin and scruffy, with his long thin face and keeping our spirits up. Not that there's much low spirits here, with the Gambian boys always laughing and joking and rushing about despite the heat. (They don't like the nights much though, as it suddenly gets cold here as soon as the sun goes down.) The sun doesn't set like at home though, not just sinking slowly over the sea but all of a sudden, it's gone and apart from a red glow, quite dark. Then you get all those weird noises, insects and screeching birds. I've told you about Major Brimshaw already and how he gets all agitated about everyone doing things by the book and how they must be smart and DISCIPLINE all the time. Well, I've got to really rather like him in a way, as he's never known anything but a soldier's life and doesn't fit in. George says it's because he's very lonely. Anyway he can be nasty with the Gambians, calling them useless blacks who won't fight when it comes to it, and then they never take offence and think he's joking with them, and even have him playing cards with them. He always tries terribly hard to win at cards and they always think it's only right for Major BLIMSAW as they call him to win as he's an officer. George says they're very fond of him and think he's a marvelous brave soldier, which of course he is. Oh, and he says can I teach him stone carving and I feebly said I would, but honestly, I have no heart or energy for even getting my chisels out, let alone doing any work.

Well, how is everyone, and Grandfather's still well, and all the animals. I expect you have lots to eat and cider, eh? Any way lots of love to everyone and write soon. Tom. PS Hope Jimmy's *well too and got lots of work.*

12th August 1940

Dear Tom, wrote Emily, *Our Sally Samson is really doing jolly well, and she's even got on the right side of Grandfather at last. It happened like this. You know how grandfather spent all that time with the maps he bought from Phelps stationers in Newmin, well, he thought he'd copy out the one you're in really large and pin it to the scullery wall. Well you know how impatient he gets and he got into such a mess and you could hear him swearing even in the bedroom. (I'm staying for a bit because Jimmys in Plymouth doing the shelters. He's very worried as he thinks the Germans will attack the docks and that and he says it's easy for them to get down here now they're all along the coast of France opposite.)*

Anyway, then Sally came in for her tea and saw grandfather doing the map and said could she help when she'd done the cows. I went to your shed, hope it's alright, Tom, and borrowed your measures and rules and promise to put them back for you safe for when you come *home. Oh Tom I do hope its soon when you've beaten all those nasty Italians. Grandfather got very teasy and said she couldn't do it properly, but Sally was SO CLEVER! It turns out she had been to an art school in London before the war and knew all about how to do it and showed grandfather how to measure and get it right and you ought to see the map, Tom! All in different colours and with grandfather's little flags. The papers say they've crossed the border into the British part but grandfather says it's very hilly where you are - just like you say, with only scrubby little bushes and rocks and sand, but nothing like our beach I know. Grandfather went into Newmin and spent all day in the library and now hes a great EXPERT on Somaliland and he says it's so rocky that the Italians won't be able to get you out. I hope he's right. Oh Tom Sally's such a nice person and she's very pretty with fair hair done up at the back and lovely face and blue eyes and quite plump not like your skinny old sister. They've given her a kind of uniform with boots and knee-length fawn socks and kind of jodhpurs and a really nice green sweater and a floppy hat and although it doesn't sound all that good, you ought to see her! and Ma is already marrying you off to her but don't tell Ma I told you! But do you know she only gets 28/- a week! And all found, of course, but Pa always finds some more extra as he says she does so much overtime, which she does, but doesn't expect anything for it.*

But back to grandfather and the map and in the end he just sat back and watched her do it. Then she told me that she turned round once to ask him something and she saw him looking at her with large tears rolling down his cheeks and she couldn't help herself giving him a little kiss and hug and he was crying and said that Steve had never come back and he didn't think Tom would either. Sally said of course he would it wasn't like France and the trenches when no-one ever came back. And besides Tom was in charge of a big gun and bound to be in the background even if there was a battle. He thinks there will be, judging by what the papers say.

Oh Tom I'm just rambling on as if we were sitting out on the cliffs with the seagulls swooping all about us. And the skylarks way up over. One day it will be like that again, I know, everyone sends all their love and we all go to church now and pray to keep you and George and the Gambian boys safe and that Major Brimshaw and Sergeant Jock too of course.

Your loving sister
Emmy

* * *

Emily's letter was destined to be stuck in the Aden Field Post Office for some time after August 12th, but at the moment she was writing Your loving sister Emmy, Sergeant Jock was already dead, and Bari Din was racing across the slope to Major Brimshaw's rocky outcrop.

Tom watched as Bari Din called to the Major. The Gambian stood to attention and saluted as smartly as on the parade ground - exactly as Brimshaw had coached him in the drill of "delivering a message to an officer". Brimshaw made no attempt to return the salute but snatched the message and hastily dragged Bari down into the cover of his position. Then Tom saw that Brimshaw, grinning broadly, had taken Bari's hand in both his and shaken it warmly.

At last he read the message and turning towards Tom's emplacement, waved an acknowledgement.

Then Tom realized that the noise of shooting had stopped.

But in the sudden quiet a steady throb of plane engines was growing steadily louder. A flight of Italian light bombers was heading for them, at a steady 200mph at 2000 feet.

'*Take Cover! Take Cover!*' he screamed. '*Air attack!*'

George flung himself alongside Tom in the shelter.

'Savoie-Marchetti bombers: SM 79s. Three engines: bloody good machines.'

'I reckon there are nine or ten. Three waves.' Tom said.

'Fifteen hundred feet. Bugger-all we can do about it.'

'Just have to hope they'll miss.'

'They can't.' George spoke in calm matter-of fact tones. They carry hundreds of very small bombs. Or a few bigger ones.'

'And where is our Air Force?' demanded Tom sourly.

'Well, South Africans, Rhodesians. Not much use to us though. Kenya.'

The first stick of bombs fell near the Punjabi positions: the second fell diagonally across the gun emplacement, throwing up great chunks of concrete and metal and a choking cloud of sand and smoke.

They could hear more explosions in the hills behind them before the bombers banked and flew back overhead as they made calmly for their airfields in Ethiopia, quite unscathed.

It took some time for the dust to settle. A heavy bomb had smashed through the side of the gun pit and the gun had lurched half onto her side. Clearly the right wheel and axle were beyond repair, but what damage there was to the breech and barrel was less clear.

No-one was hurt, and apart from a small fire in a food store, there was no serious damage to the emplacement itself.

Lamin Bar held a roll-call: all present and correct. Save Bari Din.

'All members of the crew will report to Major Johnson who will inspect the 25pdr for damage and see if it is reparable. I will contact Major Brimshaw, Sapper Lyons and Bari Din to see they are unhurt.'

But Tom knew that they were not.

He scanned the hillside for any signs of Somali irregulars, but the whole terrain was obscured by lazily drifting clouds of dust. Brimshaw's position - or where it should have been - was itself now completely obscured by swirling smoke and red sand.

Tom drew his pistol and crept cautiously from the emplacement. The approach to Brimshaw's position was pitted with small craters and Tom found himself slipping and sliding on the loose shale. Groping his way forward, nearly blinded by the dust that floated into his eyes and mouth, Tom tripped and stumbled forward. The revolver flew from his grasp as he fell flat.

To Tom's horror, a turbaned Somali figure swathed in bandoliers emerged ghostlike from the smoke and stood over him.

'Captain Jorret?'

The sound of his name frightened Tom even more than the carbine that was pointed at his head.

'Yes.' He tried to control the quavering in his voice. 'Who is this?'

'I am sorry, Captain.' The Somali drew back the scarf that hid his mouth, but it was the voice rather than his now bearded appearance that Tom recognized.

Relief flooded through him. 'Rachid!'

'I am sorry, Captain,' Rachid said again, with the half-smile that Tom remembered well, 'I took charge of this section as I knew all about you and the gun. I hoped, Captain, that we would not have to shoot at each other.'

'Well, we have lost a bren-gunner - '

'I know. And you are searching for the other one? Major Broom-'

'Major Brimshaw, yes. And two soldiers.'

'I am sorry, Captain Jorret,' Rachid said again, his face impassive. 'We are close by their position. I found where I think it was. Over here, sir,'

The smoke was clearing a little as they made their way across a pile of rocks, some still hot to the touch.

There were no signs of Major Brimshaw or Sapper Lyons or Bari Din, only a crater where the Bren had been and where the rocks had been blown away down the mountainside.

'Oh my God,' Tom whispered,

'They must have sustained a direct hit.' Rachid spoke haltingly but showed no other emotion. 'My men have seen - some evidence - of your comrades. The young Gambian. Some of the clothing probably - of the other soldier.'

'You mean, Rachid - what does that mean -?'

'They could not have survived. We will see to the - remains, and mark them with our own dead.'

Tom was numbed. He could not focus on the loss of his comrades: instead, he started to grope about searching for his pistol.

Rachid put up a warning hand. 'I have found it, Captain Jorret.' He held the gun by the barrel and offered it to Tom.

'Now you may shoot me, if you should want to.'

'Of course not. Of course not.'

'Then let us sit here and parley.'

Tom scrambled to his feet. 'I should be getting back.' Tom spoke as if he were late for tea. 'To my men., that is,' he added. 'To my command.'

'Captain Jorret: it is better we talk for a moment. Better for us both.'

Chapter 21

Rachid squatted cross-legged and gestured Tom to sit opposite him.

The Somali spoke in his perfect if rather mannered English. 'They will spare you for a moment longer, and if we sit here, out of their sight, they will not shoot at us.'

Still dazed by events, Tom sat down obediently.

'You, the British, have finished your time here.'

Tom made a feeble gesture of protest. Rachid waved it aside impatiently.

'Come, Captain, you know it, Major Johnson knows it. You have no guns but yours, and you have no aircraft, and your troops are a tenth of the Italians. It is a matter of time before they push you into the sea. All you can do is to save the lives of your men.'

'Even if that were all true -'

'-it is,' Rachid interrupted.

'Even if that were true,' continued Tom defiantly, beginning to recover his spirit, 'nothing is up to me to decide. I command the gun, that's all, and obey my superior officers.'

Rachid smiled and shook his head wonderingly.

'We shall say nothing more as to that. Let us believe what we will. Let us instead talk about us, the Somali fighters, irregulars, you call us, do you not?'

Tom shrugged and made no reply.

'We irregulars can kill more of your soldiers than the Italians do. We do not care if we die, for many believe that to die for our cause will secure our place in heaven. But I myself do not want that: I would rather live to see you take to your ships and sail from our shores.'

Tom still said nothing.

'You know, Captain Jorret, that we *irregulars*,' - Rachid spoke the word with bitterness - 'we who happen to live here, and whose country this is, for all its poor state when compared with that of England, we *irregulars* would prefer to live under the English to living under the Italians. But we would much prefer to live under neither.'

Rachid paused for a reply but there was none.

'So we will let you withdraw without impeding you and we will fight only the Italians. If you do not try to impede us.'

'Rachid, I'm a junior officer. You know that it's impossible for me to make any arrangements like that.'

Rachid gestured to the crater behind them. 'You have already lost some comrades: why lose more needlessly?'

Tom thought of 'his' Gambians laughing and yelling with the football, and thought of Terence Brimshaw and Bari Din and Sapper Lyons blown away through his incompetence. And his gun was probably useless, and the battle of Tug Argen had as good as been lost before it began…*but- how could I explain all that to a court-martial? Cowardice in the face of the enemy? But the battle is lost, and I must look to my responsibility, to get the Gambians safe…*

'Very well, Rachid. I will give orders only to return fire. But I cannot answer for what the other commanders will do.'

'You are a man of honour, Captain Jorret. But there is one condition.'

'Yes?'

'The gun. It must not fall in enemy hands, or at least, it must be rendered useless to him.'

Rachid obviously doesn't know that it can't be fired anyway.

'You realize what you are asking of me, Rachid: that I should sabotage my own field gun? They will shoot me for that.'

'Then I am afraid we shall destroy it ourselves, and,' - Rachid stared unwaveringly into Tom's eyes - 'Captain Jorret, we can take no prisoners with us into the mountains. And my men do not care how - their enemies suffer.'

Tom paused, pretending to weigh the matter up.

'If I were to agree,' he said at last, 'I must be sure that you will retire out of range. Your signal that we will have gone will be the explosion of the gun.'

Rachid said: 'You can be sure of my word, Captain Jorret, as I am sure of yours.' Tom made to shake hands, but the Somali was already moving away.

Rachid turned and held up his hand in farewell.

'May Allah be with you, Captain,' he said, and was soon out of sight behind the rocks.

Tom shook his head in bewilderment. He stood for a moment regarding the revolver he was still holding. He automatically checked the safety catch, sighed, and stuffed it back into its holster.

He trudged slowly back to the silent compound.

* * *

Annie bustled in with some scrambled eggs for Sally who had just driven the cows back to the top field.

'Sal,' she said, 'I do wish you'd write to Tom. I'm sure he'd love to have a letter from you. Tell him about your friend the old lady in Kent and the German planes.'

'Well -' Sally said doubtfully.

'No, I'm *sure* he would'. Annie smiled down at her: she was quite Annie's favourite now. No one would call Annie a scheming woman; but equally no-one could fail to see where her hopes lay.

'Well -' said Sally again. 'I suppose I could -'

'He loves to have letters, you know. Sitting out there in the desert with nothing to do. And he'll be so pleased to know you're helping so much here keeping things going. And -'

Bob looked up from his *Western Morning News*. 'He knows all that, Annie. Give her some peace, you. Let her have her tea.'

'No, Mr Jorret, Mrs Jorret's quite right.' (Sally had never allowed herself to use Christian names.) 'Captain Jorret might like a letter from a stranger.'

'The name's Tom, dear. And you are *not* a stranger.'

Bob gave a grunt of resignation and went back to his paper.

Nevertheless, Sally sat down and wrote to Tom. No-one knew if he ever received it.

She told Tom with enthusiasm how the farm was going, how kind everyone was to her, including even grandfather Jorret (and in writing this, she did not realize quite what she was implying), how she helped him with his maps, and then she relayed part of the letter her friend had sent from Kent:

I don't know whether its secret, but it can't be a secret to them that they have lots of their planes being shot down. We have SEEN them! Our Spitfires go up after them, and you can see them high over the fields twisting and turning and diving and climbing and you can even hear the machine guns firing and every now and then one of them spins out of the sky. The poor young men, not only our boys - and we cry a bit at night as some of them are shot down are our boys, although we have seen several of our boys baling out and they land in the fields but the poor Germans, and it's not their fault that Hitler wanted a war, is it? and there are FAR more of theirs come down than ours. There was a picture in the papers of some farm workers with pitchforks capturing a German pilot who was still dragging his parachute behind him as he hadn't been able to unstrap it before they arrived. Frederick says that our Spitfires and Hurricanes are much better, and the Germans use up so much petrol getting here that they often can't get home after the battles, Frederick says that he thinks its all one big battle to stop the Germans being able to cross the Channel, and he thinks we're winning THIS one even though we've lost, well, ALL the others, but he says that like Mr Churchill says without mastery of the air we can't win any battles and Frederick thinks that's what went wrong in France But I'll never forget this, fancy me seeing a BATTLE at my age! like those Victorian ladies who went and WATCHED those battles in the Crimean war! How they could DO that, though, I can't imagine. Everyone comes out here though, and all the small boys shout and cheer and they all say they wish they were old enough. There was one Messerschmidt (I don't know if its spelt right) with its tail shot right away and the two parts seemed to stop and hang in midair before they came crashing down side by side. The German airman bailed out all right, though, I'm glad to say.

Sally painfully transcribed this word for word (feeling that to do otherwise would be slightly dishonest) and added the messages of love from Tom's family and signed it *Yours sincerely, Sally Samson.*

She added a *PS: I hope you don't mind me writing to you*

without knowing you at all, but Mrs Jorret said you would like to hear from me.

* * *

They clustered around Tom as he clambered through the sandbags, but they knew the worst merely from looking at his slumped shoulders.

'We have no hope, Captain Tom?' Lamin Bar asked. 'Bari Din? Mr Sapperlines? The Major Blimshaw?'

To each question Tom shook his head despondently. 'They could not have suffered,' he said, but he wondered if it were a lie.

'Now,' he said, trying to assume an air of firm authority, 'now we have to safeguard - that is, we must, er, -'

At that moment, mercifully, George Johnson lollopped over to him, almost at a run.

'A word, Captain Jorret,' he said, taking Tom aside.

'Look, George, I've-' Tom began.

'Never mind that. We have to lose even our friends. We are under orders to evacuate. The Black Watch will cover us as far as they can, but we must get out. And leave nothing for the Wops.'

He took Tom by the shoulders.

'Look, Tom: we are neither of us soldiers. But we've got to be now.'

'I've seen Rachid.'

'What?'

'I've seen Rachid and arranged a truce with the Somalis.'

'You've done what?'

'Rachid's their local commander. He knows all our movements. They are to pull back provided we destroy the gun and get out.'

George gave a low whistle. 'God, Tom, you don't know what you've done!'

'Yes I do.'

'But they'll shoot you for this!'

'I know.'

'You can't just make peace with the enemy! No-one else must know, is that clear?'

'Rachid knows we've lost, George. He wants to save his fire for the Italians.'

'That's as may be. But you can't do that kind of thing.'

'I've done it.' Tom took a deep breath. 'Those fellows, Pete Lyons and Terence and Bari Din, they were my responsibility and I let them go and get themselves blown up. I am not going to get anyone else killed needlessly.'

'That's nonsense. Anyway,' George gave a wry smile, 'everyone's killed needlessly in this war here, Tom.'

Tom shrugged and said nothing.

George suddenly went to Tom and hugged him.

'Tom,' he said. 'Well done, old chap, well done.' He paused. 'But you are to tell no one else. *No-one*.' He grinned. 'Apart from all else, they'd shoot me as well now I know. Now we must get out of here.'

* * *

The Gambians sat cross-legged in a semi-circle around Tom. They sat silent, crestfallen, stunned by their friends' deaths.

Tom tried to appear business-like, brisk. He failed miserably.

'We must let the -er- loss of - our friends, *not* let the loss - stop, that is, us making - doing our best -' He looked about him helplessly.

'It all right, Captain Tom,' said Joni Kru. 'We are soldiers, all might die. You said, if we fight, we have pain and fright, Captain Tom, and we follow you all the time. That so, isn't it, chaps?'

He looked about him to his comrades, who all shouted their support, grinning and clapping.

The incongruous "*chaps*" made the scene unbearable for Tom and tears rolled slowly down his normally impassive face.

He swept the tears aside with his large khaki handkerchief and (thinking of Brimshaw's probable response) pulled himself together.

'Thank you, Joni Kru. Thank you all. But we now have to get ourselves to safety so that we can fight again. We cannot use the gun and it must be destroyed so that the enemy cannot repair it. We are ordered to withdraw to Berbera and allow the infantry to carry the fight against the enemy. Our comrades in the Black Watch are sending transport to evacuate all essential stores. We shall prepare to destroy all that we cannot take, and I myself will be responsible for laying the charges when our withdrawal is complete.'

There will be a massive explosion with all the shells stacked round the gun. But the motorbike should see me safely away.

'In my absence Major Johnson will be your officer until I rejoin you.'

* * *

The transport from the Black Watch with a young officer and his platoon arrived to supervise the loading of the stores and Tom ordered all the shells and other material to be stacked beside the gun.

The Gambian soldiers each in turn (to the Scots soldiers' amazement) came and hugged Tom before they climbed sadly into the 3-tonner.

When night fell Tom sat sadly on the parapet and watched the shadowy trucks edge out of the compound on their journey to Berbera and out of his life.

Chapter 22

'All it says here, Grandfather,' said Emmy, trying to keep cool and composed, 'is that there's been "heavy fighting in the British colony of Somaliland".

"British and Empire forces are checking the enemy advance and inflicting heavy losses." That's all it says.'

'Give it here, girl,' demanded Peter Jorret roughly, grabbing at the newspaper.

'You'll tear it, Grandfather. Anyway, you know you can't make the print out.'

'I've got my glass, 'aven't I?'

But the old man's eyes were too weak. 'Where's Sally? She'll read it. You keep missing bits out, don't you? Thinkin' I won't notice.' He squinted at the paper.

'Look, anyway, it's out of date!' He stabbed his finger at the headline. 'This bit's writ three days ago. Look at the date: even I can see that: the fifteenth of August! Three days ago!' He chuckled. 'The Wops'll be beat by now, you'll see!'

Jimmy and Emily exchanged glances.

'I don't think you should get your hopes up too much, Mr Jorret,' said Jimmy. 'The Italians have all their troops there from Abyssinia. And their tanks and planes.'

The old man snarled at him. 'You always say that. Eyeties can't fight, except against the natives.' He began to work himself into a rage. 'You're no better than a defeatist! Always saying how bad things are when our boys are sweating their guts out! Fifth Column that's what you are!'

Emily burst into tears. 'How can you say that Grandfather? Just because Jimmy's not in the army or something, you say he doesn't - oh- why do you say that?'

Jimmy patted her hand. "That's all right, Emmy. We all have to let fire at something, sitting here worrying.' He turned to the old man. 'We're all worried about Tom, Mr Jorret, but we just have to keep going, do our best, you know, even if it's not fighting.'

But even Jimmy Henbury was upset: his face had reddened, and he nervously took off his glasses and rubbed them with a handkerchief.

'Look, I'd better go, Emmy. There's lots to do.' He tried to smile reassuringly. 'Goodnight, Mr Jorret.'

Peter Jorret, a little shamefaced, pretended to concentrate on his newspaper and muttered some kind of reply, which Jimmy took for an apology.

Jimmy led Emily into the scullery.

'Look, Emmy, defeatist or not,' he gave a weak grin, 'fifth column, indeed! No, but I think things are going very badly out there. When they talk about *stemming*, was it? no, *checking*, the enemy advance, well, it probably means that they're already retreating. And your Grandfather knows it: that's why he lashes out like he does.'

'Yes, but -'

Jimmy kissed her gently. 'I must go. I know it's a daft thing to say but try not to worry.

We've just got to carry on doing our jobs. See you tomorrow.'

Emily saw him to his car (a somewhat battered Hillman Minx) and went into the yard in search of Sally.

Emily watched as her friend hosed down the milking

parlour, not a difficult task, but one which Sally did, as everything else, with a calm efficiency.

'I'll be with you in just a minute,' Sally shouted.

Not for the first time, Emily felt a twinge of envy. Sally, she thought, was everything she wasn't, plump but not too much so, fair-haired, rosy-cheeked, smiling. Well-spoken. Confident. Young…

'Grandfather was terrible to Jimmy, said horrid things, Sal.' Sally put her arm round Emily's thin shoulders.

'You mustn't mind. I've noticed this sometimes. Very old people lash out spitefully sometimes, especially to people they're fond of.'

'That's what Jimmy said. But Jimmy was really upset and,' Emily smiled wanly, 'I don't think he's very fond of Jimmy.'

'Oh, I don't know. Your Grandfather's used to running things, having everyone running around, and now everyone else but him is important. He thinks he's useless, and everyone is helping Tom except him. He as good as told me that, Emmy.'

'I expect you're right.' Emily smiled again. 'You usually are.' She felt a sudden rush of affection for Sally. 'I'm so glad you're here, Sally. You've made such a difference to us all. Even to Grandfather.'

Sally gave her a kiss on her cheek. 'I've loved being here, Emmy. I've felt one of a family for the first time.' She stood still a moment and looked about her at the slate-roofed, whitewashed walls of the yard.

'However awkward your Grandfather is sometimes, Emmy, he's right about one thing: it's the family that matters in the end, almost *all* that matters. Everyone takes responsibility for everyone else, if you see what I mean.'

* * *

Tom sat on the parapet. He could just make out the shape of the gun lurching on its side. *It's probably useless anyway: they'll never bother to repair it. But I promised Rachid: a man of honour, he called me. Never blown anything up before: I suppose it'll be OK. Just push down the pump thing, George said: all right for him, he knows what he is doing. Suppose it doesn't go off? Better go and check the detonators - for the umpteenth time.*

Again, Tom cautiously approached the gun. He shielded the light of his torch as he shone it on the piles of ammunition boxes and petrol cans stacked around the now useless gun, and thought of the many hours they had spent in perfecting their drill, and the eagerness with which the crew had painted and polished and greased the weapon - the weapon they never thought about as killing people, killing ordinary fellows like themselves in every respect but skin colour.

Funny thing: August, what, 25th? Where was I last year, watching skylarks, well, not in the middle of the night. Not in August for that matter. Had George recruited me by then? Or was I still doing as I pleased, not having to worry about anything. Or anybody. Sitting with Emmy watching skylarks. And letting Terry go and drown himself. And letting Terence get himself blown up. Didn't have to take responsibility for anyone: am I my brother's keeper, kind of thing. Old Brimshaw swimming out to the rock. Silly ass. Gunger Din wanted to help him and it was my responsibility to get him back and Gunger Din gets drowned as well…

'Captain Tom! I find you at last!'

Tom was jerked awake, terrified: a huge lean shape had loomed up in front of him.

'It's me, Captain Tom! Lamin Bar.'

'Lamin Bar!' For a moment Lamin Bar was part of the nightmare: then reality (almost as bad) struck him. 'What the hell are you doing here?'

'Thought I help a bit,' said Lamin, 'You might need help, Captain Tom.'

'Where are the others? You should be on your way to - wherever - *Berbera* by now. What's the time?'

Tom shone the torch on his watch. Barely forty minutes had passed.

'It all right. You must have dropped asleep waitin', Captain Tom.' He sat down by Tom without being invited, and Tom shifted to make more room on the parapet. 'They're all gone. Expect all safe now. Major George say that most of the army headin' for the coast now. D'you think battle over now?'

'Don't know, Lamin.'

Tom felt Lamin shivering, and he too was feeling the cold. Luckily, George had reminded him that he would need some blankets while he waited. Tom went to fetch some from the pile he had put by and handed Lamin a couple.

'No, I don't know, Lamin. What I do know is that our bit of it's over and in a few days all our friends will be safely in Aden. So will we, I hope.'

'The Wops are winnin', Captain Tom. No need to tell me different.'

'OK. They're winning. But George - Major Johnson - says that the Black Watch fellows are here to cover our retreat. And I know the Somalis won't attack us.'

'You know, sir?'

Tom cursed himself for his carelessness. 'Well, Lamin, not *know*, exactly: it's just that they'll wait till we've gone. At least,' he added lamely, 'that's what I think.'

Lamin seemed satisfied with that.

'Anyway, they won't come near us when we've blown this lot up,' Tom went on, 'I've a feeling they'll turn their fire on the Italians now.'

Lamin Bar has absolute trust that what I say is true and will happen. He could have - he should have - gone off with the others to probable safety, out of the battle. But he didn't: felt responsible for me. Just like old Brimshaw's Gungar Din... Didn't he realize that if this lot goes wrong we'll both be blown up with it? What if that bloody plunger don't work? Or we get caught in the blast? Just simple trust...

Tom struggled to understand why he felt near to tears at this sheer, well, simplicity, honesty, unthinking loyalty.

'Lamin, you know - there's no need- very grateful - I just -'

'It all right, Captain Tom. I told the others I am stayin', sir. They all agreed it was only right. You look after us all, Captain Tom, and we responsible to see you safe if we can.'

There was a long silence.

'Tell me about The Gambia, Lamin. While we wait.'

Lamin thought for a moment. 'Well, Gambia is hot, not like this, but always hot. Not dry an' parchin' like Somali, Captain Tom. Wet and steamy so the sweat runs off you like the river. That is, June to November, then it get cooler and dry. But the River flows deep and green with all the forest. And the birds, Captain Tom! All colours of rainbow, callin' and chatterin' and singin' louder than all our wailin' women-folk.'

Lamin told him that the great river, the River, two hundred miles long, was like a great snake twisting and turning through the trees, and every now and then there would be villages with their little patches of field and their cattle. At least, that's what he was told; he. Lamin, had never been right up the river where there were different savage tribes and (he grinned so that even in the dark Tom could see his white teeth) you never knew they might not catch you and eat you.

'No, only jokin', Captain Tom, but me an' the others live by the ocean. Serekonda a fishin' town, that's where we all come from, and where the clergyman teach us to write English. You live by the ocean too, Captain Tom? You do fishin' too?'

'Well, yes: not like you, Lamin, not by the ocean so much, but a kind of corner of the sea where it -' Tom could find no way of describing the Newmin bays.

'Look, Lamin, hold the torch a moment.' He scratched the shape of the Cornish Peninsula in the sand at their feet. Here's where we are.'

'Far away from Gambia.'

'Yes, Lamin, very far away. And it is cold in the winter, not cold like this, but wet and windy. Very windy.' He pictured himself standing on the cliff when he was a boy, the gulls swooping about him, and caught by a gust which all but knocked him down to the rocks.

'Fishing? Yes: lots of fishing. The boats chug out of Newmin harbour every day and bring back their catch to sell in the market or send up to Plymouth or on the train to London. A few years ago -' and by now Lamin had lost track and just nodded (in the dark) as if he understood it all. As for Tom himself, he was lost too, in his memories, homesick for the wind and the salt spray and the slippery rocks swamped by the incoming tide.

'You were sayin'? Few years ago?'

'Sorry, yes. A few years ago, when I was a boy, all the fishing boats were sailing boats, and in the storms, some were lost. The storms and the tides carried them away and they were drowned.'

'The same in Gambia. Great storms sweep in from the Atlantic Ocean, Captain Tom, and we never see the fishermen again.'

'Will you go back, Lamin? After the war, I mean?'

'No. Never go back. Never had such a life as now, Captain Tom, with great men like you and Major George, sir, givin' me trust. In Gambia, all my family dead, malaria, and people too poor. English governor tries, but hopeless, Captain Tom. Poor tribes, up river, all diseased and hopeless.'

'Lamin, are there skylarks in the Gambia?'

'Skylarks, Captain Tom? What you mean?'

'Skylarks. I used to watch them, climbing higher and higher, singing and singing, without a care in the world, just singing, and not responsible for anyone or anything.'

'Oh yes, we have every bird, and skylarks too. But excuse if I say you are not right. Skylark always in danger from the hawks, and always higher and higher and noisy to get hawks away from the nest and young skylarks on the ground. Always responsible, sir. Sacrificing self so that family survive, sir. Not free and easy, Captain Tom.'

'No,' said Tom slowly. 'Not free and easy at all.'

He looked at his watch by torchlight.

'Think we must make a move, soon, Lamin. First, I'll show you where our dugout is.

And you must take shelter in it.'

Chapter 23

It was Friday in the third week of September: the second post had arrived with still no news.

'You'd have thought they would have said by now,' Annie said, for the twentieth time.

Sally took her hand. 'We know that if - if it were the worst, they would have, well, notified you.'

'That's what they do.' Old Jorret held his head in his hands. 'You get a telegram. You know when the telegram boy comes up the drive on his bike, when he knocks on the door an' you see 'im standin' there, you know, it's Steve all over.'

'Don't, Grandfather,' said Emily, wringing her hands. 'You mustn't upset yourself and us all. We just got to wait. If he weren't safe and sound, they'd have said. We'll get a letter soon, you'll see.'

Bob had no spirit left even to pretend to read his newspaper. 'What we do know is that they've all got away. It said so weeks ago, and they're evacuated. It said so.'

'Inflicted heavy casualties on the enemy,' said his father. 'Our forces fought a strategic withdrawal from that barren region of East Africa and inflicted heavy casualties on the enemy. I know. I 'ave it by 'eart. But they don't tell the truth, not always. They never said, in the first lot, they never said that all those lads was wiped out, the Somme I mean. Didn't say 'till afterwards.'

'It's all different this time, Grandfather.' Sally had taken to calling Peter Jorret that. 'They don't want to tell the Italians anything, so they have to keep quiet. And they said about the Navy, too: we have control of the sea there. I showed you on the map. They would have got all our men off to Aden, you'll see.'

'Then why don't he write?' The old man brushed away a tear with his sleeve.

Sally left Annie's side with a comforting smile to her and went to sit at Jorret's feet. 'We mustn't just sit here worrying, you know. I've never met your Tom, but he wouldn't expect us just to sit here worrying, by all accounts. Isn't that so, Emmy?'

Emily nodded. 'He'd have just said don't be so daft and gone and watched the sea and the skylarks for a bit, and then he'd have gone and done a bit of stone-carving. He never used to sit around worrying about anything.'

And they're all sitting around looking at me, Sally thought, all relying on me to give them some smiles and encouragement, for they're all old - even dear Emmy, in her way, she never seems to have been young - and they've really lost heart and can't see any point in anything anymore. Even Emmy is talking about Tom as if he's dead.

She looked up at the old Cornish grandfather clock in the corner, carved with strange birds, which old Peter Jorret kept accurate to the minute from the radio.

'I could switch on the wireless: that might have some fresh news.'

She switched on the rather expensive set that Bob had bought when the war broke out: it took much less time for the valves to warm up, and had none of those annoying whistles and crackles of the old one.

But there was only some jolly supposedly morale-boosting music-hall programme on. It somehow deepened the gloom.

'Never mind: it'll be time for ITMA soon,' said Sally, somewhat desperately.

'Why don't Emmy and I go and make some tea? If I may, Mrs Jorret?' she added, smiling at Annie.

Annie smiled back. 'Of course, dear. And bring some of those scones.'

Sally led Emily through to the scullery leaving the sitting-room in a pool of miserable music-hall jollity.

Emily sat in the high-backed settle and watched Sally, her hand wrapped in a cloth, shift the heavy iron kettle along to the hotplate on the range.

'Not much tea left,' said Sally. 'It's your father, having it so strong.'

Emily laughed. 'We've got a lot from Tom. Didn't you know? He had some sent from Kenya, a present to Ma.'

'I didn't know they allowed that,' said Sally in surprise.

'Oh yes. They send parcels back on the troopships. Keeps our morale up,' she added, with unaccustomed sarcasm.

Sally shot her an enquiring look. 'We won't be able to drink it if -'

'Emily!' Sally spoke with unusual severity. 'It's up to you - to us - the younger ones, to keep everyone going. We don't know what the situation is, but we must not make it worse for them. Take the scones in and I'll bring the tea in a moment. Tell them what Jimmy is doing. Vital things for the war effort, and so is the farm, and they must be proud of it as well as of Tom.'

She laughed and hugged her friend. 'Lecture over. Take the scones.'

* * *

A letter did arrive, at last, on September 23rd. It was not from Tom, but from George.

As always, Annie was waiting at the window for the first post, and she could see the old postman with the sack over his shoulder trying to rush up the drive.

He struggled to the front door waving the letter.

'Something's come, Annie, from foreign parts,' he shouted. He hovered on the doorstep as Annie snatched it with trembling fingers. 'Annie, I'll bide here a bit, see if there be news of Tom?'

Annie didn't answer but rushed indoors leaving the door open behind her.

Sally was busy about the farm, but the others were already standing waiting.

Annie fumbled with the envelope 'You read it, Emily,' said Annie. 'I can't - can't - see what-'

'Give 'im to me!' Peter Jorret snatched it from her. 'I won't have it torn. You'll tear it.'

The family watched in stunned silence as the old man took his penknife from his waistcoat pocket and carefully slit the envelope and laid it aside before handing the letter back to Emily.

'It's typed, from Lt-Col' - she read the letters literally - 'George Johnson.'

Annie screamed at her. 'Never mind that! What's it say?'

Emily scanned the first lines.

Dear Mr and Mrs Jorret, Tom is safe. He is safe here in Aden.

'Oh thank God!' said Annie. 'Thank God! Go on, Emmy.'

There was a timid knock, and the old postman poked his head round the door.

'Beg pardon, Mr Jorret,' he said, addressing Peter Jorret, 'but we'll all be a bit anxious-like.'

Annie 'Oh, sorry, Josh: I forgot: we're all so excited. It's good news: Tom is safe. Thank you Josh. Tom is safe. We'll know more later,' she added meaningfully, ushering the beaming postman out again.

'Now the whole village will know. But do go on, Emily,' she said, resuming her chair and leaning forward, her hands clasped over her knees.

Emily went on: *we lost one of our Gambian friends but all the rest of us are safe. The navy got us away from Berbera.*

Forgive the typed message but I am in dock. Or would have written sooner. Some vile bug got me, but better now. Tom would have written of course but I'm afraid he's laid up too. The fact is he got a problem with his right arm and they didn't know if they could save it. Some fellows got caught by Italian planes, and I think that Tom was thrown from his motorbike –

'Motorbike!' exclaimed Annie. 'What was he doing on his *motorbike*?I *warned* him…' Her voice trailed off.

'I expect it was an army one, Annie,' said Bob as if it explained everything. 'Anyway, go on, Emmy.'

'I'm afraid - well, I'd better read it. But Tom doesn't sound too well, Ma.'

'Why? What's it say for goodness' sake?'

'They use them a lot,' said the old Jorret. 'Motorbikes. They had 'em in the first lot.

Steve -'

'Oh be *quiet,* Grandfather.' Emily was close to tears again. 'It says - George says - Tom had a head wound and was severely concussed and took a long time to come round and what with his arm, well - this is what it says: *it might be a while yet before he can write and tell you about it. I'm a bit tired so I'll get the lad to send this off. Write when you can to me and Tom together so I can read it to him. With love to you all, your friend George.*

'Your *friend* George!' whooped Peter Jorret. 'Think of that! And him a Major!'

'I think that's what that L-t. Col. means, Grandfather. He's been promoted: he's a Lieutenant-Colonel now. I'm sure that's it. But he's written something else here, it's terribly difficult to read, all shaky. He must be very ill.'

But the old man wasn't listening: he was muttering gleefully to himself about our friend the Lieutenant-*Colonel*...

Bob adjusted his round horn-rimmed glasses. 'Let me look, maid.' He squinted at the scrawled message.

'I think he says that's someone with him. L-A-double R-I-something,' he said. 'Helping care for T.'

'Not double-R,' said Emily, peering over his shoulder, 'It's M - Lamin, he's the Gambian boy Tom's written about sometimes. Lamin Bah. That's good, isn't it? If his friend's there to help?'

'He's one of those black claps, ain't he? What's a black man doin' lookin' after an officer?' Peter Jorret thumped his gnarled fist on the arm of his chair. 'I thought officers were treated different anyway. Separate. When Steve was –'

'That's enough!' There was a stunned silence in the room as Bob with great deliberation put down his newspaper and stood solidly in front of the fireplace. His burly red-faced figure seemed to fill the room. 'From now on, you will speak respect for Tom's friends. If they're friends of Tom, especially when he's far away and wounded, they are friends of us all. In my house.'

He had not raised his voice. Indeed, he spoke more softly. But he spoke with an intensity even Annie had never heard before.

'In my house, I say, father. If you are to stay with us, you will stop all this talk. And enough of Steve and how we have to be like him. Say nothing bad about the dead, they say, but Steve's been dead these twenty year or more and we all want to be with the living, I say, and not looking back to what -' he stumbled for some softer words -'what was a bit of a dream all those years back.'

He said no more, for at that moment Sally came in from the scullery.

'Oh I'm sorry. Am I interrupting you?' She caught sight of Grandfather with large tears rolling down the grooves in his thin face. 'Shall I - Oh God, it's not Tom?'

'No, no my dear,' said Annie, putting her arm round her shoulders. 'Tom's safe. Tom's safe in Aden. Sit down and we'll tell you what we know. I think, Bob,' she said, turning to her husband, 'we ought to open a bottle or two of that port wine we were saving, and drink to Steve's memory in the past, and to Tom and all his friends for the future.'

She went and kissed her father-in-law. He looked up and put his wizened hand over hers.

* * *

Emily tried to scrawl a letter that very afternoon but found no words to say.

September 23rd 1940

Dear Tom and George, You have no idea how we all felt so happy that you and the other friends are safe at last. She sat and sucked her pen as if she were still at school. She wrote *Hope you are both getting better,* then crossed it out and started again. What could she say? Tears came to her eyes as she wrote: *we were so sad about the Gambian boy, though, and hope his mother will* - will what? So she crossed out the last phrase and started a third time. *I'll catch the post so you know that we have got George's letter and God bless you both and send news soon that you're getting better, your loving Emmy. PS We're all well and do you know what, Pa suddenly really told Grandfather off for being silly! The cows and dogs and cats are well too. XX E PPS. The RAF has really beaten the Germans and they don't think the Germans can possibly invade till next year so that's something!*

Chapter 24

The church dated from the fourteenth century: it was small and simple with the usual tower (with its set of six bells, silent since 1939), nave and chancel. A small north aisle had been added in the 16th century as the local population had been swelled with Huguenot migrants.

The north door opened onto the graveyard where the bones of generations of Crannel villagers lay - there were Samsons by name, and Jorrets, who, did the old man but know it, descended like him from those very Huguenots.

The Sunday after George's letter, Sally Samson and Emily nee Jorret stood before Terry's simple headstone, which was already gathering a little moss and frequented by tiny stone-coloured insects. Sally knelt to put fresh flowers on the grave before the two ladies, arm-in-arm, walked up the sandy path to the South porch.

The church was packed: it had been every Sunday since the start of the war.

Bob and Annie had saved their seats in the Jorret pew, where for once even the old man sat: he stared about him balefully, dressed in a stiff collar and heavy black serge suit. The vicar was surprised, and a little disconcerted, to see him there, as Peter Jorret had attended only marriages and funerals, and very few of either.

The service ran its customary irrelevant course. Especially

irrelevant was the Old Testament lesson, which featured an obscure Jewish personage called Mephibosheth, whose name (often repeated in the extract) caused the old vicar, who had been called out of retirement as younger men went as chaplains to the forces, considerable difficulty, and a painful fit of suppressed giggles in Sally, who infected Emily too, and Sally tried to contain herself by praying that there was no verse where *Mephibosheth saith,* and was only saved when the lady organist in her sideways felt hat struck up *Now Thank We All Our God.*

Then the long prayers. Sally loved the rolling Cranmer rhythms. She loved the General Confession: *we have erred and strayed from Thy ways like lost sheep: we have done those things we ought not to have done, and we have left undone those things we ought to have done, and there is no health in us.* And as for our sins: *the burden of them is intolerable* (or was that the Communion service?).

Her attention wandered and she covertly looked about her: Mrs Trelove, a widow since the first war who ran the Post Office shop, sitting next to old Josh the postman, and behind her Beth Cummins and her two pert teen-aged daughters who had grown quite unruly with their father away in the Merchant Navy. Then Albert Penwarry, the fisherman who had been to Dunkirk, and his family, one of the boys nearly at call-up age; then a stout lady in voluminous black, Mrs Rawson, also widowed by the Battle of the Somme, who hated the French and blamed them for all the troubles that the wars had heaped on her (her son being a Sergeant in the Service Corps and responsible for driving ammunition trucks).

But for all their faults and weaknesses, *was* the burden of their sins intolerable? It seemed to Sally that the people whose sins were so burdensome were the last people to regret them, let alone repent them. *And it's really no comfort that Hitler and Goering and Himmler are doomed (as obviously the Vicar thinks) to eternal damnation. Something we'll never know about, unless we are sent to join them, which would be grossly unjust of God, as our - my - sins don't cost suffering to millions of people. Anyway, what sins? Curiously the sins of the flesh* (she relished the word *flesh* and repeated it to herself) *don't really seem like sins at all, to give love to one or two (three, actually) RAF boys who might be going off to be killed…No, my sins are of the category left undone those things I ought to have done, so concerned about myself "following the devices and desires of my own heart" as dear Archbishop Cranmer put it, that I never thought about my responsibility to - O God, does that count as repentance or do I have to give to the poor or something?*

Sally jerked her attention back to the sermon. The Vicar was still talking about sin, while every day the most monstrous *crimes* were being committed as a matter of course, as thousands of innocent folk were being blown up and burnt to death in their homes with their children and their dogs and cats and the new dining-room table they had saved up for - and Sally's imagination, and her memories, brought tears to her eyes, even as the Vicar was asking them all to pray for all our men and women in the forces and ask God to keep them in His loving care, even though in front of him sat three or four folk the war had already bereaved …

Then the Vicar read out the list of names of villagers who were serving, whom we must all remember in our prayers, and Sally squeezed Emmy's hand as he came to "Tom Jorret and his friend George Johnson, not of this village, but one whom Mrs Jorret had especially asked to be included" and the list ended with James Rawson as the black-robed Mrs Rawson sat stony-faced. People said that Mrs Rawson had been a harsh and unkind mother and that James had been eager to join up and get away and didn't even write to her. Sadness swept over Sally once again as she thought of the cold lonely and loveless life the woman had helped to build for herself.

Then at last came the Blessing. Sally, again, loved the simplicity, the naivety, of the Church of England services, the tradition, and the fact that no-one ever considered the meaning of what they were saying or singing, but just said it or sung it with the vague feeling that behind it all there was something more meaningful, beyond their daily lives. She loved too the naïve sincerity of the earnest clergyman who could not understand how anyone could doubt the truths woven, as it were, into the fabric of English life, and his baffled grief as he attempted to grasp any meaning in the daily cruelties of the world…

So she felt real guilt as the giggles welled up again: why did she *always* revert to schoolgirl when she should be at her most devout: "the piece of cod that passeth understanding"? When Emily asked her outside what had set her off again, she, Emily, had never heard it, and their laughter brought disapproving looks from the parishioners as they gathered to gossip in the churchyard after shaking hands with the Vicar stammering for their names. ('So good to see you here, Mrs Ah-um, how is, er, *he* getting along?').

Little knots of churchgoers edged slowly down towards the lych-gate. Some gathered around Peter: the village still regarded the old man with some awe and apprehension and listened respectfully to his views.

'It's those Frenchies, Mr Jorret, who let us all down,' said Mrs Ransom.

Peter nodded sagely, his expert maps in mind. 'We'd've been all right if they hadn't joined in with the Wops at

Djibuti,' he pronounced, in the three words *Gee- boot- ee.*

'Oh I know,' agreed Mrs Ransom, who of course did not, but tried to assume the air of one sharing the secret. 'Gee-boot-ee. Yes.'

'Some of 'em are alright, Tom says,' Peter conceded.

'Oh yes, *some* are. And he should know, your Tom. Of course he should,' replied Mrs Ransom, now quite befogged.

'Didn't try and stop us lifting everyone out. Didn't dare, did they?'

'You're quite right, Mr Jorret. Wouldn't dare, oh no. Not them!' She glared at Mrs Trelove of the Post Office who was trying to get a word in.

'Tom's wounded, I hear, Mr Jorret,' her little wrinkled bird-like face showing genuine anxiety.

'Wounded, when he was fightin' to get the others away.' Jorret was already building a new myth around Tom, but he had accidentally hit somewhere near the truth.

'That's Tom, always thinking of others,' said Mrs Trelove, quite untruthfully.

'Had to,' said Jorret. 'Officer, high-up, has to look after his men. I recalls how my son Steve-'

But he could not elaborate on Steve's career as Bob had taken him by the arm.

'We're off to the Britannia, Pa. Morning, Mrs Trelove, morning, Mrs Ransom. You'll excuse us, I know.'

Mrs Ransom sniffed. 'Drink. Jorret family's known for it, Mrs Trelove,' she confided to Mrs Trelove as the men made off for the Britannia Arms, which was sited conveniently near the church gate.

'No such thing, Mrs Ransom. How do you say such things, what with Tom lying wounded and all?' And Mrs Trelove turned her back on the unhappy woman and scuttled back home.

As did all he ladies from the church, it being unheard of for the Crannel womenfolk to be seen in the Britannia Arms; occasionally, one or two younger ladies might sip a small glass of sherry in the evening before going to the pictures, but never on Sunday morning. Besides, many had to prepare the Sunday dinner.

Contrary to Mrs Ransom's opinion, Bob did not drink a great deal, but enjoyed the chance to meet up with the other farmers (there were two other small farms centred on the village) and those farm workers who were left, all at least middle-aged. They sat around the small tables in the smoke-filled public bar (where the beer was a penny cheaper than the saloon). The beams were hung about with horse brasses that the Freemans kept scrupulously gleaming clean, even though the ceiling, the paintwork and the coloured pictures of the hunting fields were stained yellow with tobacco smoke.

The talk was always of the war, of the bombing that was growing in intensity.

'I has a bucket o' water outside the front door and a bucket o' sand. Regulations. Had drowned rat in the bucket the other day,' said Arthur Green.

Arthur was a farm worker, nearly sixty-three years old, who for the first time in his life had become an important figure, as an Air Raid Warden, with a blue battledress that he wore on all occasions and a white helmet with the word WARDEN painted on it that Mrs Green made him reluctantly leave at home.

'What, drowned in the sand, Arthur?' said someone. Everyone laughed.

'It's a very important responsibility,' said Arthur huffily. 'Hope that it don't come to it,' he added sententiously, 'but someone 'as to be in charge if it come to it.'

'Quite right, Arthur. We'll all rely on you.'

Arthur was mollified but remained suspicious that the others were not taking the matter seriously enough.

Someone asked Bob about Tom.

'He seems to be recovering slowly,' Tom said. 'Annie had a letter the other day, but it didn't say - well, I'll show it you and you'll know as much as we do.'

He produced the letter from his wallet. It had been laboriously and carefully written in a large round hand in bright blue ink.

Dear Mrs Annie Jorret. I sending you this message from Captain Tom, who still ill in hospital but doctor say get better and better but not use right hand much. Major George now Colonel arrange I stay with Captain Tom to help at same time I get better from little injury to ribs nothing much.

I am most respectfully and affectionately,Lamin Bah (Sgt)

The fellows around the bar guffawed at this until silenced by a withering look from Bob.

'It aint be good English, that,' opined Arthur.

'Better than yours,' said Josh the postman.

'A Bloody native, that, aint 'e?' said Arthur.

'He comes from the Gambia, an' 'es a friend of Tom's, so you keep yer mouth shut,' shouted Peter Jorret.

'Blackie, 'e is. You can always tell, from the writin,' said Arthur sulkily.

'That's an amazin' gift o' yourn, Arthur, tellin' a man's a blackie form his hand- writin', said Josh.

Chapter 25

'Emmy,' Jimmy Henbury was saying, 'I can't see how I'll be able to get back for some time now.'

She could see he was agitated: he had a way of whipping off his round-rimmed glasses and taking the silk handkerchief from his breast pocket to clean them.

'I was hoping you could spend some time here in the spring.'

'These raids: they're going to get worse. I know it: if you were the Germans, and our navy was a sitting target, and we hadn't any planes to defend it, and - well, you see what I mean.'

Emily looked blank. 'Not really -'

'I mean they'll go for the docks. Devonport. You know they've been over several times already.'

'Plymouth's nothing like London, though, Jimmy,' said Annie. 'Or Coventry. The poor people there, how can they stand it?'

Jimmy shook his head sadly. 'Annie: no-one here in the West Country thinks there's any danger. I tell you, when those three or four bombs fell a few months ago, everyone just stood round and gawped: they said it was a gas main, couldn't believe the Germans had done it, not to Plymouth. But we think these raids are just trial runs, reconnaissance, and come the spring, they'll - well, we'll see.'

Bob put his paper down. 'Who's *we*, Jimmy? *We* think?'

'Well, you know, ARP men, the Major Ack-Ack -'

'Anti-aircraft guns, Pa,' explained Bob.

'I know *that*,' the old man snapped. 'My friend the Colonel, 'e's in the Royal Artillery -'

'Quite so,' interrupted Jimmy hastily, 'Ack-Ack, yes, and balloons, and then there's us who build the shelters. And an RAF officer. *And* a Navy man.'

'Why aren't they fightin', not jus' sittin' round in committee meetin's?' demanded Peter Jorret sourly.

'They'll be fighting soon enough, Grandfather,' said Jimmy grimly. 'Fighting fires and fighting bombers. Soon enough, Grandfather.'

The old man scowled at him; he hated to be called grandfather by Jimmy Henbury. 'Committee meetin's. Like the Women's Institute. Makin' jam, I suppose,' and the old man chuckled at his own joke.

'I'll get some soup,' said Emily, and led Jimmy off to the kitchen before he could reply.

'We could do with some soup,' said Annie (who seemed to be getting old and tired). 'This wind finds every crack in this house. And in my bones.'

'They say the coal's running short,' said Bob. 'It's all going to the camps, and goodness knows when they'll send another trainload down here. We're all right for a bit, but I'll have to see about getting some wood down from the Valley for next winter, and that'll take weeks.'

'At least we've got food enough,' said Sally. 'Think of those poor folk who've only got their rations to live off.'

'There's no sugar left,' said the old man.

'You know there is. You know you have mine anyway,' said Annie. 'Sally's quite right: folks are much worse off than us.'

'Aye, we've lots to be thankful for,' said Bob. He stared into the fire for a moment. 'At least Tom's warm, eh?' he said.

'Oh, I do wish they'd send and let us know *something*,' said Annie, and tears were not far away when Jimmy and Emily came in with the soup.

* * *

"They" did not send a letter, but Tom did, in the third week of February (1941).

Emily and Annie were not sure whether to be relieved or even more anxious, as the letter was scrawled with a shaking hand, almost illegibly.

They had so much difficulty in deciphering it that Sally had to make a fair copy before they were at all sure of what Tom was saying.

Dear all,
Sorry its left hand for [first] *time, can't use the rt one yet. Lamin badly hurt in chest with* [chips?] *of rock but never complains, ins*[ists?] *on wheeling me about I* [should] *be wheeling him. Can read a bit now and write (!) but Drs say I can't come home until can keep balance. Teaching Lamin about C*[ornwal]*l. And skylarks. He says they go to Gambia after us. Hope George will come to see you soon when he has* [leave?]. *Bit tired now so LOVE, your Tom.*

'Wheelchair,' said Peter Jorret. He sometimes had a way of seizing the salient point: it reminded the others of his business acumen in earlier days.

'D'you think he's - crippled?' Annie nervously patted a stray grey lock into place: she wore her hair in a bun now.

'Nah!' said the old man. 'Wheelchair means 'e's out o'

bed. Soon be back to rights, you mark my words.'

'I expect you're right, Pa. Sounds as if he's a bit dizzy when he walks, that's all, Annie.' Bob tried to console her. 'Anyway, perhaps Major Johnson'll be here sometime. He'll tell us.'

'*Colonel* Johnson. George's promoted, he told me.'

Emily smiled, and pecked a kiss on the old man's bald head. 'All right, Grandfather! We must remember he's a Colonel when he comes.'

'He still keeps going on about his beloved skylarks,' said Annie absently.

'They mean home,' said Emily. She paused. 'And peace,' she added.

Annie gave her daughter a tender smile, but this time a tear did roll down her haggard face.

* * *

George's voice was unmistakable despite the crackles on the line.

'Won't ask you to put me up, Emily. Thinking of rations and all that. Staying at the Mess. Try to be with you Tuesday, if I may?'

Emily's voice was shrill with excitement. 'Oh, sir, we are so looking forward to seeing you. Ma and Pa - I can't say how much -'

'It's *George,* Emily. *Please.* Tell you all about Tom and Lamin. Ten o'clock all right?'

* * *

The old man, in his best black serge suit, black overcoat and Homburg hat, waited outside the front door from twenty to ten, and every few minutes burrowed through all his clothes to consult his half-hunter.

George was right on time. (He had in fact arrived at the drive a few minutes early and had waited out of sight in case he should be a nuisance.)

He lurched out of a 15cwt, and saluted Peter Jorret when he saw him standing there.

The old man was nonplussed, and waved George a kind of salute back.

George rushed up and took the old man's hand. 'Very good to see you again, sir.

Hope you've not been waiting long in this wind.'

'We Cornish used to wind and foul weather, Geo - Colonel.'

George grinned. 'Not supposed to drive me'self. Against King's Regulations, but being a Colonel has its advantages.'

Each tried to usher the other through the front door until George gave way and went on in, only for Peter Jorret to announce him with a bellow: 'Colonel Johnson!'

They stood around awkwardly as George kissed the Jorret ladies on the cheek and shook hands with Bob.

Emily introduced Sally (who suppressed a smile as she half-thought she ought to curtsy).

George too felt slightly absurd and found himself talking like royalty: 'Miss Samson: I've heard so much of how good you have been to my friends.'

Sally laughed and at once the atmosphere lightened. 'It's Sally. And it's just the same for me about you. I'll go and make some tea. Or' - she shot a worried glance to Annie - 'or coffee?' Annie nodded her consent.

'Tea please,' George said. 'Oh, I nearly forgot. Got some tea for you. And coffee. From Tom. I managed to get some too. Kenyan, you know.' He turned to Bob. 'In the truck. I wonder if you'd mind giving me a hand?'

Once outside he turned to Bob: 'Phew!'

Bob grinned. 'Well, we don't have many Colonels to coffee, you know.'

George drew back the canvas of the 15cwt and Bob saw four large cardboard boxes and a heavy army holdall in the back.

'I wanted you to come and see this: I've got Tom's tools here. He asked me to bring them. Can't use them there. Didn't want to upset everyone, so if -?'

'Thanks for that, George. I'll get the key to his shed later and we can put them away quietly. I'll tell them later.'

'Might have a chance for a walk later, Bob? Tell you about Tom? Quietly?'

They carried the cardboard boxes back, and Annie's eyes lit up at the sight of the profusion of bags of tea and coffee opened up before them.

'There are several old ladies in the village who'll go potty at the sight of these, George,' she said, suddenly relaxed. 'We'll take some round presently,' she said to Emily and Sally.

Peter scowled. 'There she goes - givin' it a-', but he was silenced by a look from Bob, and put on a sickly grin. 'That's right. Must help others. Always said so, Colonel.'

'Well, I hope there's plenty. Lamin put some in, too.' 'Lamin? Lamin Bah?'

'Oh yes. He's no family of his own, in the Gambia.'

'He's wounded too, isn't he? Tom managed a letter, you know,' said Annie.

'I know. He's recovering well, Tom I mean. You mustn't worry about him. All right in good time.'

'What did I say? I tell them, Colonel, I said, 'e'd soon be out of 'is wheelchair, and back.'

'We-ell. Let me tell you how it all happened. I'll tell you

what, Mr Jorret, what if we use your map Tom was telling me about, and I'll show you.'

Annie interrupted him. 'No, George: tell us *exactly* how Tom is first. And Lamin.' George and Bob exchanged glances. 'I'm so sorry. I was forgetting you only- well, Tom - suffered a head injury. Gets headaches and can't walk firmly yet. The doctors are really optimistic. Complete recovery. May take some time though. His hand isn't good. Crushed, and can't grip things.'

They sat silent for a moment.

'And Lamin Bah, his friend?' asked Emily. (The old man scowled at this but said nothing.)

'He was, well, thrown rather heavily onto the rocks. Very rocky there, you know. Not like here, it's sharp stones, shale, and he had broken ribs. Some stones embedded in his ribcage. Wonderful fellow, must be in great pain. He'll get better, they think.'

Annie fussed arranging chairs whilst Bob and Sally carried in the map pinned to its large sheet of plywood. George stood before it with Peter Jorret's stick, feeling as if he were running an O-group.

'If we could hold these hills,' he said, 'we could stop them from getting to Berbera. Very important. Unfortunately, the French here...'

'Gee Boot Ee' shouted Peter.

'Exactly, Mr Jorret, Djibuti…'

'The Frenchies all ratted on us, did'n they.'

'Do be quiet, Grandfather,' said Emily.

'Mr Jorret's right. We couldn't defend that corner. Sooner or later they'd come round the side. Like football. Goal's in the middle,' he said, pointing at Berbera, 'you can get at it from right flank, or left flank, or through the center.'

'But where was Tom?' demanded Bob.

George showed them where Tom and his gun crew had been sited east-north-east of the Tug Arden, and explained how exposed they were both to the infiltration of the Italian Alpine troops and to the harassment of the Somali irregulars.

When they asked him about the Somalis, George said merely that they had been a danger but, he believed, they had 'turned their fire on the Italians at the end'.

'So, you see,' George said brightly, 'what with no aircraft and only Tom's gun and few others - not nearly enough, no - with thousands of Italians coming up from Ethiopia. All their equipment, well,' he spread his hands in a gesture of resignation, 'all their guns and tanks, we decided we couldn't hold out without losing all our chaps.'

'But we had some things going for us. The mountains. We could get our chaps out gradually, you see, and then we had some Scots lads, the Black Watch, sent over from Aden to help out.'

He chuckled. 'Tom's Gambians thought the Black Watch must be another lot of Africans! Never heard of Scotsmen. Black Watch were magnificent. Covering us getting away was most difficult operation of all, and they were absolutely brilliant. Even a bayonet charge at the end. Stopped the Italian lot in their tracks. Gave us time to get all our fellows aboard the ships and safe away.'

'Yes, but *how* did Tom get wounded?' demanded Annie.

Chapter 26

George looked sadly at the five apprehensive faces turned towards him.

There's no avoiding it: they've got to know. I'll tell Bob a bit more later. Put a bit of a gloss on it for the moment.

'You can see where Tom's gun was,' he said, pointing to the map. 'Bit exposed if the enemy creeps up. Infiltrating, we call it.'

He explained that the Italian Alpini and Blackshirt brigades were excellent soldiers, whatever the papers said, tough, well-equipped and battle-hardened in Ethiopia.

'Then there's the Somalis in the hills, waiting. Best to clear out, as we couldn't risk hitting our own chaps as they pulled back. So what to do with the gun? Couldn't leave it and couldn't get it away. So Tom and I and HQ decided, blow it up and delay the enemy that way as well.'

'Couldn't leave it for the Eyeties, you see,' explained the old man helpfully. 'Of course not, Mr Jorret. 'Course not. Nor the stores and shells.'

George then explained that Tom decided to send away all his gun crew and the other soldiers in his camp. Their job was done; they were to join the road north to Berbera, and then take ship for Aden.

'I had to piece the story together. Some bits from Tom, some from Lamin. Tom wasn't fit to talk much at first. The only way to find it all out was to ask one of them what the other did. Tom and Lamin Bah, they both gave all the credit to the other.'

Bob spoke up in his slow Cornish voice. 'But what did Lamin Bah have to do with it, if he'd been sent away?' he asked.

'Ah, that's it. Apparently, Lamin got all the others on the truck, then slipped back to join Tom. Wouldn't leave him on his own. Disobeyed orders, really. But thank God he did.'

There was a murmur of approval at this.

'Tom, you see, wanted to give them all a couple of hours to get clean away. ' He paused, looking about him as if giving a lecture. 'He had to blow everything up. The method was one you may have - well, you know, he would have to lay a cable to the gun. He got the lads to stack all the ammo and stores round it.'

He began to flounder in his story 'It's like the touch paper to the fireworks. But he had a plunger thing. Works by electricity. You've seen them on the westerns, where they blow up the rocks to make the railway.'

George would have continued in his meandering style to explain how the charge was laid and how Tom had prepared a dugout to retreat to, but his audience had grown impatient, even agitated, until Sally said:

'Could you come back to that later, sir, and tell us what *became* of Tom and Lamin?' George gave her an approving nod.

'Of course. Silly of me.' He took a deep breath, then rapped out the words in sharp staccato phrases, avoiding their eyes.

'They blew up the gun.' Pause. 'They set off on the motorbike.'

He took another deep breath. 'The fact is, they were

blown off the road onto the hillside. Italian bomber. Didn't hit them. Bomb blast blew them off, bike and all.'

He went on, now speaking deliberately and calmly. 'Lamin was thrown clear. But Tom was trapped with his right arm under the motorbike. He wasn't conscious.'

'We don't know *exactly* how it happened, you understand, but Tom must have banged his head somehow. Lamin was thrown clear, as I said. Got this wound in his chest. Bleeding.'

George looked round at them helplessly, and mumbled *wound in his chest* again.

There was a long, stunned silence.

'Is that it?' demanded Annie at last.

'Most of it. But I'll pinch some of that Scotch I brought.' Sally scampered to the kitchen.

'Bring some more glasses,' Bob called after her, 'We could all do with some.'

* * *

After lunch and some of George's coffee, Bob suddenly said:

'George, I'd like you to take a walk out with me onto the headland.' Annie looked up in astonishment.

'Walk, Bob? You haven't walked out there for years!'

'Wanted to show George where Tom used to go for the skylarks and that,' replied Bob lamely.

'I could do that,' said Emily eagerly, 'or we could all go.' Bob held up his hand to stop them.

'No. I shall go with George, and that's that.'

* * *

They smuggled Tom's tools into his hut. George looked admiringly at the workshop: all the tools were neatly arranged on wall racks, and George could see that they were sharpened and oiled and in perfect order. There were benches, lathes and grinding wheels, and George, despite knowing nothing of the craft itself, could see the orderly and precise nature of Tom's expertise.

Bob saw George's admiring look. 'Yes,' he said proudly, 'Tom knows - knew - what he was about. There weren't a better mason in the whole of Cornwall.'

'I can believe that.'

Bob locked the door behind them as they stepped out into the warm but windy weather.

'Yes, I can believe that, Bob,' George said again, 'but that's why I wanted to talk. The fact is, Tom won't be able to get back to his work. Ever.'

Bob swore under his breath.

'The hand isn't completely useless,' George went on, 'I told everyone it was trapped under the motorbike, I didn't think it right to say, well, his hand's so badly crushed he can't grip things. Trapped for over an hour. And he'll take a long time - maybe years - to recover all his, well, mental powers.'

Bob gasped. 'You don't mean he's - well, -?'

'Stupid? No, certainly not. No sign of that. Just that he's withdrawn, spends lots of time just thinking. Reads a lot, serious stuff, too.'

Bob heaved a sigh of relief. 'Well, he always kept himself to himself. Never read much though, as I recall, 'cept trade journals and technical stuff.'

They walked for a while in silence, save for the screaming of the gulls wheeling below them over the cliffs.

'He may sit by himself alone a lot,' said George at last.

'Nothin' new about that, George. In fact, he often used to come to this very spot and watch the sea and the birds. He was like me, George. I used to come here too, often.' He grinned. 'Specially when I was courtin' Annie.'

They sat down on the sandy grass. The promontory jutted out over black rugged cliffs, and thirty feet below them the waves hit the rocks with force enough for the roar to make conversation difficult. Every now and again they could feel the spray on their faces as it was caught by gusts of wind.

'Every seventh wave's the big one, so they say,' said Bob. 'Wind's getting up again, George. D'you want to be getting back?'

'No. Let's sit here a little longer. You should know something more.'

Bob made to light his pipe. A hedge of scrubby hawthorn protected the clearing a little, and Bob put his back to the wind, turned the pipe upside down and shielded the match in cupped hands to light it.

'Go on, then. It's bad, I take it?'

'He wakes up with nightmares. Always the same: how he watches someone drown and does nothing to save him. I'm like a skylark, he says, taking no responsibility, just singing my own song.'

'Always loved those skylarks. Used to watch them by the hour here.'

George was getting a little impatient with Bob's seeming obtuseness.

'You're missing the point, Bob. Tom is, well, disturbed, very down. Has black moods. Blames himself for the lad who drowned. And the Gambian boy who got killed, and the youngster with Major Brimshaw. Says he allowed Brimshaw and the others to go to certain death. Just like the drowned fellow.'

'Terry Samson. I remember. Tom brooded about that for months.'

'Well, he thinks he's to blame. I tell him it's nonsense,

people get killed in war, he did all he possibly could. Held the Italians up, saved lots of lives probably.'

'Not all in vain, then?' asked Bob. 'The fact is, it's all wearing Annie out. You must have seen: she's so much quieter, lost her fun. It's not just Tom, of course, it's everything.

She feels for those folks in London, Coventry and that, while we're, well, we're not sufferin' at all. Quite safe here in Cornwall.'

'Not so, Bob. You lost some sailors at Dunkirk, and some folks at Penhale. We're all responsible for things in our own way. Must keep the farms going, or we're really done for.'

Bob sat puffing the pipe thoughtfully for a few moments.

'Responsible, yes,' he said after a while. 'D'you know, George: he's always been wrong, Tom.'

'Wrong?'

'About skylarks. They climb and sing, right. But not carefree. They draw all the enemies away from the nest, self-sacrificing in a way. Risking their own lives for their family, you know. Tom should know that.'

This fellow sees into things far more than he lets on, George thought.

'It's a curious thing, Bob. Do you know what the plane was called that blew Tom and Lamin down the mountain?'

'Can't say I do.'

'Well, it's a three-engined job, fighter-bomber. Good plane in its way. 270 miles an hour. It's called the *Sparviero.*'

Bob said nothing.

'*Sparviero* is the Italian word for sparrow-hawk.'

* * *

They sat down to a wonderful pre-war tea when they got back. Annie had made some scones, and they spread them generously with some of the apple jam she had saved the sugar for and with some chunky and yellow Cornish cream Bob had made illegally.

'Mr Wilkinson would have us all in Bodmin gaol for this, Ma,' said Emily.

Annie wiped a tear with the corner of her apron. 'If only-'

'- if only Tom could share it,' Emily said. 'I'm sure he will one day soon, won't he, don't you think, Colonel Johnson?'

George was standing at the fireplace, plate in hand. He took another bite of his scone before replying, while they all looked up at him.

'These scones: not tasted anything like it since I was in Devon years ago.'

'Devon!" snorted the old Jorret. 'They don't know nothin' bout good Cornish cream, you.'

'Oh yes, Mrs Jorret, Tom will be back,' said George slowly, 'but *when*, I don't know. It's no secret there's lot going on in Africa and, well, even if he's fit enough, the hospital ships… Look at the map: all that fighting along the Med coast in the North there, and Italians in the Sudan, and Kenya.'

'They won't send him back, George, will they, to war, I mean?'

'No, Mrs Jorret, they won't. Tom's not, well, fit to fight now. He's done his bit.' George paused, and took another scone. 'So has Lamin Bah. Lamin's probably not going to be strong enough for a long time either.'

'So what happens to him?'

'Tom wants him to come back here, to Cornwall. To the farm.'

There was a stunned silence.

'But will he be fit, I mean, well enough to work on the farm?' It was Sally who asked.

'Probably not.' George grinned. 'Won't be able to do what

you do, Miss Sa- Sally.

But he will be mad keen to learn. If you'll all have him.'

Peter Jorret said: 'He's black man ain't 'e? Won't do here in our village!'

Annie screamed at him: 'Hold your tongue! How dare you!'

Everyone was shouting at him at once.

George silenced them with a gesture.

'Lamin crawled across and tried to lift the motorbike off Tom's arm, but he was too weak through his own wound. So he crawled up the hillside through the rocks and stones and burning sun. At last he reached the road. He got help from retreating soldiers. He then collapsed and woke up on the ship.'

Peter Jorret began a blustering excuse: 'Didn't mean, did a good job, only-'

'Mr Jorret, forgive me, but I have something else to tell you,' George interrupted, firmly but not unkindly. 'In Kenya a white corporal and a black rifleman from the KARs went out on patrol and didn't come back. No-one knew what became of them, except that eight weeks later they found their bodies in the mountains. Not their bodies, but their bones, picked clean by the vultures perhaps.'

'Do you know,' George went on, 'they didn't know which was the rifleman and which was the corporal. All their khaki drill had been shredded and scattered by the wind. They found their KAR badges, but which was which?'

He looked hard and unsmiling at Peter Jorret.

'Well, they couldn't tell, could they, not…' stammered the old man.

'No, not…' said George. 'Exactly.'

Chapter 27

There were tearful goodbyes when George Johnson left them. They could not know when - or if - they would ever see him again, and he was their only link to Tom. He would be unlikely (he said) to be going back to Aden,

'No doubt they'll send me off to Africa again. No secret that: that's where the fighting is. Unlikely,' he added with a wry smile, 'they'll want the likes of me in the War Office. Only smart polished chaps there.'

Nonetheless he promised to "pull a few strings" to get Tom and Lamin back. They were bound, he said, to be invalided-out "in a few months". It was already March (13th) and they had been wounded in the previous August.

As they sat round the stove in the kitchen (it was the only draught-free room in the house) they fell into a despondency that even George's whisky could not relieve.

'They must have been terribly seriously hurt,' said Annie. 'They've been in that hospital for months.'

'Seven months,' said Bob.

'They're walkin' about,' said Peter Jorret cheerfully. 'Be right as rain, you mark my words.'

'You're probably right, Grandfather,' said Emily. 'Only even when there's room for them on the ships, they've still got to go right through the -er-'

'Through the Med,' said Peter Jorret scornfully. 'Everyone

knows that. There's the map, you.' (They had brought it into the kitchen on the old man's insistence.) 'George tol' me the Navy had it all sorted. Sunk lots of Eyetie boats.'

Peter Jorret's map went no further north than the Mediterranean so Emily could not argue further. She just felt in her bones that Tom would have to be lucky to get home safely…

A little later the old man returned with the papers. He refused to pay the eightpence a week for them to be delivered, and (rain or shine) took a daily walk down to the Post Office to collect them. He then spent the two hours before lunch reading the war news. Annie was relieved for him to do so: "Don't want him under my feet all morning".

She was startled by a sudden whoop of excitement from the old man.

'What did I tell you? Didn't I say it all? There's General Cunningham done it! All the papers 're sayin' it! He's gone right up from Kenya, look! An' swep' Eyeties right across there.'

He pointed to his map where the South African troops had taken the greater part of Italian Somaliland and were striking into Ethiopia.

'Look at these papers! Mail says Eyeties runnin' for their lives!' They stood there bewildered.

'So what's it all for, Pa?' Annie demanded despondently. 'What are they all doing down there in Africa when the Nazis are bombing London and everywhere every night?"

* * *

A week later Emily was, as usual, sleeping badly when she became conscious of distant thunder. In fact, they had heard the distant rumbling roar even before they had gone to bed, and assumed it was a storm in east Cornwall. When the wind got up again, the noise grew more insistent, the more so as at midnight the village itself was so silent.

Emily put on her dressing gown and crept downstairs. It was still warmish outside despite the wind.

It took some moments for her to make sense of a flickering red glow in the sky to the east.

Plymouth!

Jimmy had said ages ago that they would be going for Plymouth docks. But in London and Bristol and Coventry and Hull and everywhere they just bomb everything, houses, schools, hospitals even.

Emily was a gentle person, who in some people's opinion, was too ready to see the good in people and ignore the bad: but she was stirred to a burning, illogical hatred of all things German by the destruction that was raining down on all the cities.

Why do they have to bomb all the ordinary folk out of their homes?

She had heard how the Stukas had screamed down on a terrified Warsaw, but she didn't know much about Poland and it was all a long way from Gustory Farm and the sea-girt village of Crannel.

But Plymouth!

How she had loved to go on those trips to Plymouth when she was ten or eleven just after the last War riding on the trams on Union Street and (once) being taken to a new Cinema to see Charlie Chaplin as a tramp…

And then taking the train from Newmin with her mother on those rare shopping expeditions when Annie made the excuse of someone getting married to go and buy some new clothes…

That was after I'd got married to Mr Harris but he'd

already gone away…

Oh God! Now Jimmy's there! He won't be in one of his shelters, he'll be out trying to help the poor people who were being bombed out and he'll be… Oh God don't let him be killed…PLEASE God…

She sat there in the wind, gradually getting colder and colder, until gone midnight, when the roaring ceased but the glow in the sky only slowly died.

She dozed off and woke shivering. It was nearly half-past five when she at last she went indoors. She stoked the dull stove and boiled a kettle. She hesitated about using some of Annie's hoarded tea and decided to put up with the herbal mixture they had contrived.

'Emmy! What is it? You poor thing, you're frozen! I thought I heard you moving about,' said Sally, who had appeared at the doorway, also in her dressing gown.

'Oh dear! I hope I didn't wake you?'

Emily gave her a wry smile. Sally looked as fresh and bouncy and rosy-cheeked as if she were sitting on the beach on a summer's day.

Emily could not resist looking up at the great square mirror on the kitchen wall: she saw a reflection of a lined, thin face, pale almost to greyness, framed by ill-combed hair which had long lost any youthful life.

Only a few years younger than me and I'm an old lady compared…

But what Emily did not see was what a discerning eye could see: the sweetness and goodness that shone through the tired face…

'Well, you did actually.' (Sally, like Emily, was incapable of telling the simplest untruth.) 'But I'm jolly glad you did: can't have you sitting here alone all miserable. Is that tea you've made, Emmy?'

Emmy gave her wry smile again. 'Kind of. I'll pour you a cup.'

'Right. And we'll have some toast,' and Sally bustled about making some.

'It's Plymouth, Sally. They must be destroying our lovely Plymouth. It's all in flames. And Jimmy's there, and you know him, he'll be out in all the bombing and the fires…'

Sally could find nothing to say: *what's the use of saying, don't worry? I know just what it's like for her.*

She tried to push the memories to the back of her mind again, and simply went and held her close and let her friend's tears run onto her dressing gown collar.

After a while, Sally suggested that they went and washed and dressed, came down and cooked some eggs.

'Then it'll be time for the cows, Emmy. I could do with some help.'

* * *

There was no word from Jimmy Henbury all day, and then at 8.30 in the evening, it all began again, as squadrons of Heinkels flying high over the anti-aircraft barrage plastered the unhappy city with a mixture of High Explosive and incendiary bombs, the latter by the thousands.

The center of Plymouth was aflame for the second night.

Emily waited by the telephone all morning. (Bob had had it installed just before the outbreak of war.) But there was nothing.

'It's just like waiting for news of Tom again,' she said. 'We just sit and - we just, oh I don't know…' She twisted her handkerchief in her thin hands.

'There are thousands and thousands like us, Emily dear,' said Annie.

'Well, you knows what George says, just 'ave to get on with things,' said old Peter Jorret.

Sally thought: *We've only got prayer left. Please God keep Jimmy safe. And -but what can God do about it? If he'd wanted to do something, we wouldn't have had a war at all. Perhaps lots of German women are saying the same things and praying too. But then, what have they got to pray about? It was their army that smashed up France, and Holland, and Belgium. And Poland of course. I don't suppose the German women thought much about what all those people were going through at the time. Anyway, they've got nothing to worry about, some bombs on Berlin, but their soldiers are all right in France and all those other countries. I'm wrong, hating them all, but I can't help it.*

The German planes had left at just after midnight on Friday morning, and as far as anyone knew they went back to the French coast without any damage.

They still had heard nothing from Jimmy Henbury. Bob called the switchboard girl at the exchange,

She was hardly a girl, despite the customary description, as she was nearer sixty than fifty, but she manned the switchboard with an assumed voice of brisk efficiency. But her news did very little to relieve the anxiety at the farm.

'Oh, 'tis you Barb,' she said, lapsing at once into her village accent. 'No, m'dear, we're getting nothing from Plymouth. The loins are all down, my love.'

'You'll let us know, Juliet, just as soon as you hear anything.'

'That Oi will, Barb, sure as eggs. How's Emmy an' the others, then, Barb? Tom's on the mend, bless him, thank the Lord.'

'We're all keeping going all right, Juliet, thanks. Mustn't hold you up, Juliet. Give our love to Harry.'

* * *

On the following Wednesday, Emily was churning butter in the scullery. She always had an ear for the phone when Juliet rang through at ten o'clock.

'Crannel four-two,' Emily shouted.

It was Juliet's official voice. 'I have a call for Emily Jorret.'

'This *is* Emily!'

It was Juliet's Cornish voice. 'Just hold on for a moment, dear. I'll put you through just as quick as ever I can, my love. It's good news, I think. Not *bad* news, anyway. I was just telli-'

'Oh, *do* hurry Juliet.'

But there were anxious moments of pauses, distant voices and cracking sounds before it was Jimmy Henbury, faint, crackling, weak, exhausted. But Jimmy.

'Emmy. I love you Emmy. I'm all right. Safe.' She could not reply for tears.

'I can't say much. I'm writing. Emmy, it's been terrible. Ghastly. Much worse than -'

Emily at last gasped out: 'You sound so worn out, my dear, dear Jimmy. Are they coming back? The Germans?'

'Who knows? They think we're going to be left alone for the moment. That's what the top people think, though how they know- we're safe for the moment. *Safe!*'

He spat out the last word with unexpected bitterness. 'Safe! If we're not dead or buried in our homes, Emmy. Oh Emmy: I'm done for. My shelters - *safe?*'

'Are you coming home? I love you, Jimmy. *Please* come back.' 'Can't. Not yet. Too much - clearing up. Love -.'

'I regret we have lost the connection. The line is occupied, caller.' Juliet's official voice had cut in but quickly gave way to the other one 'Sorry, dear, but it's such good news isn't it?

He does sound tired, though, doesn't he? Must have been through such a lot, dear.'

'Yes. Thanks, Juliet.' Emily slumped back in the chair, jerking the phone off the table as she did so. She fumbled to replace it. 'Goodbye.'

But she had already been disconnected.

Chapter 28

Emily heard no more until Jimmy's letter arrived three days later.

When she opened it, it took some time for her to realize that it was indeed from him, the writing was so changed. Instead of the meticulously neat well-framed writing, it was in painfully careful shaky large lettering on two rather grubby sheets of paper.

Emily waited until Sally could join them at breakfast before reading the letter aloud to everyone (apart from a line or two of endearments that Emily had no intention of sharing).

'It's obviously written in a terrible hurry or something,' she said, trying to conceal her anxiety. 'I'll have to read it to you, as I can only just make it out.' (For once she was *not* truthful, as the childish script was all too legible.)

I cannot begin to describe the horror of what they have done to Plymouth, she read haltingly. *Whole streets have been reduced to piles of smoking rubble, and we have been trying to dig out poor people from the ruins only for the bombers to come again, many bombs falling on or near the same places. Everywhere as daylight broke - sometimes we did not need daylight, the fires were burning so brightly - we came across bodies, men, women, children - horribly burned, with great wounds. And then poor people sitting by the roadside, some in their pyjamas, sitting staring at us in such a state of shock that they could hardly speak. We could get no sleep. Nor could we have slept. Bill Treadwell - you remember, he was my foreman who retired and then came back for the duration, well, Bill was so exhausted that he collapsed and we fear for his life.*

I'm afraid that I've been hurt too- not badly, and not by the bombs! I'm a bit ashamed as I was helping the firemen get an old fellow out from the rubble when I stumbled over a block of concrete and fell on my arm and now it's in plaster. Strange to survive all that bombing - and all that falling shrapnel from our own guns, which is very dangerous - and then fall over and have to be a casualty and take up valuable time of the first-aid people. But Commander Pearson has said that I and my whole team must go home for a week, as we would be no use to anyone after these last few days, exhausted and bruised as everyone is. They think the Germans will be back after they've done a reconnaissance of the damage to the docks, but not for a few weeks: that's what they've done with other towns. All the hospitals and clinics are full for miles around so I am coming back to the Headland Hospital in Newmin with some walking wounded. Try to visit me, Emmy. I must close, as I seem to have run out of energy. You won't believe it but it has taken me nearly two days to write this letter!

'There are a few more bits and he sends his love to everyone,' said Emily.

They sat in silence for a few moments.

'Must be hurt, with that writin',' said the old man, peering over her shoulder. 'But I 'spec he'll be back on the job soon enough.'

* * *

The Headland Hospital was a hastily converted hotel. Before

the War the hotel itself had been regarded as by far the best (and most expensive) in Newmin. It stood in its own grounds on a majestic site on its headland and had been built in massive Edwardian style a few years before the first War. As sailing and golf holidays had become more and more sought-after in the Cornwall of the thirties, and the train connections of the GWR had been so much improved, Newmin had become a favourite resort for the wealthier holidaymakers. Accordingly, the hotel had been completely refurbished in 1936, with extensive new kitchens, and new bathrooms that served only four rooms. Not least, there was land enough for a 9-hole golf course, albeit on the wind-swept headland where a sudden gust might carry your sliced drive right out to sea.

After Dunkirk the Penhale camp had been hastily fitted out for hundreds of returning BEF soldiers and the Headland Hotel was requisitioned to cater for the ill and lightly wounded. The few remaining permanent residents were moved to a separate wing to be shared (much to the annoyance of some of them) by the medical and nursing staff.

Now there was a flood of civilian casualties from the Plymouth blitz, including Jimmy Henbury (feeling shame at the inadequacy of his injury) and his friend Bill Treadwell. The latter survived only two days in the hospital. Bill had literally worked himself to death in his efforts to rescue the victims of the bombing. Jimmy was a far younger man, but his state of exhaustion was not much better, and in fact the doctors had used the excuse of the arm to insist on hospitalization so that he could recover physically and, hopefully, mentally.

Emily took the ferry across the Crannel estuary to the landing stage at the foot of the headland.

It was Isaac, the old man, who rowed her across, not his son Peter, who had taken over from his father some years before.

Emily thought Peter had gone into the Merchant Navy, and she was fearful of saying the wrong thing.

'I suppose Pete's in a bigger boat than this, Mr Jones,' she blurted out, with a nervous giggle.

'Why, bless ye, Miss Emily, he's 'alf-way 'cross the Atlantic now, I should imagine. Don't suppose he'll be back to ferryin' when it's all over,' he added sadly. 'Not now he's been to sea proper.'

Isaac was much slower but hadn't lost the skills of letting the tide do most of the work. He climbed expertly but creakily onto the jetty to give Emily a hand and tugged an imaginary forelock as Emily fumbled in her purse for the sixpence.

'Thank'ee, Miss.' He patted her hand. 'Missus, I should say, Mrs Harris, isn't it?

Sorry to hear of your loss. But so many folk -' His voice trailed off.

She gave him the grateful, shy smile that almost made her look pretty again.

Dear Mr Jones, I expect he's thinking whether he'll ever see his Peter again. Beastly, beastly war…

Using the ferry meant a steep climb up the rock path, but it saved the long walk along the peninsular if she were to use the bridge further up-river.

It's strange, she thought as she climbed the stone steps, but there's Tom hurt in the head and the arm fighting somewhere I've never heard of, and then there's Jimmy near a nervous breakdown and also hurt in the arm in Plymouth! Thank God though they're both alive, when so many people are dead and hurt much worse. Now it's almost safer to be fighting in Africa than to be living in Plymouth with the bombing.

Jimmy came down to the reception lounge to meet her. He was a small wiry man and was known for his strength, but as Emily saw him gingerly coming down the stairs, his arm in a sling, he was noticeably thinner and weaker. *He looks the same, but different. It's his eyes, glazed, shocked and he's got those huge round glasses on…*

He tried to greet her with a breezy toothy smile, quite false, as she knew. But there was nothing false at the way he clung to her with his good arm and, to her consternation, burst into tears. He had still said nothing.

At last he took off his glasses and held them in his injured hand while he wiped his eyes.

'So sorry, Emmy.' He smiled at her, more in his old way. 'No way to greet someone - who's - the dearest, gentlest, -' He nearly broke down again.

Emily took him in her arms again. She could think of nothing to say. She was near to tears herself but told herself that she must be strong for him.

'Shall we sit here, Jimmy, or should we go and walk around for a bit?'

He looked hard at her, surprised, after all the bombing, at the banality of her first words to him.

'Walk.' He suddenly looked about him and gripped her arm. 'Walk. Outside. Can't stand being indoors now, the ceiling might not hold up, you know. Safer outside even if…'

He just as quickly came round and apologized. 'Sorry, Emmy. I was just thinking how - Think aloud sometimes now, Emmy. Doctors say it's only temporary, 'til I've had some rest.'

They walked round the edge of the golf course, the wind gusting in their faces, until they reached something of a windbreak where the ground dipped below the cliff edge. Scrubby bent hawthorns gave the golfers something of a chance as they teed off from the green, and Emily and Jimmy sat down on a wooden bench the hotel had provided for spectators - not that there were likely to be either spectators or golfers until the March-April winds had dropped a little.

Jimmy stared at a patch of wet mud where feet had trampled the grass.

'They dropped one-ton bombs in the last wave. A one-ton bomb would destroy the whole village of Crannel. Everyone would be killed or injured. All the cows and the dogs and the chickens would die.'

Emily could do nothing but put her arm about his shoulders.

'That was after they had blown the houses up and then burned the survivors to death.

How did the aeroplanes get off the ground with *one-ton* bombs aboard, Emmy?'

'I don't know, Jimmy.' She shook her head despondently, 'But *how* they did it's one thing: all the experts'll know *how*. But *why*? Someone tell me that.'

Jimmy leant to pick up a stick and drew a line with it in the patch of mud at his feet.

'People are either above or below the line, Emmy. That's what I think. I like to believe that most people are well above the line. Some, like you, are so far above that the rest of us can't catch up.' Emily shook her head vehemently. 'Some are not quite so far above as they could be,' he went on, ignoring her protest 'like Grandfather, say.' He gave her his quiet smile, again in his old way.

Then his expression hardened. 'But many are below the line, some so far below that they hold everyone else in such contempt that they don't care whether they suffer or survive or not.'

They sat in silence for a while.

Jimmy took off his glasses and looked straight into Emily's eyes. She saw there a look of more than sadness: of despair.

'*It's my responsibility*, Emmy. The shelters - some of them. Couldn't stand up to the bombing. They collapsed. People were buried - *in my shelters*.'

She took both his hands in his. She was not given to philosophising, nor would she ever claim to be very wise. But her pride and confidence in this outwardly insignificant man would not let his spirit be crushed like this.,

'No, Jimmy. It is the Germans' responsibility. You did your utmost -'

'Utmost!' he broke in bitterly. 'What use was my *utmost*?'

'Your utmost to save them. And you must go back and try again, for everyone's sake. Don't think of those who've been lost but think of all those you've saved. And my dear, those you are going to save!'

* * *

Jimmy Henbury was a tough character, and five or six days later he was able to contact Commander Pearson to say that he wanted to come back and begin the rebuilding.

'Take a few more days, old boy. We'll be needing you soon. Between you and me' (a phrase much frowned on by the authorities, for *walls have ears*, as the posters said) 'there's a great deal going on in the Pond, and Jerry wants to get at the Navy to stop us knocking off those bloody U-boats. Ergo, old boy, he'll be having another go at our ships here, and if the last lot's anything to go by, the whole town'll take a pasting again.'

'Well, sir, I'm ready to -'

'Good lad, good lad. We're clearing out as many of the youngsters as we can into the countryside. Bad for them, missing school, but can't be helped. How's the arm then?'

'It's on the mend, thanky-'

'Good show, Jimmy. You and your fellows can't praise you all enough. You can rustle up your chaps again?'

'We've lost Bill Treadwell, sir, and-'

'Yes. I heard. Great hero, Jimmy. Deserves the VC in my view, out in all that bloody mayhem at his age. Got to press on, though, Jimmy.'

'Quite so, sir. When d'you want us?'

'Tuesday all right for you? Mid-day?'

'Certainly. I'll get them -'

'Bloody good. Bloody good. We reckon the 20th April. That's a Sunday. Huns are like that: clockwork. Big attack on twentieth March, next on twentieth April. That's the way they think. That's why we'll beat the bastards if we can hang on, Jimmy. They'll crack when the clock goes wrong. Must go. Tuesday then, Jimmy. God bless.'

Chapter 29

A letter arrived at last with news of Tom.

Dear friends at Crannel, wrote George on the 12th March, *I am afraid that you may have been waiting in vain for news for a long time. One of our ships carrying mail was lost. Now they are sending a lot more via the Cape. Some of the South Africans wounded lads or who've finished their marvellous tour are returning home. Other troops are stopping off in Mombassa. Mr Jorret can explain on his map how our sea routes are safer now we've captured Mogadishu. We've taken ALL Italian Somaliland and have cut off ALL the Italians in British Somaliland AND we're coming at them in Ethiopia. (The papers have said that Haile Selassie's there.)*

Anyway, Tom should be well on his way home. He's bringing Lamin Bah with him to see how he likes Cornwall. Lamin and Tom are still serving but I expect will be discharged on medical grounds. So they at least will be safe.

Emily thought how strange it was that Tom who had fought in battles would be safe while Jimmy who was at home in Cornwall would risk his life every hour of the day…

I can't tell you more, George's letter went on, *because I'm on my way out again, being thought unsuitable for a Staff job, thank God. But if I say to Mr Jorret it's on the*

Northern Front…

I cannot say when next we shall meet, nor when next I can write, but please send to me at the BFPO address and it will catch up with me.

God bless you all, and thank you for your friendship, George.

* * *

Jimmy was not a churchgoer, but Emily was especially keen that he went with her the Sunday (the 13th April) before he returned to Plymouth.

The little medieval church was, as usual, packed, and the aged vicar was, as usual, inept, sincere, and moving, reflecting the hopes and dreads of his simple and uncomprehending flock.

Sally sat there uncomfortably, as usual loving the quaint uselessness of the ritual prayers and the hopes of salvation and even eternal life (*how terrible!*) if one were reasonably good.

She switched off as the Vicar stumbled on. She thought of George's letter. She had a sense that it was - for him - so *un*carelessly phrased, that it sounded like a farewell letter - an *Adieu* rather than an *Au revoir…* Despite herself, she phrased a little prayer to say it wasn't so.

The Vicar was making a little joke concerning the evils of drink: *Whilst we are proud that Britannia rules the waves about our shores, we hope that the Britannia does not rule the shores about the Crannel!* This *bon mot* was received with a subdued titter in the congregation, who considered it unseemly to laugh too much in church anyway.

Emily whispered to Sally: '*I'm* going to the Britannia afterwards. Why shouldn't I? To see Jimmy off.'

'Shocking! What would Mrs Rawson say? I'd better come as well, den of vice or no.' *Maybe I'll have a little goodbye drink, too.* 'Better tell Annie,' she added.

Annie frowned her disapproval but merely whispered to them not to be late for dinner.

* * *

The landlord irritably told Arthur Green to remove his tin hat from the bar.

'What d'you bring that thing in here for anyway?'

The Air Raid Warden gave Jimmy Henbury a meaningful look. 'We'll be next,' he said. 'Look what's been 'appening up Plymouth. Weren't ready for it, were you?'

Emily put a restraining hand on Jimmy's arm. 'There's been a great deal of suffering there, Arthur,' she said.

Jimmy put his beer-glass down and looked Arthur Green straight in the eyes. 'No, Arthur, we weren't ready. We weren't ready for thousands of tons of bombs. We weren't expecting one-ton land-mines floating down on parachutes landing anywhere. We weren't ready for hundreds of people dead and hundreds more injured. We'll be a bit more ready next time, but no, we weren't ready.'

He turned back to the landlord. 'Give Mr Green another beer on me. On condition he keeps his mouth shut. But there was one other thing, Arthur,' he added, staring at the latter's reflection in the mirror behind the bar. 'Six of our wardens were killed, going out in the raids. I'm afraid their tin hats didn't save them.'

'Steve's on 'is way back,' said old Peter Jorret suddenly. 'All the way from Africk.'

'Tom, Grandfather, 'said Emily. '*Tom's* on his way back.'

'I said that, didn't I?' said Jorret. 'They've nearly beat the

Wops in S'malia,' he said, addressing the drinkers at large. 'So Ste - Tom an' the others can come back. Hilyslassy's back, too. Won't be long.'

'What's Hilysl -whatever it is?' demanded Albert Penwarry.

'Hilyslassy. Everyone knows about Hilyslassy.' He tugged a copy of the *Sunday Express* (that he had tried to read covertly during the sermon) from his heavy black serge suit. He pointed to a headline on the inside page. 'There: *Haile Selassie's Triumphant Return to his People*, that's what it says. *The rout of the Italian forces in Somaliland and Abyssinia continues apace before the British and Empire forces, and soon nothing will remain of Mussolini's boasted East African Empire.*'

'No worth fightin' there, that's my view an' don't mind who knows it,' said Josh the postman defiantly.

'Then you're a bloody fool,' old Jorret shouted at him. 'Saves our oil an' that, my friend the Colonel told me, an' he should know, high-up in the Army *and* 'e refused to stay runnin' things in London and went back to fight.'

'Anyway, they says Tom's bringin' a native with him,' Arthur Green spoke up again, staring at Peter Jorret defiantly. 'Won't like that 'ere in Crannel, that's for sure.'

Jorret this time said nothing, and just swallowed back his beer.

'He saved Tom's life,' said Sally.

'Crannel will welcome him, he's a hero,' said Emily. 'Anyway, Jimmy's got to go back Tuesday and Annie'll be waiting us for dinner.'

* * *

Commander Pearson had warned his Civil Defence

committee that the Germans were planning new raids on Plymouth; how he knew this, Jimmy had no idea. But it proved only too correct, even down to the date, Monday 21st - and if the Germans kept to their rigid timetables, the actual hour, i.e. sometime after 8.00 pm.

As far as he could, Jimmy tried to keep some record of the bombing. But he did not reckon on three consecutive nights of it, or the fact that when he did get back to the underground shelter, the pencil would scrawl scarcely legible marks as he slumped to sleep over the notebook.

Nonetheless, the marks he later deciphered were:

21st - 22nd	*120 planes.*	*6 hours 8.20 - 2.00*
22nd - 23rd	*120 planes.*	*hit communal shelter Portland Sq 70 dead*
23rd - 24th	*120 planes.*	*hit naval barracks nearly 100 dead.*

The incessant crump of the Ack-ack guns and the almost rhythmic shattering crack of the bombs could no longer wake him as he slumped over the pine table of the Control center, and when it was his turn to go out again, he had to be roughly shaken awake and revived with scalding tea laced with rum in a huge enamelled mug.

Jimmy's senses were numbed: he had lost any sense of fear: he knew that survival was a matter of chance: even the best-built shelters could not stand the one-ton bombs should there be a direct hit (as in the Portland Square), and even to go out into the rubble-strewn streets risked dangers from the rain of jagged shrapnel falling from the Ack-ack barrage.

He had (quite illegally) carried with him a service pistol borrowed from an elderly client in Newmin. He used it to shoot pitifully wounded animals when came across them in the rubble, and more than once he had been tempted to use it similarly when they had dug out living but hopelessly maimed people, but he left it to the medics who, he knew, would administer a lethal overdose of pain-killers.

He had used it too when, after the bombers had gone, they came across a row of terraced houses in Fore Street where the front walls had been blown clean away. Three men were openly going from house to house removing all they could find, clocks, china ornaments, radios, rugs, even armchairs, and stacking them in a small truck.

Jimmy was a quiet man, never known to show anger. But dazed by lack of sleep and weariness, scarcely knowing what he was doing, he suddenly gave way to a trembling rage. He drew the pistol from its holster and fired wildly at the looters before his new foreman, Sam Shaw, could restrain him. But the shots missed, and the men ran off, terrified.

Jimmy sat down shaking on the smoking rubble. 'I should have killed them,' he said.

Sam gently took the revolver from him and used the two remaining bullets to shoot out the tyres of the truck before handing it back.

A relief crew from the RASC took over a little later.

'There's not much you can do,' Sam told the Sergeant-Major. 'Not much point in going through that lot,' he said, pointing at the ruined terrace. 'They hit this row last time a bit further along, and everyone cleared out, thank God.'

* * *

Sam Shaw took Commander Pearson aside to tell him about the looters.

The Commander, ashen-faced and red-eyed, nodded

glumly. 'I'm afraid it's not the first lot, Sam.' He glanced over to the huddled figure of Jimmy Henbury, who had not spoken since their return to base.

'He'll crack up, Sam. So will we all. Get the hell out of it until I call for you again.'

Sam looked at him enquiringly.

'Oh yes, they'll be back. Next month, I should say, when they've done a recce. Hardly touched some of the dock area, you know. You can tell Jimmy. We managed to get most of the folk away before this lot began, out to Devon. God knows what they'll come back to.'

He clapped Sam on the back. 'Tell Emily to get Jimmy to bed for a week, and that goes for all of you. I'll let you know when and if. Bloody well done, everyone,' he said, raising his voice. 'It's our battle, chaps, and we've shot lots of the buggers down. Can't re- build much more now so we can leave these army chaps to clear up for a bit.'

But he could not hide his own weariness, and even despair.

* * *

In fact, Jimmy only had two days before Commander Pearson summoned him back.

They got home late on Thursday the 24th, the journey from Plymouth having taken well over three hours; they had found several of the local roads pot-holed by stray bombs.

Jimmy would say nothing to anyone, not even Emily, except that he would go to bed. 'The spare room, Emily,' he said. 'Just keep away.'

Emily made up the room for him and once he was settled, came down and burst into tears.

'It's a nervous breakdown, Ma. He won't talk to me.'

'Let him rest, Emily.'

'Feed 'im some eggs and milk an' he'll be as right as tuppence, maid,' said the old man. 'Seen it hundreds of times when some fellers from office jobs get a shovel in their 'ands.'

Emily shot him a look almost of hatred. 'But he's always - he's strong - he's never- you don't know what he's had to- 'and she broke down again.

'We'll see how he is in the morning, Emily,' said Annie. 'Don't you mind your Grandfather, my dear. He don't understand.'

'Oh don't understand, is it?' Jorret began.

'Hush up! Go and help Sally or something, will you?' Annie turned back to her daughter. 'Take Jimmy up to the green tomorrow where you and Tom went. See if the skylarks 've started, so Tom can see them again when he's back.'

She exchanged glances with Bob. 'He'll be back soon, and then everything'll be right again, you'll see,' she added unconvincingly.

There were no skylarks, but there were stonechats in the gorse and, of course, the screaming gulls dipping and diving over the cliff edge.

Jimmy stared at the gulls as they soared and swooped, wheeling and screaming.

'They're just flying for the sake of it, Emmy,' said Jimmy. They were the first words he had spoken save for a few grunts. 'D'you think they are enjoying it, flying like that, completely free?'

'I don't know. I just enjoy watching them.'

'Or are they Spitfires and Messerschmidts just out to destroy each other? Then will the Herring Gulls come and destroy their nests, just for the sake of it?'

Chapter 30

They were still on their cliff walk when Commander Pearson rang the farm.

'Hallo. Crannel Five-three.'

'Hallo. Pearson here. Is that Emily?'

'No, Commander. She's out for a walk with Jimmy. It's Annie Jorret. Can I take a message?'

'Beg pardon, Mrs Jorret. Get Jimmy to ring me, urgent, I'm afraid. How is he?'

'Well, sir, he's not right. He needs to rest.'

'Fraid I can't spare him more than tomorrow. Need him back by the weekend, Mrs Jorret.

Get him to ring, please.'

She had hardly hung up the phone before there was a thunderous knocking at the door.

Josh the postman, breathing heavily, had thrown down his bicycle and had rushed up brandishing an ominous sickly-yellow envelope.

Annie went white and grasped the hall table to steady herself.

'Oh my God!'

'Telegram for Mr Robert Jorret,' panted Josh, wild-eyed.

Annie stared at him stunned. 'Robert? No! It can't be! He's on the farm! Give that to me!'

She snatched it from him.

Josh stood there staring back at her.

Annie slammed the door in his face and fled ashen-faced into the kitchen.

Old Peter Jorret scrambled to his feet. 'NO! NO! It be a *telegram*! It's Steve!'

Annie ripped open the envelope.

'Regret to inform you that Colonel George Johnson was killed in action 24 mar 41 Stop Letter to follow Stop Signed David Swallow Capt RA'

The old man sank back into his high-backed settle chair.

'First Steve now my friend the Colonel.'

There was a timid knock on the front door.

Josh was still standing there. 'Annie: be it *Tom?*'

'No Josh, it's -' she stopped, horrified at what she had nearly said, *no Josh, it's only the Colonel. My tears are tears of relief.* 'It's our dear friend, Colonel Johnson, you've seen him often in the village, Tom's great friend, he'll be heart-broken, we all will…' Her voice trailed off as she suddenly felt a wave of genuine grief.

In his high-backed seat before the stove, the old man was bending forward holding a huge white handkerchief to his eyes.

They all sat in silence until Annie remembered to tell Jimmy he had to ring Commander Pearson.

'Hallo. Henbury here. Jimmy Henbury.'

There was a long pause whilst all they could hear was the faint crackle of, presumably, the Commander's voice

Finally: 'Yes. Right. Goodbye.'

Jimmy slumped into one of the kitchen chairs. 'The truck will be round for me tomorrow, early.'

Emily knelt beside him and took his hand. 'You *can't* go. You're ill!'

'They've got wind of another attack. Next few days.'

'You *mustn't* go! You'll -' she thought wildly - 'you'll be no use to them like this!'

He patted her hand. 'Of course I must go. George did: he could have got out of it.'

Emily nearly screamed at him. "And see what became of it! What was the use of him being so - so -?'

'I'm sorry, Emmy.' He smiled down at her. 'I'm only going to Plymouth, for goodness' sake, not to darkest Africa.'

'It's just as bad! Worse! You won't come back either, and - ' 'I'll be back.'

Annie and Bob exchanged glances. 'I'll go and make some tea. George's tea. I saved some back for when Tom comes.'

* * *

A few days later, the news they dreaded headed the six o'clock bulletin. (The radio had come to dominate their evenings.)

This is the BBC Home Service. Here is the news, with Alvar Lidell reading it. Three nights of heavy bombing have inflicted more severe damage on Plymouth residential districts. Seventeen enemy aircraft have been destroyed.

Emily put her hands over her ears. 'Switch it off!'

'They would have phoned, Emily, if there was anything…' Annie paused. 'But do as Emily says, Bob.'

Bob nodded, and switched off the wireless set just as the telephone rang again.

They all sat like stone images as Bob hesitated, then slowly lifted the phone.

'Hello, yes?' he said, in his heavy Cornish accent, 'Crannel Five-Three?'

'I can't stand any more,' cried Emily, close to tears again.

'Is that Mr Jorret? This is Juliet, at the switchboard.'

'Yes, yes, Juliet. What is it?'

'I have a long-distance call for you, Mr Jorret. Will you accept the charges?'

'Yes. Of course.' Even Bob was losing patience. 'For God's sake, Juliet, get on wi' it!' He turned to the room. 'Long distance. Can't be Plymouth, Emmy.'

Someone was already speaking. 'Hallo, Pa. It's Tom.'

'Who?'

'Tom. Your son, Tom.' There was a hint of laughter in the voice, but it was tired. 'Remember me?'

'TOM!' Bob screamed at them all: 'it's TOM!' They crowded round, trying to hear the crackling voice.

'Tom! Where the devil *are* you? Good Lord, Annie it's Tom! Are you all right? Where are you?'

'They keep moving me about. Bit of treatment. Sorry to make you pay for this. I'm at Hartpury now.'

'Where?'

'Hartpury. Convalescing. Bored stiff. It's by Gloucester.'

'Where's that? Doesn't matter. Are you coming home?'

'Soon I think.' Tom's voice was flat and unconvincing.

'But listen, Pa. I'm going to be all right. But I'll be pretty useless. Can't take any more - responsibility.' He gave a hollow laugh. 'Never could, I suppose.'

'*Responsibility*? For God's sake, Tom, we just want you home...'

'But listen. Lamin Bah. He might arrive before me.'

The line became very faint and Bob could scarcely hear him. Several times he had to ask Tom to repeat what he was saying and had to jot down what he could make of it so that he could relay it to the family later.

Tom had said that Lamin Bah was being transferred to the Royal Artillery as a gunner; he would get more that way when he was eventually invalided out. The War office could not be bothered to sort out a stray wounded Gambian KAR soldier, and he had been in danger of having to spend the rest of the war in some out-of -the way barracks.

'Tom said that George arranged it all before he went to Africa,' said Bob. 'Lamin Bah's been declared unfit for active service.'

'Does Tom know about George?' demanded Annie.

'Apparently not. But Tom sounds all confused. Kept on about being responsible for Lamin. Then said summat about looking forward to going out with Emmy to watch skylarks.'

'Skylarks!' snorted the old man. ''e's got skylarks in 'is 'ead, that's what.'

'Then he carried on about Lamin Bah again,' Bob went on, ignoring the old man. 'He says Lamin is to have his room and he'll sleep in the hut.'

'He can't do that,' Annie said, 'not when he's been away at the war. Whatever next!'

'Anyway, Lamin Bah will be arriving and we've been told to look after him, and that's that.'

'What on earth will we do with him? He'll be quite out of place here after Africa, that's certain, what with the wind and cold.'

'Oh yes, Tom said he's been issued with all the battle-dress and greatcoats and things, so he'll be warm enough.'

'So he should be, in May-month.'

'It be very 'ot in Afric,' said Peter Jorret.

* * *

'I tell you this, Mrs Trelove,' the acid Mrs Rawson was saying in the village Post Office gossip club, 'I tell you I saw him in the village just looking about him, great black bean-pole with long shorts and huge red hat like the gyppos wear.' She grimaced. 'I gave him a wide berth I can tell you.'

Mrs Trelove looked up from the screen at her counter with a little smile of triumph.

'That's right, Mrs Rawson,' she said, 'and he's been in here already, had to bend his head in the doorway there and knocked that silly hat off. And what's more, Mrs Rawson,' she said, 'I can tell you where he's off to.'

'Where's that then?'

'Nice manners he had, and good-looking,' Mrs Trelove added, rather wistfully.

'Good looking indeed!' snapped Mrs Rawson. 'And him black as the ace of spades!'

'With great deep voice, spoke English alright,' Mrs Trelove went on, ignoring her. 'But, d'you know, he couldn't understand a *word* I was saying.'

'Natives offen speak English right,' ventured Beth Cummins. 'Leastways, that's what Stan says, an' he should know, being in the Merchant Navy and that.'

'Anyway,' continued the Postmistress, 'he called another young soldier in, the driver, laughin', and I told them where the farm was. I think they were just going to have a look. The young fellow said the sergeant were still in the army for a bit.'

Josh the postman came in and dumped his empty sack on the counter. ''e's goin to stay up at farm, Gustory, when e's out. Wi' Jorrets. Said so in *Britannia* th' other day.'

'Oh ye-es. He's that black man going to stay with Jorrets.' Mrs Rawson sniffed. 'Learning to drink, I'll be bound,' she added under her breath so they could all hear.

'A hero, Ma Rawson, that's what he be, saved Tom's life 'e did,' said Josh.

* * *

'We are never going back. The Commander is going to be posted somewhere. They say we can't do any more, even if the buggers do come back, though why they should I can't think, they can only bomb rubble unless they try for the hospitals, there aren't any schools left…'

Jimmy Henbury, the quiet, measured, confident, calm builder-architect had hardly stopped talking since they had brought him home after the last terror raids. Occasionally he would sink into a short reverie before he started again, and sometimes would revert to his old thoughtful manner; but then the flow of disjointed memories would start again.

'The whole city's wrecked, in ruins, hardly any houses left fit for living in…we all knew when they'd come, half-past eight, and then go about 2o'clock in the morning…five nights out of nine.'

He took off his glasses and cleaned them with his handkerchief for the twentieth time. 'Saw a bus, Green Line. Hardly damaged.'

'That was good, then,' said Emily soothingly.

He stared angrily at her. 'What? Good? Perched on the roof of a terrace of houses?' He laughed. 'No, not much good.' He took a sip of the SDI orange squash and for a moment his mind cleared. 'So sorry, Emmy. Got it all muddled, forgive me my dear.' He fell back into a reverie.

'Gi' 'im' some time, lass,' said the old man. 'Needs to get it orf 'is chest.'

'You know Mr Churchill came?' Jimmy resumed. 'He has a special train from Paddington and they all sleep in it. He arrived in a launch at the dockyard and we met him then took the truck ahead to clear a way. He walked for miles along the quays waved everyone away when they said it was too dangerous for him and clambered over the rubble and ducked into the ruined workshops.

'It was terrible, Emmy. You know that beautiful Georgian terrace near the North yard. Completely smashed. Some of the chaps were still searching for bodies.' He slipped back into semi-incoherence. 'We kept him away from the barracks. Naval barracks. Direct hit from one-tonner. 50-odd fellows killed and lots wished they had been. There was hammering.'

'Hammering?'

He stared at her unseeing again. 'They had to make the coffins in a gym next to where all the wounded were. Just a curtain between. They could *hear* the hammering. As forty young fellows lay there, crying in pain. Hammering the coffins. We could do nothing. Had to keep Winston away, he'd have died of grief.'

'Oh my God!'

Emily gasped in horror as she saw Jimmy Henbury's gentle face suddenly distorted in rage.

'I now know, Emily, what hatred is. I never thought about revenge 'til then. Now - now I want every, *every* one of their towns to be left a smoking ruin like Plymouth.'

Old Peter Jorret broke a terrible silence. 'You ain't tol' us what Winnie said.'

Jimmy relaxed. 'Winston? Oh, he kept muttering *I've never seen the like, I've never seen the like.* Then as he was getting on his train, he said - I noted it down - he said *The staunchness of our Plymouth brethren will not go unwritten in the annals of our victory.*'

'Now want to rest, Emmy, and if I don't wake up, it will be a blessing.'

Emily choked back her tears. 'No! You will have to build again when peace comes.'

They heard her coaxing him up the stairs, then *No, Emmy,* he was saying, *not for me, just ordinary homes for ordinary folk like us, the great dreamers will build a golden city, splendid white halls and tree-lined avenues on the ruins of our lovely city…*

Chapter 31

For months now, Emily had been putting off her decisions about Jimmy. Partly it was out of pointless respect for the memory of Mr Harris - whose very Christian name she struggled to remember - but she knew that her indecision arose out of her own timidity, her refusal to believe that her true role could only be a minor one, helping out where needed, an inessential but worthy cog in the Jorret family machine.

Now she *was* really needed and she could dither no longer, or Jimmy (whom she loved so dearly) would crack up completely. All memories of the shadowy Mr Harris had faded into nothingness: a different time, indeed, Emily said to herself, a different world.

No doubt the Post Office gossip club would disapprove: *fancy that! That Mrs Harris, poor husband hardly cold, going off to live with that builder man! I 'm sure I didn't go looking for a fancy man when I lost mine in the last lot…*

'I'm going back with him,' said Emily firmly. 'I shall stay there, in Newmin.'

'Well, I don't know-,' said Annie doubtfully. 'Perhaps he'll be better if he stays here.'

'No. I shall live with Jimmy from now on.'

'I know times are changing, but - well, it would be different if you were married.'

Emily's lips pursed in a hard straight line: for a moment Annie could see her grandfather in her.

'No, Ma. He needs me there. When he's better, well, we'll think again. I'm going to phone Sam and he can collect my things in the truck tomorrow.'

'You're still - Mrs Harris...'

''arris!' old Peter Jorret snorted. 'Dead and gorn long since an' good riddance. You go, where you're needed, lass.'

'But you're needed here, Emily. Helping Sally on the farm.'

Bob went and put his arm round Annie. 'Emmy's right, my dear. Where she's needed. Besides,' he added, 'it'll free up a room for when Tom comes back.'

'I've decided, anyway,' said Emily. 'I'll be able to help at the Hospital a lot more too.' She crossed to the door. 'I'll go and sort out some things.'

The old man chuckled. 'Didn't know she 'ad it in 'er,' he said.

* * *

The top of Lamin Bah's fez was level with the guttering of the grey slate roof of Gustory farmhouse.

Lamin sounded the clapper of the bell under the porch and stooped to greet Annie as she looked up at him, beaming.

'You must be Mr -er- Sergeant - Bah,' said Annie, rather as if she were expecting several other giant Gambians to call.

'That's right, Ma'am,' boomed Lamin. 'Afraid there's some kit, Ma'am.'

'Bring it all in,' said Annie. 'Would you like to stay for some tea?' (This to the driver who was struggling with two of Lamin's kitbags and a large cardboard tube.)

The driver refused politely and turned to Lamin and

shook his hand as the latter thanked him.

'It's been an honour for me, mate,' he said.

* * *

'Mrs Jorret, Ma'am,' said Lamin, courteously trying to like the 4 o'clock cup of tea, 'I has documents relating to the Colonel George that I was ask to give you when everyone is gathered.'

The old man perked up: he had hardly uttered more than a grunt or two to Lamin since he had arrived.

'The Colonel was 'special friend o' mine,' he said.

'I know, sir, an' I've been given special things for you. Captain Swallow from the War Office give them to me fo' you.'

'Captain Swallow sent the telegram,' said Bob.

'The Captain another frien' of the Colonel, sir,' said Lamin. 'The Colonel's executive, for his will, sir.'

'Executor, Lamin,' corrected Sally.

Lamin beamed down at her. 'Thank you, Miss. Seein' things legal.'

'Exactly,' Sally smiled back. 'The name's Sally.'

'Sally.' Lamin savoured the name slowly. 'A beautiful name for a beautiful lady,' he said without the slightest awkwardness.

Sally blushed and for once was lost for words.

'Who's this Swallow, then? Lawyer is 'e? Not fightin', then?' demanded Peter Jorret querulously.

Lamin frowned down at him. 'Not right you say that sir. Excuse me fo' sayin' but the Captain has a medal for his bravery, sir, an' lost a foot in France an' said he'd stay on an' help as he was a lawyer man before the war and knows about wills.'

'All right. Go on, then. You should have said,' Jorret

muttered shamefacedly.

'There's a message from the Captain Swallow sayin' about the Colonel.' Lamin's voice faltered. 'Can't read it. Someone else read it'

He handed Bob a large brown envelope marked *On His Majesty's Service,* and sat down heavily in an armchair, his long legs stretched out.

'You read it, Sal,' said Bob.

Sally slit open the envelope with a tea-knife and took out several foolscap sheets and another sealed envelope marked *Col. George Johnson, RA: Last Will (Feb 3rd 1941).*

'Captain Swallow's letter is first,' said Sally.

To the Jorret family and other friends of my uncle, Colonel George Johnson.

Before setting out to Africa again Colonel Johnson asked me to draw up another will and asked me to arrange for some of the things to be sent straight down to you in the event of his death. He sends his warmest good wishes to you all and thanks you for your kindness and friendship that, in his words, "meant more to me than words can tell". There are some large War Office wall charts of North Africa and the Mediterranean (no longer Restricted *as not up-dated) for Mr Jorret; sets of books on architecture and sculpture for Captain Jorret; books on old farming methods and tools and on Cornwall for Mr and Mrs Robert Jorret; some poetry books for Mrs Harris. I have been asked to arrange legacies for the Gambian soldiers and/ or their families, including seven hundred and fifty pounds sterling for Sergeant Lamin Bah "to get him started" and other sums to be made available for the family in accordance with a private arrangement with me. I have enclosed a copy of the will with of course details of the other legatees, including charities.*

The circumstances of my uncle's death are as follows. The battle of Keren in Italian- occupied Ethiopia -

'I know!' whooped the old man. 'Battle of Keren. Knocked the Wops right out of Ethiopia. Hilyslessy back in charge.'

'That right, sir. You know it all,' said Lamin admiringly. 'But many think, Eyeties didn't fight. That quite wrong, brave, tough defence in great rock fortress.' He shook his head sadly and his large black eyes began to water.

'Terrible battle. Thousands soldiers die.'

There was a long pause.

'Go on, go on, Sally,' said Annie.

Sally read that some of the Italian guns were brilliantly dug in and our spotter planes could not find the sites. So George climbed up the mountainside to try to identify them visually. He took a radio operator but left him under cover whilst he climbed into a better position to observe the Italian guns. He got back to the radio and sent the co-ordinates but must have been seen by the Alpinist snipers and was killed as he scrambled down the mountainside.

'Captain Swallow puts a note in writing at the bottom of the page,' said Sally. 'Colonel Johnson was Mentioned in Dispatches for this outstanding feat of bravery.'

'Should 'ave 'ad a medal,' muttered Peter Jorret.

'That right, sir,' said Lamin. 'Bravest man, the colonel, like Captain Tom, sir.' 'And like you too, Lamin, by all accounts,' said Annie.

Lamin laughed. 'Oh *no,* ma'am. I jus' follow.'

'I'm sorry, but I really ought to go and do the cows,' said Sally. 'I'll leave the rest of the stuff on the table.'

'I like to come, Miss, see the cattle. Only,' Lamin added, 'a bit cold outside.' (It was a warm spring day towards the end of May.)

'Gi' 'im some sacks o'er 'is shoulders, maid,' said Peter Jorret. 'Best thing when I were a lad, were sacks on shoulders.'

Sally was doubtful. 'We-ell...'

'Go on, Sally. That'll do for the moment,' said Annie, laughing. 'We'll find some great thick seaman's sweaters for Lamin later.'

They could hear Lamin's great bass voice booming in the yard. 'Do you know, Miss Sally, first thing I see in the farms, great fat cows on green grass. Our cattle all thin, bones stickin' out.'

'I should have asked him what he wants to eat,' said Annie.

'Won't have much choice,' said Bob dryly. 'Rabbit stew, rabbit pie, and turnips. And porridge.'

'Go on with you,' said Annie.

* * *

'Emily and I used to do some of the heavy work between us,' Sally explained, 'when Bob was busy, that is.'

Lamin beamed. 'Now I can do it all,' he said eagerly. 'No need to worry longer.'

Sally laughed - Lamin was beginning to believe she was always laughing - and said that she had been managing for months and was getting really muscular.

Lamin looked at her rounded figure in her Land Army green pullover and said that she was very beautiful in face and form.

'Then so are you, Lamin,' said Sally, looking up at him, and thinking that she could detect a blush under his coal-black skin.

'Ah, Miss Sally, I am damaged, in my side here.'

'Does it hurt, still, Lamin?' asked Sally, a concerned frown on her face.

Lamin shook his head vigorously. 'Ah, noh, noh, Miss Sally, the MO say I use it much as possible, Miss Sally, get muscle working full pelt.'

She laughed again. 'Then we'll get it working full pelt with the cows, Lamin. *Do* call me Sally.'

They had arrived at the gate and the Jerseys had already gathered at it. Lamin stared at them open-mouthed.

The cows, less than Sally's height, with their sleek, tan-brown hides and their black noses appeared to welcome him with wistful large black eyes.

'Everything so beautiful in this country, the ladies, the cows.'

Sally giggled. 'It's never wise to compare ladies and cows, Lamin.'

Lamin looked alarmed: 'Noh, I did not mean, oh, noh, Mis-sally -' and seeing her rosy happy face, he suddenly tipped back his head and bellowed with such a laugh that the cows reared away in alarm.

* * *

Josh at last bought Annie the postcard: 'Tom's a-comin' home Annie!'

'That's *my* postcard, is it, Josh? Not for you to read!'

'Leastways, Annie,' said Josh lamely, 'that's what we 'ope it say.'

'That's just what it *does* say, Josh,' said Annie, with a tear rolling down her cheek.

'He's coming next week, and you can tell everyone - that is, those you ain't told already.'

* * *

'Ma'am Annie, I don't like stayin' in his room, in Captain Tom's own room, an' not makin' way for him comin' home, an' I been tryin' to fine a room somewhere.'

'Why, there's no need, Lamin. Tom said especially that you were to have the room.

It was the least he could do, he said.'

'Noh, ma'am.' Lamin's gentle features were set in a firm line.

'Grandfather won't have it. You know he relies on you.' (Peter Jorret was spending hours with Lamin, discussing the war in North and East Africa. The old man had plastered George's maps over the walls of the front room and he sat in his rocking chair directing Lamin where to move the flags and tapes.)

'I'm very grateful ma'am for Misser Jorret's kindness, and yours too ma'am, specially, but must go.'

'Well - I'll talk with Bob about it, Lamin. And Sally might help you find a place. If you're sure.'

'I'm sure, ma'am Annie. Sure.'

Chapter 32

'Two places I try, Missally,' said Lamin, disappointed and a little bewildered, 'and they both say sorry no rooms.'

I was afraid of that. 'Where did you see the notices, Lamin?'

'Post Office window. Like you said.'

'Did they say why?'

'One said room already taken. But her son away at the war.'

'Mrs Rawson?'

'Right. Mrs Rawson. The other put a little chain on door and said sorry no room after all.'

Sally did not know whether she were angrier or more ashamed. She swallowed hard and tried to appear nonchalant.

'Never mind: you wouldn't have liked those places anyway. We'll sort something out, Lamin, on Sunday at church. Perhaps when we get Miss Jenkins.'

Miss Jenkins was a shrivelled but sharp old lady in her early seventies, fiercely independent in spirit but grateful for the way in which Annie and Sally (now Emily couldn't do it) would "pop in to tidy up a bit and bring her her rations" and a few eggs and cream and, no doubt, some of the rapidly diminishing tea George had left. She loved to go to church and it was a struggle for the ladies to wheel her up the gravel paths so Lamin had added that task to his list.

'I've spoken to the Vicar, young man,' she said, staring up at Lamin through her gold- rimmed pince-nez. 'He has just the rooms for you in the Rectory and I've told him to get them warm for you. You're to be sure to look at all those books there and improve yourself.'

'Ma'am, you very very kind to me.'

She leant forward and patted his hand. 'Nonsense. You deserve everything, so far from home, and fighting for us as you've done.'

She looked away, remembering how in her forties she was to marry a navy Commander only for him to go down at Jutland…

'No, young man, you make the most of every minute of the life that's spared to you.'

Lamin was never ashamed to let his tears show, and he bent down and kissed the old lady.

'Yes, yes, I know,' she said, brushing him aside with her crooked gloved hand.

* * *

Major Brimshaw had had no idea how he had arrived there. One moment he had been snoozing in the sun while Sapper was minding the Bren, when Bari Din had screamed at him that the plane was coming straight for them and Sapper started blazing away.

Now Brimshaw had found himself lying nearly naked and staring up at, not exactly a tent, more a canvas sheet, insufferably hot. A young Arab boy was squatting beside him waving some leaf or other to keep the flies away from his bruises, bruises he began to feel all over him.

He tried to sit up, but his head hurt so much that he

slumped straight back on the litter.

The small boy leapt up and rushed from the shelter shouting something unintelligible except for "Engleesh, Engleesh!".

Brimshaw dozed off for a few minutes. He woke up with a start to see a turbaned figure - Rachid - sitting cross-legged beside him.

'So you have come round, Major? I must apologise that our medical facilities are not as I would wish for you.'

'Rachid! What the devil's going on? Where am I?'

'Major Brimshaw, I have ordered my men not to kill you, as is usual for our prisoners.

We cannot afford to feed them and watch them.' Brimshaw lay back silent, completely bemused.

'But I will give you a simple choice: to die or fight on our side.'

This time Brimshaw did sit up, nearly bumping his head on the awning.

'What! You ask me that!' His face was purple with rage. 'Take your pistol and shoot me now, if that's what you want. Do it!'

Rachid showed his teeth in his icy smile. 'To fight, Major, against the Italians.'

Brimshaw stared at him stupidly. 'I don't know how you came to make me your prisoner, Rachid, but I tell you this, I will do my utmost to evade you and rejoin my own army.'

Rachid shook his head slowly. 'That, Major, will be impossible. They left days ago in full retreat. The gun is destroyed. You will have to swim to Aden to catch them.'

'But - Tom - Captain Jorret. The gun destroyed you say?' Realization horrified him. 'But what of Gung- Bari Din? And Sapper Peters? Rachid! You haven't killed them?'

'I did not, Major; the Italians did.' Brimshaw buried his

face in his hands.

Even Rachid's expression momentarily softened. 'Major Brimshaw, I am no longer your enemy. We are allies, against the Italians. You can help us, teach our brave young men how to fight. They are ignorant and stupid and prefer to die fighting rather than live fighting longer, as you have done.'

Brimshaw was not really listening. 'Tell me, damn you, what *happened!*'

'Sparvieros. Three of them. We had been watching you for days. We thought to seize the gun but could see the Italians were driving you out for us. So we waited.'

'I still don't see -'

'The Italian planes were heading for the road at Tug Argen across your position. Then I saw through my binoculars the Gambian soldier throw himself at you. He pushed you down the gully just before the bomb fell. My men found you by chance the next day half buried in shale and stones.'

'Captain Jorret probably survived. But your men were killed.' He shrugged. 'That is war. They died bravely.'

* * *

'He got up in his suit this morning, Bob,' said Annie. 'Did he say anything to you?'

'Old Jones brought his taxi round quite early.'

Annie groaned. 'He must be changing his will again.'

'I made Grandfather some breakfast and he said he was going in to see Emmy and Jimmy. Something about cottages,' said Sally.

'He's got a pair of old cottages out Pentire. Pretty poor state,' Bob said. He shrugged. 'I don't really know what he's got. Some fields out there, I think. Used to be part of the -' He broke off at a warning glance from Annie.

'Part of the Samson farm,' said Sally. 'It's all right. I know.'

* * *

The Vicar climbed unsteadily up the pulpit steps.

'My text for today, er, um, or rather,' (beaming) 'two texts, as does not only Exodus tell us, as you, er, all know, in verse 22 of the second chapter I have been a stranger in a strange land, but also St Matthew has it,' and at this point the Vicar suddenly spoke with fire and conviction, just as he had done years ago when as a young man he had burned in the spirit with the fires of Faith, I was a stranger and ye took me in. I was a stranger and ye took me in!'

He paused and looked about him at the crowded congregation, seeking out one or two faces, his pale watery blue eyes for once animated, even fierce.

'Yet there are some among us who shun the stranger, who close their hearts to those from far away - even one amongst us who has fought gallantly and suffered wounds to keep our homes safe. That angers Our Lord, and we who strive to follow the Lord must hear Him scolding us.'

The poor old man's concentration just as quickly slipped away again, and his gaze lost its intensity as if the cloud had covered the sun.

'No, we welcome among us one who, er, has left those arid desert sands, um, so like the sands - where Our Lord lived nineteen hundred years ago - '

'No, NO,' whispered Lamin, in a whisper that carried to the choir stalls. He was sitting in the back pew with Sally (as anyone sitting behind him would not have been able to see past him). Miss Jenkins in her wheelchair sat in the aisle beside him. Lamin was muffled up to the ears in his army greatcoat, whilst Sally sat neat and cool in her smart well-cut suit and summer straw hat (which ensemble caused some of the Post Office gossip ladies to mutter about all that get-up having cost a pretty penny mark my words - and the time those two spent together in the cow sheds! She was no better than she ought to be. They say he's a war hero, and all that, but fancy a Cornish woman throwing herself at, well, a black man).

'The Padre don't know about it, Missally,' Lamin grumbled, for once a little put out. 'The Gambia a mighty great river and on both banks green jungle, and -'

'Sh-sh,' said Sally.

* * *

A half-circle of whitewashed cottages, some with slate roofs and some with (much cheaper) thatch looked out over the Crannel village green, and scrubby oaks and sycamores formed a windbreak around the other side. The green was hardly big enough to allow for more than a patch of grass where the children could pile up their coats to make goal-posts, and a little bus shelter for the elderly to sit and wait for the bus which never seemed to come.

Tom climbed down from the 15cwt to survey that familiar scene, too nervous, as he was, to go straight home and face the family after what? -getting on for two years?

The RASC corporal who had driven him down from Gloucestershire had gone over to the Britannia to book himself in for the night and to get some Woodbines.

Tom decided to sit in the bus shelter and, well, there's no hurry. Not after two years.

The children were not kicking their leather ball about, but were gathered clamouring around a lean black figure squatting on the ground, beaming at them and spreading his hands drawing pictures, surely of boats, in the air...

Lamin looked up and his face lit up with joy as he saw Tom approaching.

He leapt up and rushed over to Tom as he stood there, tears in his eyes.

Neither could speak as they clasped each other, but the children gathered round, all talking at once.

He's a Captain, look, three pips. Who is it, Lamin? Why're you cryin' Lamin? Was he with you in Africa, Lamin?

Tom was of course much changed, stouter, sun-burned, with thinning greying hair cut short, and with the scar running down the side of his face, but one of the older boys thought he recognized him.

'It's Mr Jorret! Is Lamin a friend of yours, sir?'

Tom found his voice. 'Yes. Yes: my dearest friend. Without Lamin, I would not be here.'

'And without Captain Tom,' said Lamin, 'I would be - nobody.' He brushed away his tears with his sleeve. He beamed at the children. 'Look, I come back again some other time and tell you some more, eh?'

Lamin's tellin' us all about Africa and when he was where the Italians were.

'I never seen a black man before,' piped up a small girl earnestly to Tom. 'Lamin says they're all like him. Very tall and very nice an' kind.'

Tom took a shilling from his pocket and offered it to the older lad.

'Run and knock on the Britannia door and ask for Corporal Sims and ask him to bring all the stuff up to Jorret's Farm in half an hour. Lamin and I want to walk up to the Farm.'

Can we come, can we come, please!

'No,' said Lamin. 'I said I come back to talk some time. The Captain and me, we must talk now.'

Chapter 33

Old Peter Jorret had mysteriously ordered them all out onto the front drive. He was strangely dressed in collar and orange bow tie, thick woollen cardigan (despite the August heat), plus- fours and boots.

'Got you all together 'ere,' he said pompously, 'cause I 'ave somethin' important to show you, affect all yer futures. Young ''enbury's drivin' over his lorry with Emmy, an' we'll all squeeze in. 'Emmy says his 'ead's all right for drivin' jus' as I said. You come up front wi' me, maid' (this to Annie), 'an' you all get in th' back.' He leered slyly at Lamin. 'You won't mind givin' the Miss 'ere an' 'and?'

Lamin never understood sarcasm. 'Of course I help her, sir.'

'Yes, now we're all 'ere, includin' Ste- the Captain, that is - back from the wars an' 'e'll soon be right as rain, an' with that arm 'e'll never be chippin' stones again, an' good job too, says I, 'e can get on lookin' after the estate like 'e should've bin doin' in the first place.'

There were murmurs of disapproval at this, but Tom merely shrugged and said nothing, as he had always done.

Jimmy drove up with the truck and jumped down from the cab. Apart from the white fringe of hair round his bald head, dark shadows around the eyes behind his round-rimmed glasses, he looked as he had always done, calm and neat in his manner and movements. Tom noticed, however, how his hands shook a little as he undid the tailgate chain.

Lamin grinned as he lifted the ladies (not without some squealing from them) bodily into the truck, then scrambled up to give Bob and Tom a hand. At last they were all loaded, with the picnic baskets Annie had prepared, and a crate of light ale, for a ride, which Peter Jorret had promised to be rough and bumpy, and you'll all have sore bums.

So it proved. They arrived at length after a winding drive along a sandy track round the coastline (passing on the inland side of Tom's private promontory) and continued along a sandy path, barely wide enough for the truck, to a clearing in which two large cottages stood side by side.

They were of rough stone much in need of re-whitewashing. The roofing was also in need of repair where the slate tiles had slipped, and the French-style heavy oak shutters were eroded along the edges by the salt wind. High overgrown Cornish hedges marked the edges of the fields that extended to the track they had driven along.

Peter proudly produced an enormous key with which they forced open the front door on its rusty hinges. But the interiors (the one house being the mirror image of the other) were surprisingly large: four rooms only but of the standard sixteen-and-a-half feet square with high ceilings, through which could be seen the joists of the attic floors, where on occasion the plaster had fallen.

Peter marched them through each house in turn as briskly as his wasting leg muscles would allow to the sculleries with their large open sinks and huge taps.

'There you are!' he said triumphantly. 'Water laid on, and the electric,' he added, pointing with his stick to a black fuse-box festooned with cobwebs. 'Bit of work soon 'ave these ship-shape.'

He turned to Jimmy Henbury and Tom. 'What d'you think, eh? Soon 'ave 'em ship-shape?' he repeated. 'Give you somethin' to do, stop broodin' an' that?'

They exchanged glances, and both burst out laughing together.

'Yes, Mr Jorret,' said Jimmy. 'We'll have them ship-shape for you. Not soon, though: it's a long job.'

'You got all the stuff in your yard?'

'Ye-es. Most of it. Have to get some permits, though, and get the electricity wired up properly.'

'Good. 'Cos they're for the girls, one for Emmy, an' one for my Miss Sally *Sam-son*.' He put a slow emphasis on the surname. 'They can have them for nuffin, 'cept signing the papers.'

* * *

October the fifteenth. The weather always used to change on the fifteenth, or thereabouts, before the War, so nothing changes. Anyway, the west wind is bringing the first winter chills: it's certainly getting to be uncomfortable sitting here watching the waves breaking over the Gull Rock. Skylarks are all finished, of course, beginning of August. Never really knew what became of them in the winter: just stayed here on the ground, I suppose. Some from up-country were supposed to migrate. Perhaps to Somalia, poor devils. Or to the Gambia.

Nothing's changed: the waves still crash over Gull Rock and the wind gusts the spray in my face. Two and a bit years, and nothing's changed. But everything's changed really. Somalia: never even heard of it two years ago, let alone been out and back to build gun emplacements (without any guns).

Funny to know Somalia better than lots of Cornwall, and Berbera better than Plymouth. Or Plymouth as it was before the War. Jimmy says I wouldn't know if I was in the centre of Plymouth or the centre of Devonport. Jimmy: God, yes. Can't concentrate for more than ten minutes at all. Well-organised, steady chaps like Jimmy crack up much quicker than sloppy chaps like me: they care more, or used to…

Tom took out a packet of Woodbines and shielded the match to light one. He laughed to himself. *That's changed, anyway. Ma was quite shocked to see me smoking. Not nearly as shocked as when she saw the scar on my face. Told her how lucky I'd been, compared with so many others. Lucky to have had Lamin by me, that's for sure.*

All the way to Somaliland to build gun emplacements without any guns. Get shot at and bombed and what nearly killed me? Bloody motorbike. Can't ride now. Never again, not with this arm, can't grip anything. The old bugger's pleased *about it! Thinks he's got his own way at last; he has, I suppose.*

But old Terence, he'll do better than me in the end with mason work. What a shock! Somehow, though, I never quite believed that he'd gone. Not like poor Bari Din and Sapper. And George… Best man I ever knew and he gets killed…

Tom turned up his coat collar and put his cap on against the wind, trying to conceal even from himself the tears that came at once to his eyes as he thought of his friend. But Tom was incapable of self-pity: if he hadn't known it before, he knew it now, *he* was all right.

I can always just swan on, in a place I like with people I like. Or love, *really. Most poor sods in this world are born in stinking dumps like Berbera or Calcutta or wherever. Or if they're in beautiful old Plymouth they're bombed to smithereens…*

Don't know why but felt in the guts that George was kind of doomed…He was always a bit unreal, floating in and out of my life. As for Brimshaw, just the opposite… Terence

Brimshaw is - what's the word? - indestructible. Rachid just said that there was no trace of him. Just as well I never did anything about what he called his "affairs". Even so, what a shock, him turning up at the door like that! "Someone at the door for you, Tom. Says you knew him in the army." Couldn't recognize him, short hair gone white, moustache gone white, glasses, face all lined and sunburned. Not 'til he spoke.

"You promised to show me how to cut stone, Tom. Rachid told me to go and join our lads when they broke through, and he just vanished: shoved off north again, I suppose. Tell you all about it sometime. Anyway, you said you'd show me how to do stonework. I'll get a place in the village."

But I must say, he's bloody good with the chisel. Pleasure to watch him, he's so keen. Bit excitable, though. You've got to take it steady. Can't afford slightest slips with the stone.

Nothing's changed, yet everything's changed. All the dunes have shifted, and they've mined the beach right up to Crannel Cove. Have to go careful across the rocks to the crab holes now. Can't imagine why they've mined these beaches, though. Can't see the Germans going round Land's End to invade Cornwall.

Yes, everything's changed, or rather, everyone's changed. There's Emmy, firmly in charge, and Jimmy quite content bricklaying and whitewashing and so on. Anything so he doesn't have to think. Pa and Ma - well, they're slower. He seems happy leaving the farm to Sally and Lamin, and just help out and working down at the cottages. Ma's in the kitchen cooking for everyone and managing the rations, but she's sadder, lost her fun. Wonder if she's ill. Dreamed that I'd marry Sally. But anyone could have seen Sal's hooked on Lamin anyway.

God! That really was a shock, when the Vicar - he's not much better in two years, either - on Sunday.

Tom laughed out loud, and assumed a bleating voice in

caricature of the unfortunate clergyman: "I - er - publish the - er - Banns of marriage!' Long pause while I shuffle papers. 'That is, banns of marriage between - er - Lemmin Baa, bachelor, and Anne Sally Jane - er - Samson, spinster, both of this parish." Stares about him. "If there be - just- er- *cause or impediment* why these two persons should not be lawfully joined together in matrimony, ye do now declare it."

(At this there had been a loud whoop of "Hooray!" from Miss Jenkins, but as it was from that doyenne of Newmin society, no-one dared to show disapproval.)

Tom was still shouting his vicar's voice into the wind when Terence Brimshaw appeared before him, shaking his head sadly.

'Bang on the head still bothering you then, Tom,' he said, grinning. 'Thought we might go and help at the cottages.'

He stood beside Tom looking out at the Gull Rock. 'Wonder if anyone's swum out there,' he said.

'Too dangerous, with undertow and that,' Tom replied. 'But we'll get Lamin to row us out there one day. We'll take a stone: it's time you did some lettering: GEORGE JOHNSON and BARI DIN and in fifty years' time, no-one will have a clue who they were.'

'Nor Brimshaw or Jorret, for that matter,' said Terence.

He put his arm about Tom's shoulders and they walked off round the cliff path to the cottages.

Printed in Great Britain
by Amazon

58163502R00156